The Duke of Pain

Rakes of Regent's Park #4

By

Karyn Gerrard

Table of Contents

The Duke of Pain (The Rakes of St. Regent's Park #4)

KG Publishing

Vers 1.4

PRINT ISBN: 978-1-7386845-0-2

Cover art by © The Write Designer

Summary

The oldest and only remaining original member of The Rakes of St. Regent's Park, Gideon Broyles, the Duke of Watford, has grown weary of his debauched escapades. Due to his wretched past, he often refers to himself as the Duke of Pain. He selfishly breezed through life with no thought for anything or anyone. All that changed when Gideon met Olivia Durham at an exclusive club. The passionate encounter has him reeling, as he never experienced these powerful emotions before.

Olivia also has a dark past. Hiding behind a fictitious persona, she provides a particular service to her clients. One that doesn't involve physical intimacy, for Olivia cannot stand to be touched. In all her years at the club, no man has sparked her interest—until Gideon. Despite trying to ignore the intense feelings swirling between them, Olivia finds the darkly handsome duke hard to resist. When secrets from her past come to light, the complications become insurmountable.

There are multiple obstacles to overcome, including shared doubts about their capacity to feel—anything. For two emotionally closed-off people to find and accept enduring happiness? Gideon and Olivia must believe that love can conquer all.

Rakes of Regent's Park Series

IN A PRIVATE MEETING place, in an old bank office behind Colosseum Terrace on Albany Street, a group of gentlemen attended a gathering. It had nothing to do whatsoever with financing, investments, or stocks—unless you counted moral bankruptcy. The central rules of this club: no serious attachments to anyone, and the pursuit of one's own pleasures, especially of the carnal variety, were to be of the utmost importance.

But weariness and boredom were setting in. Along with something more worrying: loneliness. A disquiet of the soul. These bad boy peers of Victorian London were damaged, hiding their inner torture beneath a thin veneer of devil-may-care dissoluteness.

It takes an exceptional group of women to capture the hearts of such men. To see past the outer shell. The ladies are determined to live and love in their own way, with no relinquishment of their independence and no compromises. How satisfying to find that deep down, these progressive men are in total agreement.

Author's Note #1

SECTIONS OF THE DUKE of Pain were previously published nine years ago with a digital publisher under another title. These sections have been completely revised, rewritten, and expanded to fit The Rakes of St. Regent's Park series. It's mostly new material.

The Rakes of St. Regent's Park consist of the following books (so far)

Book 1: Protecting the Duke

Book 2: The Baron and the Mistress

Book 3: Knight of Christmas

Book 4: The Duke of Pain

Book 5: The Not So Perfect Duke

Book 6: COMING SOON! The Viscount of Shadows

Each historical romance author does their own world-building, much like authors in fantasy or other genres. Each author has their own set of characters and peers. That is why many of my characters from other books pop up in the stories I write. They are all part of my particular historical romance world. See the author's note #2 for historical facts in this story.

Prologue

FEBRUARY 1898

London, England

Boredom. That word summed up Gideon Broyles, the Duke of Watford's, life for decades. Turning 40 years old should have him utterly depressed. But the only emotion he felt—and had felt—for as long as he could remember—was boredom. It was the only emotion he allowed himself to feel.

However, annoyance had started to creep in.

As Gideon looked around the table, his mouth curled slightly. It was the monthly meeting of The Rakes of St. Regent's Park. The gatherings used to be weekly, but with a shift in membership and leadership, they were monthly.

Gideon was the leader of this motley crew back in the day. Back when there had been twenty-one members. He was the only original member left. Rather pathetic that he was still sowing oats that had long grown stale and moldy.

"Brookton, either call the meeting to order or dismiss us. I've better things to do than sit here for hours on end," Gideon declared.

The room grew silent.

Damon Cranston, Marquess of Brookton, and heir to the Duke of Chellenham, gave Gideon a sly smile. "Perhaps you would like to take over."

"I've done that, thank you. Can't be bothered."

"Before I take the roll call, Allenby has an opportunity he wishes to lay before us. I said we would take a vote. There are shares available in the Daimler Motor Company Limited, and he wanted to give us the first option to buy," Brookton concluded.

Those motorized vehicles were the wave of the future. The prospect appealed to Gideon. Even though he didn't show it outwardly, Gideon admired Christian Bamford, Duke of Allenby. Or he never would have handed over leadership of this group to him some months back. But Allenby had recently married and moved on. Allenby was also a man of vision. He kept his dukedom afloat by investing in the burgeoning auto industry, which was good enough for Gideon.

"I am all for it," Gideon stated. "All in favor?" A series of grunts and affirmatives came from the other men. "It is so carried. Have Allenby come in next week; the sooner, the better."

"Very well. Then let us take the roll call." Brookton dipped his pen in the inkwell. "Tolwood."

"Here."

Gideon rolled his eyes. Why Brookton insisted on a roll call when only seven were in the current group was beyond him.

Merritt Redfern, Viscount Tolwood, was busy looking for a bride and not having much luck. In the past four months, three members—or former members—had married and left the club except for the occasional dinner or game of cards, which reminded him.

"I've heard from Brandon Knight. He will not be returning to London or this group," Gideon declared. "He is off to Canada for two years, where he will be married. When he does return, he will take up residence in Herne Bay, though he mentioned setting up an office here in London. We may see him on occasion."

"Oh, I say," Tolwood exclaimed. "Who is the lucky lady?"

"A widow, late wife of the Earl of Oakby," Gideon replied nonchalantly. "He will also be stepfather to the young earl. A lady he knew in his past. Let's move on."

Gideon did not want to answer questions about Brandon. Or about the recently deceased Oakby and the scandal surrounding his lurid death.

To say he was hurt and disappointed about Brandon's new life would be admitting he had feelings. Though Gideon wished his friend well, he would miss him. Brandon had been the closest friend he'd ever had; even Brandon wasn't all that close.

Brookton ran a line across the paper. "Knight is out. Shinwell?"

Troy Buckingham, Viscount Shinwell, grunted in response.

"Linton?"

No reply.

"Rome Linton had another engagement," Gideon replied. "As does Gregory McFadden. If you looked up from your papers, you would see that."

"Then that leaves Wollstonecraft," Brookton said.

"Yes, I'm here," Oliver Wollstonecraft replied, looking almost as bored as Gideon. Oliver was the heir apparent to his grandfather, Aidan Wollstonecraft, the Earl of Carnstone.

"Then let's begin," Brookton declared, closing the journal. "I think we should reiterate what this group is all about: the foremost pursuit of one's pleasures, especially of the carnal variety. There is time enough to settle down and see to responsibilities; meanwhile, we will enjoy all life offers affluent men of considerable means."

Again, Gideon struggled not to roll his eyes.

"And in that vein, we share our experiences, recommend clubs, or warn against others," Brookton concluded.

"The Chrysalis has closed its doors for good," Wollstonecraft interjected. "I thank you all for the warning. Despite assurances, word circulated about their shabby practices, and the madam sold the place. A new club is opening in its stead, I hear."

"I have heard of a new club opening in the East End. It is called The Velvet Vine and Tackle, and I will make a cursory visit when it opens," Gideon volunteered.

"Very well. You know what we all like, see if the place can accommodate us. Wollstonecraft, when you hear what will be replacing The Chrysalis, do let us know," Brookton exclaimed. "I have also heard some news. The Blind Cupid, which changed hands last summer, is about to be sold again."

"It is just as well," Wollstonecraft sniffed. "The new owners let it go to seed. The standards there now are deplorable. What happened to the red-haired madam who ran and owned the place?"

"She married a copper. Keep us informed of any further changes," Brookton replied. "Meanwhile, we will avoid it unless it improves."

"I know of the copper," Gideon interrupted. "Rory Kerrigan, Detective Sergeant. He assisted in Allenby's business last autumn, and I've also had a couple of dealings with him. A good contact to have on the Metropolitan Police."

"Perhaps you would like to take over this group again, Watford?" Brookton said sarcastically.

"Never. Pray continue."

"Has anyone heard from Huxley?" Brookton asked.

Warren Cowley, Viscount Huxley, had been in and out of a sanatorium since last September. In late October, he had attended a farewell dinner for Christian Bamford, the aforementioned Duke of Allenby, former leader of this coterie of clowns. The duke was one of three who had left the group after finding their true love. Brandon and Asher Colborne, Baron Wenlock, made up the other two.

Gideon nearly scoffed aloud at the prospect.

True loves.

Allenby married a bold lady detective. Wenlock married some street waif he had known years before. And Brandon? He married a woman from his wretched past, a lady he originally wanted to take revenge on. It was all too ridiculous for words.

How clever that I stay above such dubious and unfortunate entanglements.

If Gideon married at all, which was highly unlikely since he remained set in his ways, it would be someone above all reproach. Someone safe. Someone Gideon couldn't care less about, one way or the other.

What was the original topic? Right. Huxley.

Gideon looked at Brookton. "I haven't heard a word."

Brookton sliced a line across the page. "Huxley is out."

It may be time Gideon was out. What did these men mean to him? Nothing.

"I would wait on Huxley, allow him to withdraw," Gideon said.

"Very well, we'll keep him on the books for now. Huxley is *not* out." Annoyed, Brookton scribbled furiously.

Yes. Maybe Gideon should have his name stricken from the records. He should start making it known that he was ready to consider marriage. Forty was such a stark number with life more than half over and all that rot.

Perhaps by the summer—which is what he had said last summer. And the summer before and the one before that.

All he knew? Gideon had no heart to give to anyone. If he were honest, the only other feeling he experienced beyond boredom was—Pain.

In his maudlin moments, he called himself The Duke of Pain.

No one knew of his past.

When Brandon revealed his secret past of anguish and hell, Gideon had not revealed anything at all of his.

Well, he hinted, but that would be as far as it would go.

No one would ever breach his heart enough for him to speak of the past.

No one.

Chapter 1

EARLY JUNE 1898
London, England

THE NIGHT WAS A TYPICAL one in the East End of London. Thick, coal-laden fog blanketed the cobblestone streets of Whitechapel. Laughter and raucous merriment poured out of the many pubs lining the narrow lanes and alleyways. A noxious odor of gas and stagnant water filled the air.

As his carriage traveled to a new and exclusive club, Gideon Broyles, Duke of Watford, held a linen handkerchief to his nose. It recently opened on Poplar High Street, called The Velvet Vine and Tackle. Gideon grunted with amusement at the name, for "vine" was a euphemism for lady parts, and "tackle" was a euphemism for male ones.

He had arranged to make a preliminary inspection of the club with the owner/host and later report back to his acquaintances at their meeting place on Albany Street near Regent's Park. If The Velvet Vine and Tackle passed his exacting standards, he would add it to their list of favored carnal haunts. They had quite an exclusive list of varied places to satisfy their myriad preferences.

Sexually active for several years, more than he cared to count, there wasn't much Gideon hadn't experienced. Since his brief tumble with an under-house parlor maid at age sixteen, his sexual escapades increased as time passed.

The monotony was the main reason he had sunk to such dissolute levels. But he hadn't examined the motives all that closely.

When the mood struck him, Gideon played the game, attended assemblies, and occasionally danced with the eligible daughters of the *ton*. None had ever sparked his interest or, more importantly, his lust. In reflection, he wondered if he even felt anything resembling feelings of any kind.

Moving aside the red velvet curtain on his carriage window, Gideon glanced at the alley. A couple of men were copulating with shilling prostitutes against the brick walls. Yawning, he sat back. Anonymous alley sex was not to his taste. That particular predilection had belonged to Asher Colborne, Baron of Wenlock, one in his tight group.

However, the man was disgustingly and happily married, as were two others in their company. There was hardly anyone left in The Rakes of St. Regent's Park. What once was a thriving group of twenty-one now stood at three active members. Four men recently joined as prospects and potential full members, but Gideon was not overly impressed with any of them.

The carriage came to a halt. Gideon clasped his walking stick and waited for his man to unfasten the door. The door opened, and the wrought-iron steps snapped into place. Flicking his long cloak, Gideon slipped into the adjoining alleyway.

His man understood that he was to return in one hour, and Gideon allotted that block of time for the inspection. Once he knocked on the oak door, the small window slid open, and a pair of sinister, blood-shot eyes glared at him in question.

"Password?"

"Lord Craven."

"Welcome."

Gideon inwardly cringed. The password annoyed him. By no stretch of the imagination was he a pusillanimous man. The name referred more to his cravings of a sexual nature. The decadent adventures he pursued had earned him the alias. When he first started his sexual journey, the prostitutes at one of the more famous brothels had said, "Lord, he be cravin' more!"

And that is why he had the name: Lord Craven. Still, the moniker grated. Recognized at various clubs across London, there was no use in changing it now. The window slid shut, and the door opened. The rather brutish doorman stepped aside, and Pan, the host, immediately greeted Gideon.

Rumors abound that Pan was a eunuch. He was well known in these debauched circles, for he had been the manager and host at The Garrison Gate before recently opening his own house of vice.

"My Lord Craven, Ready for your tour?"

Pan was well aware that Gideon was the Duke of Watford. For privacy purposes, Pan would not acknowledge him as such. Besides, having everyone "Your Grace" -ing him annoyed him to the extreme.

"Yes, I am ready. If you please, no names or titles, not even the coded one."

"As you wish. Shall we begin?"

Pan gave him an admiring gaze, taking in his form and formal evening dress. Gideon removed his kid-leather gloves, then his hat. He passed his hat and gloves along with the walking stick to Pan. He decided to keep his cloak on.

Pan momentarily ducked into the coatroom, then rejoined him. The host then led him into a large room across the way. The interior resembled a photographer's studio, with the walls adorned with framed prints showing the attractions available within the brothel. It allowed the customer to compare the goods and services offered before choosing.

"In these pictures are the lovely ladies available for various assignations," Pan said. "Next to that are the few men I have available. All my employees are clean and treated by a physician, and the rule of the house concerning sheaths? They are required for whatever act, included in the price, and are abundantly available throughout the brothel."

Gideon nodded his approval. Using protection was a strict and non-negotiable rule among The Rakes of St. Regent's Park. He'd witnessed the effects on others of various diseases and poxes from indiscriminate sex. He was never without protection.

Rumors flourished in certain circles that the Earl of Oakby had recently succumbed to syphilis. Not an outcome Gideon wished for himself.

The debaucheries were all part of the quest, reaching for the next thrill, and he was willing to try anything to react, a stutter of emotion, a hitch in his heartbeat.

Alas, he remained stymied for years.

He glanced at the photos. The women were generally attractive and posing in provocative undergarments. All different sizes, ages, and races. Quite the varied selection indeed.

"We also offer photographic services for all of your erotic needs. By appointment, of course."

Although fascinated by photography, this type of thrill was not to Gideon's taste, but he would inform Viscount Shinwell, a new prospective group member.

"I believe I will start with the third floor," Gideon answered. Pan sent a layout and general description of the club in advance of his visit.

"A good choice. Our voyeur area is quite popular. Please, follow me."

Pan led him through the narrow, darkened halls. The hiss of gas from the wall sconces intermingled with groans of ecstasy emitting from the many closed doors.

The third floor consisted of small rooms with secret alcoves. The voyeur floor also gave potential customers a clear idea of the offerings at the club. Each door leading into a private niche had a sign. The red side indicated customers occupied the alcove, and the blue meant it was vacant. The first door showed blue. Gideon had received a full accounting of the services and rules of the club before his appointment.

"Do call on me when you are ready to proceed." Pan bowed elegantly and disappeared into the shadows.

Gideon opened the door and slipped in. A small shelf held numerous pieces of flannel and a basket underneath. A porcelain bowl of water sat nearby. Gideon dipped his fingers in, finding it pleasantly warm. He would give The Velvet Vine and Tackle their due; the den of sin was well-equipped, clean, and discreet.

For one's voyeur's pleasures, there were various peepholes. Curious, Gideon peered through one of the highest-situated holes. Two men sat on a padded bench. They were young, well-built, and quite beautiful.

Gideon watched as the two naked men roved their hands over each other. Exploring muscled biceps and tightly packed pectorals, the two young men moaned with desire. This particular activity did not appeal to him personally. But to each his own. Once the men started to kiss, he exited and slipped into the adjacent vacant recess.

He glanced through the peephole and was shocked to see the Duke of Glenholme and his pretty auburn-haired wife. Gideon shook his head in disbelief.

Now he had seen everything.

Of course, dissipation ran rampant through the aristocracy. How many orgies had Gideon attended at various manors and country estates through his early years? Gideon also had a few short-term affairs with the wives of earls and viscounts—with the men's knowledge—since they were usually off pursuing their carnal delights.

This situation was surreal, as he had just attended a ball at the duke's London town house, not one month past, where everything was in strict propriety and decent society. What manner of perversity would the duke and the Duchess perform?

He watched as Glenholme deliberately and reverently disrobed his wife, laying affectionate kisses on her bare shoulders. They removed layers of clothing and tossed them aside. The Duchess was attractive; Gideon had always thought so, and the duke was surprisingly fit.

The couple lay on the wide settee, and Glenholme proceeded to make love to his wife—nothing untoward or sinister in the act. The duke was skilled and thorough, leaving no part of his wife's skin untouched by his hands or lips. The Duchess arched her back in ecstasy as Glenholme's head disappeared between her thighs. The scene riveted Gideon.

The couple's deviant thrill was performing for an audience. Gideon never guessed it of the very proper duke and his Duchess. Weren't they concerned about the gossip? Though there was an unspoken rule of privacy to some degree. The aristos had a pact of not revealing each other's secrets, although they managed to slip out in certain circles.

How strange.

Gideon had never performed oral sex on a woman. He never saw to their needs, touching, embracing, and kissing. Far too intimate and negated his own pleasure. He did not make love.

To him, it was fucking. Nothing else.

I am a selfish bastard.

The Duchess cried out, her head back, her long reddish-brown hair touching the wood floor. The duke then proceeded to make a meal out of her breasts. A low, simmering flame grew and slowly spread through Gideon. This scene was exquisitely erotic and damned desirable to observe.

There was no frantic rutting. The duke made passionate love to his Duchess. The look on the duke's face, as he thrust deeply, was akin to awe and what Gideon supposed could be love. He felt ashamed for observing such an intimate act. Stepping away from the wall, he felt heat flushing his cheeks.

Good God, an emotional response.

Not just arousal, for he experienced that as well, but a rush of emotions he could not name. A sense of loss that perhaps he was missing out on something quite profound.

What utter bollocks.

Gideon exited the small room and stepped into the next alcove. His hand shook as he reached for the door handle. Taking a deep breath and exhaling, he walked in.

The stark contrast between the tender lovemaking he had observed to this torture chamber scene was hard to fathom.

Sir Anthony Tollingham, Knight of the Realm and a respected judge at Chancery, was completely naked and restrained by chains hanging from the ceiling. His arms elevated slightly; the older man glanced toward the door. Mixed with his look of trepidation was also expectation—the man no doubt waited to be birched or flogged.

The door swung open, and a woman strode confidently into the room.

Gideon's breath caught in his throat.

She was exquisite.

Her golden-honey hair hung in thick waves down her back. Lush and shapely, she wore a black lace bodice with knee-high boots a pirate might wear. Along with black leather gloves, she held a riding crop, which she tapped absently in her palm as she walked around the judge as a lion would stalk its prey. Her light blue eyes were hard and cold. The look on her beautiful face was furious and determined, and Gideon simultaneously felt the blood rush to his head and cock.

"Do you wish me to commence?" she asked the judge in a tone she might use to ask him if he wanted sugar in his tea.

The judge closed his eyes and smiled. "Oh, yes, please."

"Yes, please—what?"

"Yes, please, Mistress Birch."

Gideon choked back a snort of derision. These types of games were fascinating to him, and he indulged a few times to be sure. Gideon had once used a cat-o-nine-tails but hardly made a mark on anyone. He just reveled in the role of master in complete control.

Come to think of it; he was authoritarian in all his salacious sex play. Could he submit to this beautiful woman and her riding crop?

Not bloody likely.

An almighty thwack filled the air as Mistress Birch laid the riding crop across the judge's back. The man howled, but the cry ended in joyous laughter. She slid the crop along the man's back, and he moaned in ecstasy.

"One more, where do you want it? Chest? Back? Your buttocks?" she demanded.

He had seen enough. Gideon stepped into the hall, buttoning his long coat to hide his stiff-as-a-pike cock.

Pan bowed slightly. "Did it meet your expectations?"

"Depends. Just how depraved is this place?"

Pan's long lashes fluttered coquettishly. "The light birching is as far as we go. No violent acts result in bloodletting or worse. We also do not deal in the abhorrent acquisition of virgins. No children. All here, male or female, are aged eighteen or higher and have specific duties. My employees, when treated with respect, will act in kind. They also are clean, inside and out. As I stated previously, I have a physician on retainer."

"Orgies?"

"I can arrange for private groups that I approve of."

Gideon nodded. "I will return later with a few of my select friends, and I will ensure that they follow your rules to the letter."

"Do you wish to know the price?" Pan asked.

"Price? It is no object, and you will find that my friends and I are generous if satisfied."

"Forgive me, but I asked about your group, The Rakes of Regent's Park. I received a most favored recommendation. I hope I have not offended you with the *non de plume* you have in these circles."

"No, I am not offended. I'll send word when we are ready to make an appointment."

After heading downstairs, Gideon collected his hat, gloves, and stick. About to depart, he hesitated and turned to face Pan.

"I want—her."

"Mistress Olivia? With the riding crop, you mean?" Pan asked innocently.

"Yes. Make the mistress available tomorrow night. For me alone."

Pan bowed. "I will do what I can to arrange it. Where shall I send word of the appointment?"

Gideon reached into his pocket and gave Pan his card. "Send the information there."

"Good evening."

Satisfied, Gideon exited the building. There was his carriage waiting on time as usual.

He tried to think of anything else but was still hard as oak. Gideon's thoughts were filled with Mistress Birch—Olivia.

Gideon had never experienced such a swift reaction to a woman, one so vivid it caused his heart to stutter in his chest. It was beyond her beauty; it was the look in her eyes, as they were as lifeless and cold as his own.

What possessed him to request her?

Guess he would soon find out.

Chapter 2

OLIVIA DURHAM STEPPED out the side door into the private passageway. With the riding crop tucked under her arm, she peeled off the leather gloves and handed them to Pan, who stood nearby.

"The judge is unconscious and needs attending to," she said without emotion.

Pan's eyebrows rose. "My dear Olivia, did you again beat him into submission?"

"The old reprobate wished for me to flay his skin. His request was tempting. However, the mere threat was enough to send him into a swoon. As usual. I'm going to my room to rest."

Pan reached out and laid a hand on her arm. The contact made her cringe.

"Lord Craven has made a request specifically for you tomorrow night. I believe the gold room will suffice for the assignation."

Lord Craven?

She knew he was a duke. Olivia had heard the idle gossip, for he was known far and wide in the trade. "Oh Lord, how he craves!" the women had tittered. The ladies also claimed he was tall, imposing, dark, and dangerous. His glare could cause ice to form around one's extremities. Of course, the same could describe herself—the ice part, at least.

Olivia frowned. She had also heard he was a beast in bed, not that she planned to fornicate with the depraved duke. None of her encounters had anything to do with sexual gratification. Not for her, at any rate.

"He will pay a great deal of money to be in your company," Pan urged.

"From what I hear, Lord Craven does not strike me as the type to surrender to anything."

"Agreed. The duke observed you with the judge, so he knows what you offer. I am surprised he would subject himself to a submissive position, but there it is."

"His real name?" Olivia asked.

"Gideon Broyles, the Duke of Watford. You might have heard of his stepfather, Sanford Ellingford, the Duke of Whinstone. His reputation eclipses his stepson's. Cruel bastard. I won't have him here."

Olivia was secretly grateful Pan ensured a safe environment for his workers; she had been with him for years at other establishments.

"I haven't heard of Whinstone, but then I don't pay close attention to most of the gossip. I find dukes too superior to deal with, and I'm not interested."

Olivia turned to head to her room, but Pan reached for her arm again, then pulled back as if remembering she loathed to be touched. It was not so much that she abhorred physical contact; she would just *prefer* no contact.

"All the safeguards will be in place. The room is private, but the hidden bells are in working order should you require assistance. Colin will be down the hall in case you need him."

Olivia exhaled. "A lot of money, you say?"

"Yes, your share will be quite substantial, I assure you. More than you made all of last month."

The offer was too good to pass up. Olivia needed and wanted the money. Poverty and the ever-lurking specter of living in the streets caused her to consider the arrangement.

Why not, indeed?

"I will agree to a thirty-minute block. No more."

Pan handed her the gloves, then bowed slightly. "As you wish, my dear."

Olivia took the back stairs to the enclosed walkway linked to the house directly behind The Velvet Vine and Tackle. This space was exclusive to the sex workers as they had their own private rooms. Pan ensured the area was neat, clean, and entirely livable and insisted that the staff keep it that way. Her room was her home, and she had nowhere else to go.

Once Olivia entered, she turned the gas on the wall sconce, and with a decided hiss and pop, luminance filled the space. Pan had electric lights installed in the brothel's main entranceway and parlor, but the rest of the establishment, including the living quarters, still had gas illumination.

Her room was cozy, consisting of a single bed with warm blankets and feather pillows. In the other corner stood a plush chair that she used for reading. Further along, was a small fireplace for warmth and heating water for a cup of tea when the mood struck.

Olivia removed her clothes and slipped on her flannel nightdress. She then pulled open the top drawer of the bureau.

What to wear for Lord Craven? Something to titillate but nothing more. Olivia held a sheer coral peignoir with a matching coral and gold corset. Might as well give the duke his money's worth, for he would be looking and nothing else.

As Olivia did her ablutions, she pondered her fate and what led her to the life she led. If Pan hadn't found her that night—she shuddered. Pan had become her dear friend and confidant. His real name was James Sidle, and contrary to tittle-tattle, he was not a eunuch. He played up his role around customers.

James had confided to her one night over a bottle of port that his gate swung both ways, as he put it. "In this cold world, it behooves one to discover warmth and affection where one can find it," he explained.

The observation made sense to Olivia, even though she never would find warmth and affection with anyone, regardless of gender.

James was a hopeless romantic who found a profit in the vices of others. There was more to his past, but that applied to all working and living at The Velvet Vine and Tackle.

James knew some of her past; he was the only one she had confided. Her long-term plan consisted of making enough money to live quietly in an isolated cottage far north or south of London.

It would take a few years to have enough money, but she planned to live frugally, planting herbs and vegetables in a garden and sewing or baking on the side for the extra coin.

As long she was alone—and left alone.

After lighting the fire, Olivia curled up in the chair and wrapped a blanket around her shoulders. At thirty-two years of age, there was no reason not to achieve her goal in five years. Then Olivia could have that quiet and solitary life that she hungered for.

If it meant servicing a decadent duke, all the better.

Money is all that matters.

"YOUR GRACE, YOUR MOTHER awaits you in the parlor. Her Grace is alone."

Gideon handed his cloak to Hobson, his butler. "We are not to be disturbed."

"Of course, Your Grace. I have brought a tea tray already."

Gideon stood before the parlor door, trying to regulate his breathing. Why had she come here this morning? They were not close, and Gideon held a vast amount of resentment toward her for her marriage to Whinstone—and more.

Swinging open the double doors, he strode into the room, not bothering to take his mother's hand or give a perfunctory kiss on her wrinkled cheek.

"Why are you here, Mother?" he asked in a dull tone as he sat opposite.

"Not even going to ask how I am?"

"No, not even."

"Still the cold and implacable automaton, I see," she murmured as she sipped her tea.

"You had a hand in making me this way."

His mother visibly winced. "Hasn't this gone on long enough? How long do you plan to hate me? And your father?"

"Whinstone is *not* my father; how often must I say it? Stop referring to him as such. Why do you bother? You're not even living with the wretched man. Speaking of which, I want him gone from Foxmont. It is the Watford country seat, not Whinstone's. Which means it is mine to do with as I please."

"You know Sanford has no country seat; his dukedom was and is in poor straits. There is no entailed property and hardly any money," she sniffed scornfully. "Besides, you spend all your time in London chasing one debauchery after another. Someone should live at the place."

Hardly any money—that was an understatement. It was why Whinstone had latched on to the older widow—his mother—the previous Duchess of Watford. The Whinstone dukedom had entailed property at one time. But the House of Lords had taken the estate many years ago for reasons Gideon had no idea. Why take the property and not the title? And how was that even legal? It must be a juicy tale, but he didn't care to know the details.

At age ten, Gideon became the Duke of Watford. The duke's untimely death had changed Gideon's life forever, and not for the better. In the will, beyond what Gideon inherited, the late duke had settled a good amount of money on his widow. Again, one of the main reasons Whinstone had latched on to his mother.

It had been a shocking turn of events within the family and society. But none so startling as finding his mother had remarried a mere five months later, creating quite the scandal. The then thirty-eight-year-old duchess married the ten years younger Whinstone.

Yes, it had been quite the disgrace and still tittered about in certain circles.

"He has enough ready coin to rent somewhere else, considering you are still financing his lifestyle. Whinstone has taken advantage for too long, and I will no longer allow him to stay there rent-free. It is bad enough I've paid his gambling debts through the years. Tell him to be gone in ten days," Gideon stated, his voice firm.

His mother shook her head. "No. You must do it yourself if you want Sanford to vacate the premises, as I am through acting as a mediator between you."

Gideon laughed bitterly. "You never acted as a mediator. You always took his side."

"He was my husband. I had no choice," she said matter-of-factly, reaching for a raspberry tart.

"When has he ever been a husband to you? You've been living separate lives for years," Gideon snapped.

His mother's eyes welled with tears.

Oh, God, not again.

The duchess used tears as an effective weapon, and because of it, it had ceased impacting him.

"I still love him," she whispered. "I am in misery; you don't know what I suffer."

Gideon had a rough inkling. When home from school, he had witnessed the overwrought drama. His mother's querulous begging, Whinstone rebuffing her advances. The noisy but sporadic times they did have sex were enough to scar Gideon for two lifetimes.

But it wasn't only his mother and Whinstone's twisted relationship; it was Whinstone himself. Considering Gideon was well into middle age, why did the miserable bastard still affect him, causing him to feel like a helpless boy?

Gideon shook the horrible reminisces from his mind. "Mother, why are you here? You obviously want something. Why else would you deem to visit?"

The duchess made a show of dabbing the corner of her eyes with her silk handkerchief. "You are still a cruel boy. Can't a mother wish to see her only child?"

Gideon stood. "Get to the point, or I am leaving."

"Very well. Please, sit. Sanford needs money. No, it is not a gambling debt. A woman has stated she is with child. Sanford says it is his as she is his mistress and has been with him exclusively."

"I thought you said you were in agony over your love for Whinstone? You speak of his mistress and supposed by-blow without any drama. For once."

"What am I to do about it? Men have mistresses, and it is the way of things. Your father had one," his mother replied.

"I don't doubt it," Gideon murmured under his breath.

"Speak up. I cannot hear you," the duchess admonished.

Gideon sat and shook his head. "I will not support one of his bastards."

"He wants to recognize the child, at least, as far as society and the law allow. Granted, I know that isn't much, but I feel I owe him since I couldn't give him a child. I lost my babies." The duchess sniffled and dabbed her eyes once again.

His mother had two miscarriages in the first few years of her second marriage, and it was the cause of the final break between her and Whinstone.

"You mean he wants to recognize *this* particular child? What about the others? There are rumors of more. Between him and the Duke of

Chellenham, illegitimate children must be scattered everywhere in the city and beyond."

Gideon was affluent enough but not excessively so. To keep Whinstone, mistress, and child in comfort? It turned his bile to do so only because he loathed the man.

"Perhaps I can make an arrangement," Gideon murmured as his mind crafted a cunning plan. This scheme would be one way to extricate Whinstone from Foxmont permanently. "If I proceed with this undertaking, Mother, you must give up your house rental, as I cannot afford to keep numerous households."

His mother gasped. "Where am I to go? Not here, with you."

"God forbid," Gideon stated drolly. "Stay with your sister, or after Whinstone vacates Foxmont, you may stay there in the east wing, well out of my sight."

The duchess jutted out her chin and pursed her lips. "I hate Foxmont; you know that. The country? I cannot abide that sort of dull life. All my friends are here."

"Stay with one of your many friends if Aunt Mirella will not have you. Aunt is a widow and all alone in that huge town house. Uncle left her a nice nest egg. I will set you up with an allowance and pay a yearly stipend to Aunt for your upkeep. Granted, you will have to tighten the belt, as it were—"

"How dare you," his mother interrupted, her eyes narrowing in annoyance. "I am a duchess."

"Then have your duke husband pay your bills. Oh, wait. He cannot as he is as poor as a church mouse." Gideon sat forward. "You listen to me. It is my price. Do you wish for me to consider doing Whinstone this favor? A man I loathe with every fiber of my being? A man who beat me on a near-daily basis while you stood nearby doing nothing? I have the scars to prove the abuse, inside and out. How dare *you* come here and make such a request. Have you no shame, madam?"

"But Mirella lives in Lambeth," his mother whined.

How typical that his mother did not even acknowledge what he had said about the beatings. She always looked the other way. When had she ever cared about him? Why would she change now?

"There are sections of Lambeth that are respectable enough; get used to it."

"You are so harsh and unyielding; no wonder no woman will have you, no wonder—"

"Is there a time that you ever loved me, Mother?" Gideon interrupted. "Because I cannot recall one kind word or show of affection, even before Father died."

"Oh, poor you," his mother spat venomously.

Gideon stood. "This conversation is at an end. You have forty-eight hours to give me your decision. Send a message to my steward, Mr. Chapman. And a word of advice, you do not wish to anger me because I will stop the rental payment on your accommodations, regardless." He bowed stiffly. "Good day, Your Grace."

Annoyed beyond belief, Gideon strode from the room, his fists clenched. His insides were knots, as always when dealing with his mother. He cursed himself for mentioning the loving detail.

With such a blackened heart, he was not supposed to care—about anything.

Revealing that vulnerability would be a mistake he would never make again.

Chapter 3

GIDEON PACED THE ROOM for the twentieth time, a brandy snifter in his hand. The Gold Room—he could understand the reference. From the gold brocade curtains and matching silk bed linens to the fleur-de-lis gold wallpaper, the room was plush and Georgian in its decor.

He had barely any sleep last night in anticipation of this meeting. The thought of being with this Olivia had him as hard as stone, and the arousal was damned uncomfortable. He had never experienced such a swift reaction to any woman in all these years. The fact he still felt desire at his advancing age was a relief. Not just lust but an actual physical yearning.

Quite astounding, really.

Olivia's cold, implacable gaze countered with the soft, feminine body intrigued him. Gideon wasn't exactly sure how to approach this situation.

Submit, or demand that she submit to him?

He downed the rest of his drink and placed the snifter on the table. If he were smart, he would not pursue this unknown attraction. But he was drawn to it like a moth to a flame. Gideon had to know more. Frustrated and warm, he tore off his coat and waistcoat, pulling his cravat from his neck. He unbuttoned his shirt to his waist, reached for one of the towels, and wiped the perspiration from his torso.

Get control.

But how could he?

He was hot, bothered, aroused, and pacing like a restless lion kept in a cage. The conversation with his mother yesterday also was the cause of the uneasiness. But the last place he wished to think of his mother was at a brothel. Gideon would deal with that particular drama later.

The door opened, and he whirled about to find Damon Cranston, Marquess of Brookton, standing before him.

Brookton chuckled. "I'm in the wrong room."

"What are you doing here? I said that I would be the one to inspect and test this club," Gideon barked irritably.

Brookton leaned against the doorjamb, crossing his arms. "Made yourself at home, I see. Are we awaiting someone? Male or female? Or both? Maybe I could stay. It's been a while since we indulged together."

It had been years ago and not an experience Gideon wished to repeat. While involved in a few ménages in years past, he found that he didn't like to share. It was also the reason Gideon no longer participated in orgies. However, he inquired about them for the other members, specifically Brookton. Gideon was about to push Brookton into the hall when he heard the door open on the opposite side of the room.

Brookton stood up straight, and his look turned heated. "Well, I am even more inclined to stay now. Good evening, my dear," Brookton purred. He moved toward Olivia, but Gideon halted him, placing his hand on Brookton's shoulder.

"Mistress, will you give us a moment?"

Gideon had his back to her, his gaze firm on Brookton, who looked bemused by the situation.

"Yes, of course," she replied. The door closed softly.

"Mistress? I saw the riding crop in her hand. Of course, this is your preference, isn't it? Perhaps I will return another night and request her. She's coldly beautiful, just my type, and yours, I imagine. All that golden hair—"

Gideon grabbed a fistful of Brookton's coat. "Stay away from her. She is mine." In speaking the words, Gideon had shocked himself.

"Get your fucking hands off me," Brookton hissed through clenched teeth.

Further stunned at his emotional response to Brookton's interest in Olivia, Gideon released Brookton and stepped away. "Get out."

Brookton smoothed his collar. "We will be discussing this."

He shoved the marquess into the hall and slammed the door. "But not tonight."

Once he heard Brookton's retreating footfalls, Gideon headed to the sidebar and poured a whiskey. He had lost all restraint, and it unnerved him.

Best to gain control and do it now. What possessed Gideon to act in such a predatory manner?

With an exhale, he lay on the bed. "You can come in," he called out.

OLIVIA OPENED THE DOOR to the gold room and locked the door behind her. Slipping the key into the side pocket, she removed her gold cloak and laid it across the nearby chair. She turned, and the sight of Lord Craven made her gasp softly.

The duke lay on his side, propped on one elbow, a tumbler of whiskey in his hand. The duke had removed his coat and waistcoat and unbuttoned his white shirt to his waist. A muscled chest with black hair and a flat stomach was evident. Long, graceful legs stretched past the end of the bed, and his feet were bare and elegantly shaped.

This man was, in a word—splendid.

A lock of his dark hair hung over his forehead in a carefree manner. Thick black brows only enhanced the obsidian shade of his eyes. Judging by the few threads of gray at his temples and the fine lines fanning out from his eyes, he was not young. The duke was handsome, with a sturdy, well-shaped jaw and sharp, high cheekbones. Though his nose had a long, tapered point, it suited his looks.

The man's eyes narrowed as he looked her over quite thoroughly. His gaze met hers, and a frisson of heat trickled down her spine. The face, beautiful in its masculinity, showed no warmth at all.

Olivia did not look away. The duke's intelligent and frosty gaze did not intimidate her. She tapped the crop against her white leather-gloved palm.

Lord Craven sat the glass on the table, swung his long legs over the side, and stood. Tall and athletically built—but of course, he was. Broad shoulders tapered to narrow, muscular hips.

How remarkable to discover he appealed as no man ever had. Olivia tamped down the spark of attraction. Merely the twitching of a corpse, she reasoned.

It had to be.

"Mistress Birch, I presume?" His voice was deep but raspy.

"Yes. And how shall I address you?"

"Gideon Broyles, the Duke of Watford, at your service. I cannot abide the Lord Craven sobriquet." He bowed slightly.

"I rarely take on appointments at short notice, Your Grace."

"I am honored, then." He swept his arm toward the nearby chair. "Shall we discuss terms?"

Taking a seat, Olivia watched as he sat opposite on the edge of the bed. Clearing his throat, the duke crossed his long legs and gave his complete attention.

"What terms do you mean, Your Grace?" she asked. "I am sure Pan informed you that I allow a maximum of three strikes. How hard and deep I wield the crop is up to you. There is no bloodletting. As he no doubt told you, you will not touch me, nor will any sexual congress pass between us."

His eyebrows arched in question. "Indeed? Is that why your photograph was not on display with the others? Fascinating. It seems to me I paid out a vast amount of coin for the privilege of being whipped like a naughty schoolboy. I have another proposal in mind."

Olivia could tell by the determined set of his jaw the duke was used to getting his way. His onyx eyes glittered with interest.

"Pray tell me what manner of perversion you require. I have heard of your reputation, Your Grace."

A deep laugh rumbled in his chest. "I can well imagine. Let us disperse with 'Your Gracing' as well. My name is Gideon. I want you to use it. Do you agree?"

"As *you* said, you are paying a good deal of coin. So yes, I agree."

"This is not my chosen form of pleasure, submitting in this setting. Agreeing to this was the only way to see and talk to you. If I must endure a flogging, so be it. I propose this: You will give me something in return for each strike. But not all on the same night."

This man was beyond arrogant. She heard that he reveled in being in control. Be damned if she would let him wrestle power away from her in this situation.

"Explain what you mean, Your Grace."

"Gideon, please. I want to visit you for consecutive nights. One strike each night."

Olivia crossed her arms. "I do not make those types of arrangements. This club is not the marketplace at Bethnal Green, where we will haggle over the price of fresh fish or a loaf of bread. Take the offer, or I am leaving."

He smiled a predatory grin of a crafty fox.

"Why do you flog men?" the duke asked. "If you do not allow anyone to touch you or engage in rutting, then sexual gratification for yourself is not the goal. Do you seek to punish them—or all men in general?"

His clever observation hit too close to the mark. Olivia struggled to hide her reaction but knew she had revealed her conflicting emotions. This dark duke threatened her shielded reserve. She remained silent.

"Come. Think of the contentment you will derive in bringing such a supercilious man to his knees. You will be the first to make me surrender," he crooned, his deep voice causing sparks to ignite along her spine.

She cocked her head as if studying him. "I have brought many such men to their knees. That is hardly an inducement."

Gideon strode toward his coat, pulled out a velvet pouch, and dropped it on the bed.

Yes, she was thinking of him as Gideon. *That* was not wise.

"Then perhaps more money will convince you. There are thirty gold sovereigns in the sack. All yours, no splitting with Pan. A side exchange only between us. I propose sharing: for every strike of your crop, you will allow me to touch and kiss you. We will also share something of our lives. Imagine neither of us in control, neither of us submitting. We will both give and take."

What on earth was this nonsense?

"You cannot be serious. I'm not interested in such games. I do not make multiple appointments with the same client over consecutive nights. It is *not* how I do business." Olivia frowned and met his intense gaze. "You *are* aware this is a business exchange? Share? Give and take? This appointment is not an affair of the heart."

Oliva's gaze slid toward and locked on the bag of gold sovereigns. The temptation of it swayed her thoughts. For a woman who remained reserved and collected, a wide range of conflicting emotions coursed through her. Doubt, confusion, and wariness, to name a few. Such emotive games were beyond her knowledge.

"Of course, this is business," the duke sniffed. "The heart does not even factor into this, as mine had been blackened years past. If I were to guess, so has yours. We have nothing to fear in that regard. As for the touching, does it make you nauseous, or is it a personal preference here in this room?"

"It is a personal preference."

He took a couple of steps closer. "Say my name, Olivia. I want to hear it upon your lips." He gently took her gloved hand.

Olivia struggled to pull her hand away. The duke laid a polite kiss across her knuckles before releasing it.

"I didn't say you could touch me now," she snapped. "And I did not give you leave to use my name."

"My apologies," the duke murmured.

In truth, Olivia felt rattled. Heat traveled through her at his nearness. When the duke took her hand, she was not sickened at the contact. Not at all. How disturbing, yet exciting.

Gideon exhaled and tsked. "Nevertheless, that is not part of the agreement I have put before you. I will touch you, and I will use your name. Are we agreed, then?"

"You ask too much."

"I ask for trust."

Olivia's laugh sounded bitter to her own ears. "I trust no man. I never will."

Gideon took another step forward. "Why not? The men who submit place their trust in you."

Her mouth quirked cynically. "Those sexually corrupt men are not putting their trust in me. They are putting their *lust*. It is what all men feel, at any rate. Present company included."

"I cannot argue that fact, and I suppose I am one of that large group of sexually corrupt men. Regardless, the deal is before you. Take it or leave it. Tell me now."

The top of her head barely grazed his collarbone. Olivia had not stood this close to a man in years. His assessing and heated gaze had her heart slamming against her ribcage. Not a reaction she thought she would ever experience.

Perhaps it was a warning that this could be the one man to slip behind her barriers.

How laughable. *But the money.*

Taking his coin would place her goal of retiring even more within reach. Besides, when had any sex worker ever become seriously involved with the upper crust? Well, there was one example. The story had traveled to all parts of London. About seventeen years ago, in late '81, the madam and owner of the brothel, the Starling Club, was hired as a birthday present for an eccentric hermit professor, the third son of a duke. Beyond all imagining, they fell in love and eventually married.

Olivia had scoffed at such an outlandish fairy tale, but James confirmed the story was indeed true. Philomena McGrattan and her Lord Spencer Hornsby husband lived happily ever after on a semi-isolated estate with children and wolfhounds.

Regardless, such a rare occurrence was not likely to happen again, not that Olivia wanted it.

Olivia met his gaze. "You are unhappy," she whispered. Did she speak that aloud?

"As are you. Perhaps we are fated to end such a state together."

Olivia stepped back and keenly felt the loss of his closeness. The money was too good to pass up. But a tiny part of her was also curious about where this would go. If anywhere.

Such a bizarre request: give and take. Was Olivia exposing her past for this duke's twisted entertainment? Well, Olivia would make damned sure that he revealed his past as well. What caused the shield of ice to form around him?

Yes, she was undoubtedly curious—and attracted to this duke.

"I agree to three strikes on three consecutive nights. Give and take. I will allow certain touches and kisses, but no actual sex. You have a deal—Gideon."

He moaned. "Repeat my name,"

She gave him a puzzled look. "Gideon."

"Very well, Olivia. We have a deal. Should I remove all my clothes?"

She ran her crop over his exposed nipples, and he shuddered. "There is no need unless you would rather have the strike across your bare buttocks."

"I think not. However, feel free to birch me good and proper across the back. Do not draw blood."

"I never do. Grab the bedpost and hold on."

He removed his shirt and tossed it onto the bed. Gideon clasped the bedpost as she had commanded.

The crop flicked across his back, and the slight sting caused air to hiss through his clenched teeth.

"Jesus!"

Chapter 4

OLIVIA OBSERVED THE play of muscles as he flinched from the impact of her crop. A red welt rose on his flawless skin. It would be a sin to bloody such masculine perfection, not that she ever would. She had learned just how much of a flick of the wrist to apply to avoid permanent injury.

As it always had, a tight ball of satisfaction pulled at her insides from the strike.

"Aren't you supposed to speak soft words of encouragement to me?" Gideon said. "It is what I've observed with others in this situation."

"I do not play that particular game."

Olivia laid the crop on the bed as Gideon turned to face her. His dark eyes were ablaze.

"Then I was right. You do this for vengeance. Give and take, Olivia. Tell me what happened to you."

She should have never agreed to this. Did she want the money so desperately that she would sell her soul and reveal her darkest secrets?

Yes, it appeared so.

Olivia could fabricate a fiction; how would the duke know the difference? It would be easy to spin a woeful tale if that was what he wanted to hear. Perhaps he gained excitement from other people's tragedies. But there was something about this man beyond the handsome face and athletic body. She recognized and felt his deep-boned unhappiness.

This man fascinated her. And because of it, she would be as truthful as possible. To a point.

"Perhaps you should go first. You are trembling, and it is not from arousal. At least, not completely," Olivia mused.

"How astute of you. But I would prefer that you begin."

Well, he *was* paying for this. "How can we know if the other is even telling the truth? Is this just another game for you? Men become aroused at all sorts of odd things."

"I think we will know if the other tells the truth. I intend to. And no, this is not a game. I cannot explain why I made the request, only that I want to know you better. Don't ask me why. I have no rational answer to give." His voice was low and intimate, and she could hear the sincerity in his words.

"Fair enough. I cannot explain why I am allowing this beyond the money. I also will tell the truth." And she meant it.

With a jagged sigh, she sat on the edge of the bed. Gideon stood, facing her, and leaned against the bedpost. He cringed in pain. She may have wielded the crop too deftly, or her trembling comment hit close to home.

Olivia would get to the bottom of it. But first, to gather her courage for the narrative ahead. Taking a shuddering breath, she exhaled. "Twelve years ago, I came with my father to London. I was barely twenty. I lived in Hertfordshire with cows as neighbors. To say I wished for adventure was an understatement. Against my father's warnings, I ventured out onto the streets alone, curious to take in all the sights and sounds, and two men cornered me."

"Damn it all," Gideon murmured. "I can well imagine what occurred next. How horrible."

"Yes, horrible. Those drunken men dragged me into an alley, leaving me beaten and bleeding. When I managed to make my way to the inn, my father slapped me, called me a harlot, and locked me in my room."

"Damn the man," Gideon snarled.

"The next morning, I awoke and found myself alone. My father had left me nothing but a letter saying that I was not to come home."

"My God. He left you with no money, alone in a strange city?"

"He left me with nothing. The letter stated that I was no longer his daughter. Not that I was in daughter in truth."

"What do you mean?"

"The previous night, after he slapped me, he informed me that I was not his. That my birth mother, alone and starving, wound up at a convent. The kindly nuns took her in; tried to nurse her back to health, but to no avail. After I was born, she died."

"Do you believe this story?"

"At first, no. I thought my father made it up to punish me, to make me feel worse. But he claims he and his wife took me in and raised me. I don't remember his wife, my supposed mother; she died when I was four. However, two years ago, I contacted the nunnery. I traveled north of London to see them. A couple of the sisters remembered a young woman who had given birth to a baby girl with golden hair at that particular time. The story fit, so it must be true."

"Did you ever try to go home?" Gideon asked, clearly caught up in her story.

She had never told anyone outside of James. And not even he knew all the facts.

"My father is a very pious man, a vicar. He would never forgive me. I knew it deep in my bones. I will not return to him, ever." Olivia met his gaze. "Is that enough for you? Is my tale tragic enough to satisfy your curiosity? Are you not entertained?"

"What I am is sorry for your tragic past. As I told you, I do not revel in the misfortunes of others. And what of your real father?"

"The nuns gave me the name of a man. It was one my mother had repeated over and over. She had begged the nuns to take me to this man, that he would see me well looked after. But the nuns remained dubious, for society knew this man's reputation across London and beyond. He is a peer, a reckless and cruel one. The nuns believed he would never acknowledge me or see to my care. Eventually, they contacted him and made arrangements with the vicar and his wife."

Gideon's eyes widened. "My God. A peer? Who?"

The revelation lightened her burden somewhat. Why she could not be sure. Is confession good for the soul? What poppycock. But she would only go so far with this.

Olivia shook her head. "I will never reveal it."

OLIVIA'S REFUSAL TO be touched spoke of her utter disgust with the male species. The look on her face when she struck the judge with her crop, would be forever etched in his mind. To be attacked and abandoned, he could not imagine.

Satisfaction and vengeance.

The depth of her emotions made her all the more mesmerizing. Yes, she wore a frosty outer layer similar to his own, but underneath?

Damn it all.

Gideon wanted to dole out retribution on her behalf to all who had harmed her. Without knowing it, he clenched his fists. Exhaling, he tried to calm his anger.

Gideon sat on the bed next to her. "Answer me this, is it the Duke of Whinstone?"

"No. And that is all I will reveal on that matter."

There's a mercy.

A reckless and cruel peer? That could be at least half a dozen that Gideon knew of, maybe more.

"I ask because the reprobate is my stepfather, be thankful you have no blood ties. And you never tried to approach the peer who had sired you in all those years?"

She shook her head. "I have never contacted the man, and I never will. My pride will not allow it. Besides, I don't want to know him and want nothing from him."

"I'll change the subject; how long have you been with Pan?"

"More years than I care to count. I take on a couple of clients a week and assist Pan in running this club. I am very good with mathematical figures." Her luscious mouth drew into a taut line. "That is enough questions."

"For tonight," he interjected.

She sighed. "I am sorry I agreed to this. Yes, for tonight."

He turned to face her; his hands framed her face. Gideon gently stroked her cheeks with the pads of his thumbs. Heat and flame spread through him, causing his heart to stutter. At least she didn't pull away.

"Have you ever been kissed?" he asked softly.

"Do not mock me," Olivia admonished.

"Look at me."

He didn't hide behind one of his many masks of indifference for once. He showed as much gentle empathy as he could muster.

"Gideon," she whispered as her gaze met his.

His name on her sensual lips caused his prick to pulse in time with his rapid heartbeat.

Gideon leaned toward her. His lips brushed past hers in a fleeting movement. With tender compassion, he showed her how a kiss could sear one's soul. Or at least, he imagined it so. His tongue teased the corner of her mouth, so she let him in.

Trust: a new concept. Perhaps for us both.

His probing tongue tasted every part of her mouth, but he was not aggressive. Olivia soon followed his motions, and when Gideon groaned, a flicker of flame ignited deep inside his darkened heart. He pulled back and stared at her with amazement. His thumbs brushed her swollen, well-kissed lips.

"Shall I confess?" he murmured. "I have only kissed a woman a few times in my life. Never had it felt so—real."

What possessed him to say that? The cynical part of him dismissed it immediately. But deep down, he couldn't deny the impact of the kiss and how it made something shift inside him.

"Lord Craven? Hardly kissed? That cannot be right," Olivia said, her voice low. "Do not lie."

Gideon continued to stroke her plump, sensitive lips. "I am *not* lying. My many encounters resulted in my gratification, no one else's. Kissing seemed too intimate, and it appears I have missed out on an incredible occurrence."

Speaking this truth opened the gate to many complex emotions—ones Gideon never wanted to examine or experience. But they were rushing out of their hidden compartment now.

Olivia glared at him questioningly. "And why have you pursued these many encounters?"

Gideon stood, stepped toward the fireplace, and absently stirred the embers with the poker.

"I no doubt came out of the womb bored. Tedium drives my desires. I am a spoiled and pampered son of the aristocracy who was never told no in the entirety of his life."

"There is more to your story, surely," Olivia scoffed.

"Perhaps you are correct. This was a mistake."

"Turn and look at me. You wanted the truth, and now you must reciprocate. You are wealthy and titled and never wanted for anything in your life. As you said, no one ever said no—at least not by women. What about your parents? Your stepfather?"

Anger and disgust moved through him at the mention of his stepfather. He placed the poker back in the stand.

"You called Whinstone a reprobate, but he was much more than that, wasn't he?" Olivia stated. "I can see how you hate him by the expression on your face."

Again, he hid nothing, another disturbing revelation. That fact that she had so deftly skewered his weakness had him thinking he should walk away. He remained silent.

"Deciding just how much to reveal?" Olivia said sardonically. "Or if you should reveal anything at all. Give and take, you said."

She threw his words back at him.

"You didn't tell me everything," he accused.

"No. But I told you more than I have told anyone, save one other person."

"Pan?" A sudden and swift stab of envy caught him under the ribs that she should share any type of intimacy with another man.

"Yes, he is my protector as well as my good friend."

"But nothing more?"

"No. Your stepfather?"

"I became a duke at the age of ten with my father's sudden death. I assume he knew he was ill, for his will and estates were all in order. My father left my mother a hefty inheritance. That is when Whinstone entered the picture. At twenty-eight and ten years younger than my mother, he used his good looks and faux sympathetic ways to wheedle his way into her heart. They were married a mere five months after my father's death."

"Faux?"

Gideon sat next to her on the bed once again. "Yes. Once he was firmly ensconced in the house with my pathetic mother wrapped around his finger, his true character came to light. He is a cold, implacable man. I was small for my age—" He paused, for he could hear the pain in his voice.

Olivia gave him a look of empathy and waited to see if he would continue.

"He beat me," Gideon whispered miserably. "On a near-nightly basis."

Those first three words chilled his heart. Never had he said them to anyone before.

The abuse had scarred him deep within and on the outside as well. The proof? There were marks all over his body, faded with time. Olivia would see the faint cigar burns on his chest and back if she looked closely and in better lighting. And that was just the beginning.

"I am sorry. No child, no matter the circumstances, should ever be beaten," Olivia whispered.

"I agree."

"And your mother? Where was she during all this?"

Gideon scoffed. "She took his side, naturally. My mother walked away, telling me I was an unruly boy who needed Whinstone's firm hand to teach me a lesson."

"Oh," Olivia said softly. "So, she was an accomplice in the abuse."

"In the fact that she didn't care what happened to me and looked the other way. I begged her to send me away to school. That didn't happen until I was thirteen. I arrived at Eton, a sullen but dangerous animal. Making friends was—difficult, and it still is."

"That is enough for tonight."

The relief that tore through him was potent, for he could say no more. Not now. The confession had ripped him to shreds. He couldn't tell his friend, Brandon Knight, about any of this, but he tells a stranger? What in hell was the matter with him?

Olivia picked up her crop and cloak and headed toward the door. "Tomorrow night, Your Grace. At the same time."

And with that, she was gone. The door closed softly behind her.

Gideon sat on the edge of the bed for a long time, and he wouldn't leave until he had his emotions safely tucked away. Or until his hands had stopped shaking.

Close to an hour later, he rose, dressed, and departed.

Chapter 5

OLIVIA DID NOT GET much sleep the night before.

He beat me.

Gideon's misery-laden words tore at her soul. After all these years, the duke was still affected by his past.

The situation was so emotionally similar to hers that anguish, an emotion she thought was long gone and—empathy—had surfaced.

Olivia didn't want to feel. But she did.

After a quick breakfast, she retired to the office to tally the earnings from the previous night. Gideon said not to share the money, but that did not sit well. What to do with the sack of sovereigns?

James entered at that moment, carrying two mugs of tea, their mid-morning ritual.

He sat opposite and took a sip of his steaming beverage. "How did we do?"

"Better than the night before. Word is getting around, and I expect profits to rise accordingly."

"Good. Now, I am dying to know. What of the duke? Did you birch him good and proper?" James gave her a wink.

"One strike. The duke will be returning tonight at the same time. After my appointment with Doctor Flehming."

James gazed at her over the rim of his mug. "Will he, indeed? Isn't this against your strict parameters of engagement?"

"He is paying extra for the privilege. He presented me with a sack of gold sovereigns. Thirty, to be exact."

"How extravagant," James murmured.

"He said to keep the transaction between us, but I want you to have your share and keep the remaining money in your safe."

"I will have to have a stern word with His Grace about making clandestine deals with my staff and make that part of the agreement for any future customers," James mused, looking annoyed.

"And I should not have taken the money. I *am* sorry, James, and it will not happen again."

"I trust you more than anyone, Olivia. And I'm glad you told me. I will take six sovereigns as my cut and keep your coin safe with the rest of your savings. Now, the duke?"

"He wanted to give and take. For a strike, a sharing of long-buried fragments of our past, a touch, and a kiss," Olivia said softly.

"I see. Actually, no, I don't see. What a strange request from such a cold, ruthless man."

"A request made to a cold, ruthless woman?" Olivia stated sardonically.

"Have a care, my dear. These kinds of arrangements can easily slip into a deeper connection, one you say you are *not* looking for. It can happen like *that*." James snapped his fingers. "Especially between two damaged, lonely, and vulnerable people. And you both are, make no mistake."

"Don't worry. I won't allow it to progress that far."

But it had already. The duke affected a part of her that Olivia had thought long dead.

"Wait, how do you know that Gideon is damaged?" she asked.

James raised an eyebrow. "Gideon, is it?"

"He insisted I call him that; he *is* paying."

"I saw it in his eyes. He masks it well. But I saw it, nonetheless, if only briefly. I also witnessed his reaction after watching you with the judge. You have certainly caught his attention. The man was in high color, and I would bet if I checked under his cloak, hard as oak."

"James!"

"His reputation claims he is a self-indulgent, cold automaton who ruts from one end of the city to another without emotional attachments to anyone. Out for his pleasure, hang everyone else. Is that the impression he gave you?" James asked, studying her closely.

"I don't believe he is cruel at heart, so the ruthless aspect doesn't fit. At least in what I observed, who is to know? As for cold—he certainly projects a frosty demeanor. But I believe that the damage you speak of is the cause. He revealed things to me I will not repeat. And I divulged some to him."

James's eyes widened. "The intimacy has begun. After tonight, cut it clean. For both your sakes, do not continue down this road. You do not want to add to the damage. Protect your heart. Watford is not for you."

Olivia bristled. "Not for me? Perhaps sharing trauma with someone can begin the healing."

"You shared some of it with me, and still, you hide behind your Mistress Birch persona, meting out punishment to strange men. Did unburdening to me assist in any way? Begin the healing?"

Olivia sadly shook her head. "No, perhaps it depends on the person. I didn't tell you everything."

"Will you tell the duke?" James took another sip of tea, his gaze firm on hers.

"I don't know," she replied softly. "I'm in uncharted waters here."

"All the more reason to cut it clean. There can be nothing between you. You know this. Watford is a duke and beyond your reach." James stood, giving her a look of compassion. "Take it from me; peers always choose power, duty, and society over anything as trivial as *feelings*."

He left her alone. She should end this before they were hurt. Olivia took a shuddering breath, and her heart contracted in pain.

Oh, damn it all.

Feelings.

They were surfacing, and she could not allow it.

GIDEON'S NERVES HAD been sparking since he left Olivia the night before. The anticipation at seeing her again, the yearning to be in her company. The need to hold and kiss her. All of this was beyond his experience, beyond all reasoning. As much as he tried to tuck away those rampant emotions let loose last night, he couldn't quite achieve it. It was as if Olivia had opened his soul and examined it, allowing light for the first time.

An absurd observation, but he had no other way to explain the riot within him. He could ignore it and never see Olivia again, but it caused such stark pain to slice through him he felt physically ill.

Such intense desire was not wise. It was also perilous.

With a turn of the door handle, she entered the room, taking his breath away again. Tonight, she wore a burgundy corset and stockings but no thigh-high boots or riding crop.

Olivia lifted her head and gave him a look bordering on pity.

Oh no. Not that. Anything but pity.

"Your Grace," she murmured silkily, causing his cock to stir.

"Olivia."

She padded toward him in her stocking feet and moved behind him, taking his coat from his shoulders. The slight brush of her fingers sent his blood to near the boiling point. Then, with the quiet litheness of a cat, she stood before him and began to slip the buttons through his waistcoat.

"I thought tonight we would forgo the agreement to an extent," she said, her voice low and husky.

"In what way?"

Olivia's fingers stilled. "After what you told me, I will not—not—"

"Strike me? Beat me?" he snapped, annoyance overtaking his desire.

She looked up at him, pinning him with her clear-eyed gaze. "Exactly that. I thought instead we could talk. We could share a few hours without any business arrangements between us. If you like, I can give you a partial refund—"

He grabbed her shoulders. "What is this, a condolence fuck?"

Starting at his crass statement and angry tone, she stepped away. "I don't *fuck*, Your Grace; I made that clear. And pardon me for expressing any sympathy. It won't happen again."

The cold shield was back in place, and Gideon didn't like it. Not one bit.

He scrubbed his hand down his face as he exhaled. "We are off on the wrong foot. I *am* sorry. As you can tell, I'm not used to someone showing me any concern. Can we continue? And no need for a refund of any sort." He spread his arms. "Please, continue with what you were doing."

She did, and after removing his waistcoat, unbuttoned his shirt. Taking his hand, she led him to the bed. They sat on the edge.

"Why did you request a touch, a kiss, a sharing of pasts last night? Is this a request you have made before?" Olivia asked. Her concentrated gaze showed her genuine curiosity.

"No. Never. Conversation was neither part of any interaction with women nor a kiss. As I said, too intimate."

"Yes," she sighed. "Too intimate. That is why after tonight, we cannot see each other again. You cannot contact or come to this brothel to hire me, as I will not be available to you."

It felt as if someone had kicked him in the gut, and Gideon did not like the sensation.

"Why, because you are feeling too much?" he exclaimed. "Shouldn't we welcome such emotions after years of living in a barren wasteland?"

What in hell had gotten into him? Had he lost his mind?

"You said that your stepfather beat you. When did it stop?" Olivia asked, daring him to reply and effectively sidestepping his question.

"At age fifteen, when I finally started to grow. By sixteen, I was well over six feet in height. And I filled out. No, the coward didn't dare strike me then. However, the verbal abuse continued when I was home from school. Because of it, I stopped returning home during the holidays. I preferred being alone, and the quiet was blessed peace."

"A soothing balm?"

"Yes. My mother and stepfather have a contentious relationship. If they weren't screeching at each other, they screamed at me. I had had enough. Once I finished school and university, I purchased a town house and effectively cut them from my life. They only come near me when they need money, and I found it expedient to give them what they wanted if only to be rid of them for a time."

"Is that when you joined The Rakes of St. Regent's Park?"

Gideon chuckled. "I helped create it. There are plenty of idle, bored, wealthy miscreants out there, titled or not." He sobered. "I am the only original member left. I turned 40 years old not long ago, and here I still am. The years slipped by."

"Yes," Olivia replied softly. "They do pass at a blur."

"Your rape—"

"I never said the word rape. You know the judge you saw me with the other night?"

"Yes."

"I asked him once what recourse a woman had when attacked, and I gave him a scenario. The judge wasn't aware that I was describing my assault. By the current legal terms, rape must consist of penetration and ejaculation. You see, my attackers didn't stick their cocks in me; they used their dirty fingers. They beat and kicked me, tore open my bodice, and held me down as they grabbed and rubbed against me. So legally speaking, not rape," she concluded bitterly.

"Miserable bastards. Damn the law. And damn the men that run it," Gideon snarled.

"The judge said even though women can bring charges of rape now, very few cases come to court. Apparently, I placed myself in a vulnerable position just by walking alone. So, it was *my* fault. At least, that is how the court would look at it." Olivia shook her head; her lips curled in disgust.

"Yes, that's what the court would say," she continued. "Here's the thing: that judge said he feels sorry for women, for they are second-class citizens and have no say. A man can rape his wife as it's perfectly legal. It makes me sick."

Gideon gathered her close, and she stiffened. Then, miraculously, Olivia softened and laid her head on his shoulder.

"No more misery tonight," he whispered as he smoothed her golden hair. "There are horrid people in the world, and we have encountered our fair share. Perhaps more than our fair share. Let us partake in something more tangible. I want you to touch me. All over. Can you do that? Will you? I do not want you to do anything you feel uncomfortable with."

Her hand rested above his heart and sped up at her caress. Without thinking, he laid his hand on top of hers, their fingers intertwined.

"I'd like to try. What do you mean?" Olivia whispered.

Gideon stood, then removed his shirt. Next, he unbuttoned his trousers and stepped out of them, kicking them aside until he stood before her completely naked. His shaft was as hard as an iron bar.

God, he was so aroused. Her gaze fixed on his erection.

"I want you to touch me. Anywhere you like. Explore." His voice sounded raw and husky. "Please, Liv."

"No one has ever called me by that name. I like it," she said, her voice soft.

At that moment, Gideon felt his heart stutter to life. Although he stood with his feet firmly planted, the ground shifted perceptively under him. The unstable sensation caused his mind to reel and his heart to beat faster.

After all this time.

Deep to the marrow of his bones, he knew there was no going back to being that selfish, entitled rake. Why now? Was it his advancing age causing this monumental shift within him? Having a woman show concern and interest in him unlocked those barriers. Perhaps they were both lonely and damaged, and he recognized they could help each other. To learn to feel. Maybe even—love.

In a mere forty-eight hours, Olivia had changed *everything.*

Chapter 6

OLIVIA HAD SEEN PLENTY of men naked. But not one so well put together. Of course, he was masculine perfection; how could he not be?

Truthfully, she ached to stroke his skin. A thoroughly strange sensation considering she avoided making physical contact with most people.

Why him?

Curiosity won out; Olivia had to explore this conundrum.

She stood, then slowly circled him, approving of his fine arse, muscular back and arms, and overall height.

Using the tips of her fingers, Olivia traced the veins running down his arm, across his collarbone, and up to his full, sensual lips.

Then she traced his other arm, across his taut stomach, following the trail of dark hair to his erection. Dare she examine him here? Would she recoil, or could she grasp this very masculine part of him—and enjoy it?

Gideon inhaled, holding his breath as if anticipating what she would do next. Olivia gripped the thickness of him, and he exhaled with a moan.

"Yes. Touch me there." His words held a pleading agony.

She gave his cock a couple of swift strokes, then a few more. It took no time at all.

Growling low in his throat, he reached his peak.

Olivia's eyes widened. To see Gideon with his head back and jaw clenched stirred the simmering embers deep inside her. His deep-throated, raspy moans caused liquid heat to pool between her legs.

She had never had such a physical reaction to a man in all her encounters.

"Blast it," he mumbled, staggering away. He headed toward the basin, then quickly cleaned up. When finished, he turned toward Olivia, hard once again.

Insatiable man.

But that is what she had heard about him. Seeing to this man's needs on a steady basis would be exhausting for any singular woman.

But beyond all that, why had she made him—what was the word—come?

In her dreams, Olivia imagined meeting someone with whom she could share certain physical intimacies.

But this debauched duke? How could it be possible?

After handing her the warm cloth so she could wipe her hands, he motioned for them to sit on the edge of the bed.

"Liv, become my mistress."

She glanced at his flushed face. His eyes shone like polished onyx stones.

"You can't be serious."

"I do not know the first thing about having a long-term mistress," Gideon said matter-of-factly. "I am not a man who believes in possessing another like a fine piece of jewelry. I would agree to whatever terms you wish."

And with those words, the duke ruined the little trust and respect they had built between them. Olivia wasn't sure what else to call that deeper intimacy James had spoken of.

Frowning, she tossed the cloth aside. "This situation is moving beyond the parameters that we have set up—way beyond. I have no intention of becoming a possession or a mistress to any man. Besides, I hear you're very commanding and demanding in your pleasures, and I will *not* subject myself to such a situation."

"Perhaps I can be as you describe. But I have proven here that I am quite capable of sharing and submitting. You, Liv, are afraid of change or of feeling and living."

The intimacy, confessions, and physical contact were too much for her to handle in this entire situation. Whatever slim thread of control she used in these situations splintered apart. A few hot tears ran down her cheeks, as Olivia had not cried since her attack and the abandonment by her so-called father.

Gideon pulled her into his warm and reassuring embrace. She laid her wet cheek against his chest, and he smoothed her hair. No man had held her this way before. James once put his arm around her briefly, but she had not been held against a man's heart, wrapped in his masculinity, or comforted as if she were fragile and made of glass.

Gideon kissed her temple and whispered words of compassion. His gentle consideration touched her deep in a place long abandoned. For a moment, Olivia savored it, etching this into her memories. For that is all it would ever be.

Slowly and a little reluctantly, she pulled away.

"I think it best that you leave, Your Grace."

She used her best detached Mistress Birch voice. Olivia could have said plenty more, like this was a business transaction and meant nothing to her but the coin he had paid. That he didn't appeal to her in any way. She played a role; he hadn't awakened emotions she thought were long dead.

But that would be a lie—all of it.

"Don't end this here," Gideon whispered. "We will both regret it."

"I am ending it, and it's for the best. Your heart has encountered a few stutters of emotions. Now, go and find someone who can bring it fully to life. That person is not me."

"I don't accept your statement."

Olivia stood. "You're a duke and used to getting your way. But not here, and not with me."

"Will you meet me outside of this brothel? Olivia and Gideon taking afternoon tea at, let's say, Brown's Hotel on Dover Street this coming Friday. Three o'clock sharp."

Olivia's jaw dropped. "Have you lost all sense? Isn't that place in Mayfair?"

"It is. In fact, the queen has taken tea there on a few occasions. Perhaps I have lost all sense. But I want—and need—to see you. Talk to you. Be with you. Do not ask me to explain, for I cannot."

Olivia picked up Gideon's clothes and tossed them to him. She couldn't think straight with him casually sitting there, thoroughly aroused. He looked magnificent.

"Please get dressed and depart immediately. Or I will have to ring for someone to escort you out." Her voice shook.

And why not? Gideon had shaken her to her very core.

Gideon slipped on his trousers and then pulled them over his hips. Instead of finishing dressing, he sat on the edge of the bed again. He put on his shirt but left it unbuttoned, then met her gaze.

"Meet me for afternoon tea as if we are a couple. Why not? And before you ask, I have never asked *any* woman to tea before. If you do not have an appropriate dress, use some gold sovereigns to purchase one. Dressmakers have plenty of afternoon gowns in all sizes ready to sell."

He's lost his mind.

"We will be seen. Speculated about. You want that?" Olivia asked incredulously.

Gideon shrugged. "You are a daughter of a peer."

"An illegitimate one!" she cried.

"That means nothing to me. You could be the daughter of a fishmonger, and I couldn't care less. Not that there is anything wrong with that, as it is a noble profession."

She scrutinized him closely, looking to see if he was mocking her or fishmongers in general and those of the lower classes, but his expression was earnest. What had happened to the perennially bored aristocrat?

Inside, she wavered.

Why? It was hard to fathom.

Curious? Attracted to him? Eager for an adventure, even if it was to a tearoom?

Perhaps all of the above?

When was the last time she had ventured out of her secure shell? Olivia hadn't stepped outside The Velvet compound since they had taken occupancy four months ago during renovations.

"Liv, please forgive me for suggesting you be my mistress. Chalk it up to my selfish arrogance to immediately voice an upper-class prejudice. I want us to see each other outside the parameters we set up here. Yes, my heart has stuttered to life. *You* did that, and I want more."

"I can't give you what you want," she whispered miserably.

Gideon stood and took her hand; then he kissed it gently. "Let us at least try."

Oh, damn it all.

"Friday. Three o'clock. I'll be there." The words left her before she could call them back.

Gideon pulled her into his embrace and kissed her. It started slowly, a thorough exploration. Then it grew fierce. Olivia's insides dipped and fluttered, and she found herself placing her arms around his neck and returning the kiss with equal intensity.

His hands trailed down the valley of her spine, sending shivers of desire all through her. Then he cupped her rear and brought her in tight against that very hard part of him. A soft moan escaped the corner of her lips, which made Gideon's kiss even more wild and desperate.

Then, in increments, Gideon ended the kiss with a gentle press of his lips against her forehead. "Friday afternoon."

He swiftly dressed and was gone, leaving her alone. Clasping her mouth with her trembling hand, she sat on the edge of the bed.

Oh, what had they done?

Chapter 7

BROWN'S HOTEL WAS A busy location in Mayfair. It opened in 1837 and quickly became a popular spot, considering it was one of the first hotels in London. Since its grand opening, it has expanded three or four times by purchasing surrounding properties. It had an elegant look, and many prominent political, royal, and otherwise societal figures had stayed here.

Why Gideon suggested it, he could not say. At least, not aloud.

To show he was serious in his intentions, whatever they were, enough to be seen in public? To enjoy an outing with a woman? Share tea, sympathy, and conversation? Get to know her better outside the confines of a brothel? All of the above?

In all these years, no woman ever moved him like this. It merited further investigation. In his strange way, he supposed this was a sort of courting. All Gideon knew is he couldn't allow things to end. Not yet. Not until they explored this intense pull. And Olivia felt it too; he was sure of it.

And sitting here in the tearoom, he wondered if Olivia would even show up. Would he be made a fool? Already a few patrons were looking his way, whispering behind their hands. For when had he ever made any appearance in decent society?

Reaching into his waistcoat pocket, Gideon removed his watch and opened the cover. Olivia was five minutes late. Could he blame her if she had only agreed to meet him in order to be rid of him?

No, he could not.

Looking at himself through Olivia's eyes, he was a dissipated and pompous man. When with her, Gideon did not want to be that man any longer. With her mesmerizing mixture of damaged vulnerability and steely will, Olivia had brought his buried emotions into the light.

He never expected it to happen to him.

Of course, if he bothered to examine his black soul, he would find enough damage. Deep scarring that he believed would never mend.

Gideon glanced toward the entrance and audibly exclaimed.

Olivia stood, resplendent in a gold and brown afternoon gown. Even with its high neck and long sleeves, she looked glorious. The garment, trimmed in gold lace and brown brocade, suited her coloring and golden hair. Across the front of the dress were embroidered gold roses. She held a matching gold parasol and wore a brown and gold bonnet suitable for a sunny spring day. Olivia looked every inch a peer's daughter.

Smiling, Gideon stood and strode toward her. Taking her hand, he kissed it, then laid it on his arm and escorted her to the table. Nearly all eyes were on them, and for once, he basked in the attention, for he was proud to be in her company.

Pulling out a chair for Olivia, he then sat opposite. Her cheeks were flushed. From the fresh air or the fact that they were the subject of attention? Or, God forbid, she was happy to be in *his* company.

The waiter wasted no time bringing over the tea service and teacups. He then placed a three-tiered silver cake stand in the center of the table. The top layer held different flavors of scones. The second contained sandwiches, the bottom tier, sweets, and pastries. A good thing he had skipped luncheon.

Olivia leaned forward and whispered, "I have no idea what to do. This excursion is beyond my experience. And we are being watched."

"Do not be surprised if this makes the society pages. 'The coldly aloof Duke of Watford takes tea with a beautiful mystery woman.' And you are beautiful, Liv. Absolutely stunning."

Her color deepened, then she gave him the sweetest of smiles.

God, he would treasure that.

It was the first genuine smile Olivia had gifted him. Sighing, she removed her gloves.

"The lady at the table presides over the teapot," Gideon suggested. "If more than one lady, the senior one. You shall pour the tea, Liv. For both of us. You can do this."

He opened the linen napkin and laid it across his hip. He then motioned toward hers, and Olivia nodded and did the same.

She sighed softly. "Here I go. Pray my shaking hands do not cause the tea to spill all over."

Olivia poured and handed him the cup and saucer. Gideon trailed his finger along the edge of her hand. Even that slight brush of skin had him reeling. Gideon wanted to swipe the food and dishes to the floor and make love to her on the table.

Make love?

When had he ever referred to it as that? Never. Best to concentrate on the subject at hand.

"Once we add the dressings, such as milk, sugar, or lemon, we can select some of the food. We start with the top tier and work our way down. Never, ever mix them up." Gideon rolled his eyes.

"Is this something taught to the upper classes?"

"Yes. Society and its rules. Comportment. It's all ridiculous beyond words."

"But here you are, following those very rules you mock." Olivia looked into her cup. "And does one add the milk first or not? What does society do?"

"I was told the milk came first to cool the fragile cups for the hot tea. Personally, I add it after."

"So do I." Olivia took the milk pitcher, added some to hers, then passed the pitcher to him.

Again, he stroked her finger with his own until a soft moan escaped her luscious lips.

"Oh, you are doing that on purpose," she said breathlessly.

At least she was not admonishing him. Instead, her blue eyes sparkled with heated interest.

Gideon gave her a teasing wink as he sipped his tea. He had requested a blend of black currant and Assam, one of his favorites.

"Help yourself. I believe there are cranberry and orange scones and ham and cheese."

Olivia took a cranberry one and split it with her knife. "I almost didn't come here today."

"But you did," he murmured silkily. "And I am thankful. You've made my day. Nay, my week. Perhaps even the month."

She laughed lightly.

"Why *did* you come?" Gideon asked as he reached for a ham and cheese scone.

Olivia spread butter on her scone, then heaped a teaspoon of orange preserves and a dollop of clotted cream. "Why did you ask me?"

"Because I yearn to be in your company. I wanted us to see each other in an everyday setting. I suppose I picked a tearoom because I thought you would enjoy it."

"You have chosen wisely, as I'm enjoying it. I suppose I came because I yearn to be in your company. But we cannot continue with this. Deep down, you know it."

Her words were like a sharp spike to his heart.

"I know that James Brown started this hotel. He was Lord Byron's valet. Mr. Brown and his wife, Lady Byron's maid, ran it together. With a little financial help from his lord and ladyship."

"You're very good at changing the subject," Olivia said as she took a dainty bite of the scone.

"I am, that. Do you know that the first phone call in Britain was made from this very hotel in 1876? And by Alexander Graham Bell, the inventor of the telephone."

Olivia smiled. "My, you are a font of knowledge."

Hell, she's gifted me with another warm smile.

"In all manner of subjects, no matter how trivial. Try a sandwich next," he coaxed. "I requested my favorite, ham and egg, and I believe there is shrimp paste and the standard cucumber."

"You planned the menu?"

"I chose the type of tea, as well. A favorite of mine."

Olivia sipped her tea. "It's lovely. Do I taste blackberries?"

"Yes, indeed. After tea, we can stroll along Bond Street and take in the shops. If you like."

"Perhaps." Olivia finished her scone and then reached for a couple of sandwiches.

"We can catch an omnibus or walk it. Or, we can go to my residence on Hyde Park Corner, about a mile from here."

Olivia's hand, holding her teacup toward her lips, froze. She frowned, then placed the cup on the saucer. "Is that why you chose the Brown Hotel? For an afternoon assignation, either here or at your house? How convenient."

"No, it is *not* why. Blast it, Liv; if it entered my mind, it was of brief duration, and I dismissed it immediately. This afternoon tea is not some sly plot to seduce you." Damn it all; he was annoyed and heard it in his voice.

"How am I to guess your motivations? I don't *know* you, Your Grace. It took every ounce of courage for me to come here. And I didn't come alone. I never venture out alone. Not anymore."

She pointed to the front window. Standing off to the side was a large man in a brown suit, trying to look inconspicuous.

"And he is?" Gideon asked, still aggravated.

"My protection, when needed. I should leave."

Gideon gently grasped her hand. The thought of her leaving him filled him with dread.

"Don't go. Not yet. Please."

OLIVIA LOOKED INTO his eyes. She saw such pain there, unfathomable hurt and loneliness. The reveal of his emotions lasted only a moment, but it was long enough to move her numbed heart. Blast the man for affecting her on so many levels.

"I want to see you," Gideon murmured. "As a man and a woman see each other. Socially. Privately. Outside the parameters of a brothel and fees. I will agree to any arrangement you wish. The occasional Sunday afternoon stroll? A ride in my carriage? Dinner at the Savoy Hotel, in the Grill Room? Anything you desire. Or am I overwhelming you?"

"Yes, you are. I'm not used to such attention, and it is overwhelming. And what am I to do as this strange courtship unfolds? Continue at The Velvet, birching my customers and collecting my fee?"

His brows knitted. "I hadn't thought that far ahead." Gideon took a couple of sandwiches and laid them on his plate.

"What would your mother think, since you are escorting a sex worker in public? You are a duke," Olivia whispered fiercely.

At the mention of his mother, his handsome features darkened. "If I don't care what society thinks, then you may be sure I do not care what my mother thinks. I also am not certain I care that you will continue your work at The Velvet, but that is not my call, is it?"

"No, it isn't. I need to make money. I have made a commitment to Pan. Obligations—and I will not abandon them on a whim."

Gideon chewed thoughtfully on his sandwich, his gaze firm on hers. "Then, by all means, continue to thrash willing men and collect your fees. And what is happening between us is not a whim." He took another bite of his sandwich. "Next Wednesday night, dinner at the

Savoy. It is formal dress, and I can give you money to buy an appropriate gown."

Yes, he was acting the imperious duke here, and no mistake.

Just like that, she decided she would meet him for dinner. If he didn't give a toss about his reputation, why should she?

"I have a formal gown. Very well, dinner at the Savoy. I am certain it will be an adventure with the place setting holding four different forks, five different spoons, and five goblets, all of which I have no idea about their usage. But you can continue instructing me, Your Grace, in the fine art of formal dining," Olivia said sarcastically. "I will be your apt pupil."

Gideon leaned forward. "Actually, some formal place settings have eight different forks. There is so much more I can instruct you on," he whispered only for her ears. "Be my apt pupil in all things, Liv."

The offer was tempting. It may be far too tempting.

Olivia was provoking fate if nothing else. One more meeting outside of their now-defunct arrangement. What could it harm? The logical thing to do would be never to see him again. But logic was not factoring into her thinking here at all. Olivia finished her sandwiches and then selected a raspberry tart.

"I do not need an instructor. But dinner it is," she replied. "And after our tea, we may take a walk, with Colin following behind. But as far as an assignation, affair, or whatever your class calls it, I'm afraid that is not in the cards."

Gideon sat back and regarded her closely. "And why not?"

"Even though I *am* attracted to you, it is not something I wish to follow through with. It is not something I think about, much less wish to do."

"You haven't had sex with anyone, ever?"

Olivia dabbed the corner of her mouth with her napkin. "No, and I don't think I can. Not for one hundred sovereigns."

"I want to make love to you, Liv. Without the inducement of coin."

The emotionally spoken words seized her breath. What could she say to such a request?

"Listen to me," he continued, his voice low. "At the club, before I observed you and the judge, I watched a duke make love to his wife. The act was a revelation to me. I have never made love to a woman like that, seen to her needs, or even cared if she received any pleasure. Not in all these years. I engaged in selfish rutting. Making love is more than thrusting one's prick into a woman's wetness. But I wouldn't know about that."

"Neither do I," Olivia murmured, looking around the room to ensure no one overheard. Thankfully, the spacing between the tables is far enough apart to afford privacy.

"Put your trust in me as I have with you. Give and take, Liv."

"You're asking too much of me. I need time."

"But you are not dismissing me outright?"

"No. I should, but—"

"But you are intrigued. You're attracted to me as I am to you. You're curious because your heart has sputtered to life for the first time. I know because it has happened to me. Neither of us can dismiss this, Liv."

"We could, very easily. But, as you say, emotions have become involved. Oh, this is all so muddled."

Slowly, Gideon reached across the table and took her hand only momentarily since others in the room observed their every move.

But long enough to send a jolt of heat straight through her.

"Muddled perhaps, but exhilarating," Gideon said.

"Yes," Olivia whispered.

Oh, she was tumbling into the unknown here.

"Finish your tea, Liv. And we will perambulate about the streets as any couple would. Onward we go."

Onward—to what exactly?

Olivia could not puzzle this out, not right now.

All she wanted was to be with him, which made her frightened and excited all at once.

Chapter 8

DUE TO WHAT WAS BECOMING known as the Fashoda Incident, the Prime Minister extended the late spring session of Parliament. It was a territorial conflict between France and Britain over land in East Africa. The French army and West African colonial troops were marching toward central Africa. From what Gideon had read in the papers, there was heated rhetoric on both sides of the dispute. This conflict could all come to a head by late summer or early autumn. The last thing the country needed was another blasted war with France.

In Gideon's mind, they should be working in partnership with France, not carrying long-held, centuries-old grudges. Gideon was also not a proponent of global imperialist expansion as it brought conflict. There were rumblings that war could break out again in South Africa and become another Boer War. But beyond all that, Gideon was concerned that lurking over the horizon could be a war that would change the political landscape of the globe forever.

However, he had always been pessimistic about most subjects, especially politics. His sporadic appearances at Parliament did not sit well with him. Another reason turning forty had been such an austere milestone. It was past time he took his responsibilities seriously in the House of Lords. What cause should he take up?

Since he was in the minority regarding imperialism, he could concentrate on problems at home, such as social reform. Gideon stood in the central lobby, watching men hurry past to committee meetings and the like.

Who to approach?

The sound of a cane hitting the tiled floor caught Gideon's attention. It was Tremain Hornsby, Viscount Hawkestone, and younger brother to Harrison Hornsby, the Duke of Gransford.

Gideon had often sneered at the brothers for assisting those less fortunate. But lately, he had come to admire their doggedness in reform pursuits. They often worked hand in glove with the Wollstonecrafts and others on such matters.

Upon returning from the Boer War in South Africa in 1882, Tremain Hornsby became Viscount Hawkestone. It was an extinct title on the mother's side, going back more than one hundred years. The queen wished to reward Hornsby for his services to the crown by resurrecting the title through letters patent. It was rare for two brothers to be serving in the House of Lords simultaneously.

"I say, Hawkestone, could you hold up a moment?"

The viscount gazed at Gideon, who stood next to the newly installed St. David statue.

Hawkstone came to stand beside him. "What is it, Watford?"

The tone of the viscount's voice was dismissive, not that Gideon could blame the man considering Gideon's abysmal voting and committee record.

"I wish to become involved in any reforms you are working on."

Hawkstone raised a dubious eyebrow. "You? A Rake of St. Regent's Park? Grown tired of haunting brothels?"

"As if you never did. I've heard of your early exploits," Gideon replied dryly, trying to hide his annoyance.

Hawkstone leaned on his cane. "The keyword there is 'early.' What are you, forty-five?"

Gideon ground his teeth, fighting back a retort. "Just turned forty. Why, is it too late to give a damn? Do you treat all who approach you with genuine intent with such insults? This conversation isn't a game to me."

Hawkestone's hardened features softened, but just a little. "It is never too late to give a damn. We would welcome the assistance. It would not be of a brief duration, however. You know how long it takes to craft bills and push them through. This endeavor would be a long-term commitment."

"I understand."

"Is it a woman?"

The question from the viscount took Gideon aback. "What do you mean?"

"It is my experience that falling in love often brings about an examination of one's soul."

"I know you were a vicar in a previous life, but don't start spouting bible verses at me," Gideon retorted. "Spare me that, at least. When one starts talking of a soul, it invariably leads to religion."

Falling in love? Was this man serious?

The viscount snorted. "I wouldn't dream of preaching to you, as my vicar days are well behind me. Whatever the reason for your turnabout, I will give you a try. Come with me now and sit in on the meeting of like-minded men. We are trying to expand workers' rights, extending the principle of government's responsibilities towards its citizens. Also, to see workers compensated for injuries at work. Giving women more rights, including the vote."

"Quite the ambitious agenda. You wish Britain to be a welfare state?"

"It is ambitious, and why not?"

Gideon sighed. "You will find me a hardline pessimist. I believe as an empire, we reached our peak last year with the Diamond Jubilee, and it will all be downhill from here."

Hawkestone placed a hand on his shoulder. "Then it is imperative we get to work and push through what we can before it all implodes." The viscount gave him a wink, then sobered. "You may not be far off in your thinking. My fifteen-year-old son, Hayden, thinks much the same as you. By the time he inherits this title, Great Britain could be very different."

"Yes, it could."

"Well, we won't dwell on it any longer. I have two years before I am fifty. There is still much to accomplish, Gideon. May I call you Gideon?"

"Of course."

"Then call me Tremain, and come along, sharply now. We have a luncheon laid out."

Gideon followed Tremain to one of the many offices on the second floor. It was easy to become lost at Westminster, with over 1100 rooms and 100 staircases to navigate.

Tremain opened the door, and around a long table were men of various ages. "My lords, Your Grace, and gentlemen, this is Gideon Broyles, the Duke of Watford, eager to join our efforts."

Shouts of the affirmative greeted Gideon, along with pounding on the table. Good God, there must be close to thirty men here; he had no idea such a group existed. The room was thick with tobacco smoke and the odor of power and influence.

"Come sit by me, Watford," Tremain urged. "I am sure you are acquainted with the Earl of Carnstone."

Gideon sat next to the older man. The earl had just turned eighty, but Aidan Wollstonecraft looked like a man close to twenty years younger.

"Yes, I am acquainted. My lord." Gideon nodded toward the earl and glanced past him. His gaze fell on Oliver Wollstonecraft, grandson of the earl and fellow member of The Rakes of St. Regent's Park.

"Well, damn it all. You found me out," Oliver stated drolly.

The earl laughed heartily. "During my father's time, you would both be called rakehells, but regardless of your extracurricular activities, we accept your assistance, nonetheless. Shall we get down to business?"

For once in his miserable life, Gideon felt a surge of purpose. And he mentally kicked himself for not doing this sooner. Yet, as platters of sandwiches and written proposals passed around the table, Gideon wondered: was this change in attitude brought about by becoming involved with Olivia?

Could he be—falling in love?

TWO WEEKS PASSED, AND in that time, Olivia and Gideon had met for the formal dinner at the Savoy Hotel. It had been an overwhelming experience for Olivia, as the menu was in French, but Gideon had ordered them a delicious meal and took the time to explain each dish.

He again regaled her with tidbits of information, such as the Savoy was the first public building in the world to be lit entirely by electricity, with electric lifts to take people between floors. The opulence of the place was quite spectacular, and the fancy meal consisting of numerous courses nearly had her bursting her stays. Olivia particularly liked the grilled salmon with dill sauce, and Gideon ensured she had some to take back to her room under the pretense it was for her fictitious cat.

Today, they were on a carriage ride through Hyde Park in a fashionable landau with a single horse and driver. The sun was out, and it was a glorious spring day.

Gideon swept his arm in an arc. "Take a good look, Liv. In five years, this will all be gone."

"What do you mean?"

Gideon pointed across the way at one of those horseless autos rattling and sputtering noisily along the main road. "Carriages will become a thing of the past, and sooner than many believe."

"Oh, surely not. Those motor cars are smelly things. A temporary fad."

Gideon snorted. “I hope not. I have invested with some acquaintances in the Daimler Motor Company Limited. With the passage of the Locomotives on Highways Act two years ago, motor vehicles have permission to travel on roads and streets, with certain conditions.”

“How forward thinking of you. Is that one of your motors?” Olivia said.

“No. The cars you see on the roads are probably German. Ours will debut next year if all goes well. So far, it has been a shrewd investment. I’ve made money already on the venture. This is the future.” Gideon chuckled. “And I shouldn’t speak of money in a lady’s presence, as it’s considered crass.”

“Society again?”

“I know. So many rules. How about some ice cream? There is a vendor there on the opposite side.”

She smiled at Gideon. “I would love one.”

He ordered his driver to pull over to the side, and he strode across the green area to stand in a queue. The duke was such a magnificent figure of a man. But it was more than his stunning looks. They spoke with ease, and Gideon felt comfortable enough to mention his investments. It proved that they were compatible. At least as far as conversing was concerned. But where could this go? It didn’t bear thinking about today. Why ruin the afternoon?

“Well, if it isn’t Mistress Birch. Have your riding crop with you today? Did you use it on the horse—or on Watford?”

Olivia stiffened, then turned toward the direction of the sardonic male voice. Golden-haired and handsome beyond words, where had she seen this man before?

He bowed. “We have had no formal introduction, but I spoke with Watford in the gold room when you walked in. He then unceremoniously hustled me out.”

Oh. Right.

She remained silent.

"Damon Cranston, Marquess of Brookton, at your service."

"My lord," she murmured, wishing him gone.

"I say, I suppose I should better phrase it to say *you* are at *my* service, for a price, of course. I want to make an appointment, Mistress Birch. With you."

Arrogant—she could hear it in his conceited tone.

"Then may I suggest you contact the proprietor, Pan, and make an appointment. That is *if* I am available to you, which I doubt I will be."

"Picky about your customers? I find that strange, considering you allowed Watford into your whipping chamber. There is already gossip about Watford and the mysterious lady he is squiring about town. One word from me to all and sundry, and your true identity will be known. But I will keep quiet." Brookton placed a finger over his lips and gave her a sly smile.

"If I arrange a meeting with you," she snapped.

"Clever girl. Now, there is no need to be annoyed. It isn't the first time Watford and I shared the goods, as it were—"

A deep growl cut off the man's sentence. Gideon had returned, and he handed her the small carton of ice cream.

"If we were not in a public place, I'd smack you one. Stay away from Olivia. Consider this is your last warning." Gideon sounded angry and entirely dangerous.

"This is farcical. A duke and a whore?" Brookton laughed.

The words made Olivia's blood run cold. It had the opposite effect on Gideon, for he grabbed Brookton by the cravat and brought him in close. Gideon's free hand disappeared below the marquess's waist. Then Brookton squeaked.

"I'll rip your bollocks from your body if you speak or approach her again. I will see to it that you will never beget an heir to the decaying and debauched Chellenham dukedom. See that I won't."

Chellenham?

Olivia covered her mouth as bile rose in her throat. She gagged once, then twice, and both men turned to look at her with puzzlement.

That name.

Oh, no. It couldn't be.

Her gaze slid to Brookton. It was as if looking in a mirror: the gold hair, high cheekbones, and the shade of blue of their eyes. It could be a coincidence. But Chellenham was the name her poor, dying mother had spoken to the nuns repeatedly.

"Take her to the Duke of Chellenham. Her father. He will see her looked after. Edward Cranston. Chellenham. Please."

Tears sprang to her eyes. She felt woozy. "Gideon. I am unwell," she croaked.

Gideon released the marquess and pushed him aside. Climbing in the carriage, he barked orders to the coachman.

Olivia swayed in her seat, and Gideon immediately sat beside her, gathering her into his strong and comforting embrace.

"What is it? Did Brookton upset you? The man is all bluster and arrogance to the core. He would not reveal your identity, especially after my threat, because he knows I mean it."

It was hard to catch her breath; she was close to hyperventilating.

"My God, Liv, what is it?" He tenderly stroked her flushed cheek, and his kindness opened the floodgates.

The tears were falling freely now, and blast it; it loosened her tongue.

"C-C-Chellenham is the peer who sired me."

Chapter 9

GIDEON COULDN'T HAVE heard her right.

Chellenham?

That reprobate? Damon's devil duke father? Of course, it all made sense. The man was an unrepentant scoundrel of the first order. The rumors of his numerous by-blows were legendary, even eclipsing Gideon's stepfather. And that was saying something.

How old was Chellenham? Fifty-five? Then he had to be twenty-two or three when he sired Olivia before he had married. Before Brookton was born.

My God, Damon was her half-brother. What a shocking revelation. And even more disturbing because Brookton had unknowingly tried to interest her in a rendezvous.

Olivia was so distressed she started to hiccup.

"Easy, Liv. Take a deep breath and exhale," Gideon urged. Blast it all; he was not used to giving comfort to someone.

"Take me home." Her voice shook. Her entire body shuddered.

"Why not come to my house? We can talk there."

She pushed him away. "I don't want to talk," she whispered harshly. "Not about this, not ever. Forget I said anything. And you are not to repeat it. Especially to the marquess or the duke."

"Olivia—"

She grabbed his arm, her nails digging into his sleeve. "The marquess caught me off guard; the words slipped out before I could stop them. Promise me!" She hissed the last two words through clenched teeth and squeezed his arm tighter.

"I promise you, but I want to hear the details first. We can discuss it at my place or yours. You choose. The coachman awaits directions."

"Oh!" she cried. "How dare you make conditions; a gentleman would give his word!"

"As you are aware, I am no gentleman." More loudly, he said, "Smithers, to The Velvet Vine on High Poplar Street."

"Right away, Your Grace." The coachman snapped the reins, and the horse bolted forward at a fast trot.

"What are you doing?" Olivia hiccupped again.

"Deep breath and hold it, Liv."

Her brows furrowed with annoyance, but she did as he had suggested.

"Now exhale. I thought you would be more comfortable in your room than in a strange house. Is there a way to enter your private room without going through the club?"

Olivia nodded. "Around back is a building attached by two hallways, and there is an outside entrance on the bottom floor."

He took her trembling hand. "You will allow me to escort you to your room so we can talk?"

"Hell," she muttered, sounding defeated. "I cannot fight you. Perhaps you can assist me in leaving the city."

Leave?

His insides lurched from the very thought of her departure. What a strange sensation. Damn his emotions. Try as he might tuck them away as he had done many times throughout his life, they stubbornly remained front and center.

Gideon pulled her into his embrace once again. To hell with anyone who could see them because of the open carriage. Olivia did not push him away but gave a shuddering breath as she settled next to him.

They remained silent the entire way to the East End.

With the carriage neatly tucked around the club's rear, Gideon instructed Smithers to stay put and wait.

"There is a small hamper under the seat," Gideon murmured to his driver. "Help yourself to the foodstuffs. Except for the wine. I want you alert and sober."

"Yes, Your Grace. Thank you."

Taking Olivia's arm, he escorted her through the labyrinth of hallways and rooms until, at her instruction, they arrived at a door tucked at the rear of the second building. She reached in her reticle for a key. But her hand shook too much to stick it in the lock.

Gideon took it from her hand. "Allow me."

When he stepped inside, he became immediately taken by the coziness of the area: the quilt, plush cushions on the bed, and the wing chair by the fire. The table and chair sat in the corner with a tablecloth and vase of flowers.

This cozy space was Olivia's refuge from the harsh world beyond. Gideon immediately lit the fire in the small hearth, then escorted Olivia to the chair next to it.

"You know how to light a fire? Sorry, I just assumed you had someone to do that for you," she said.

"I do, but since I keep late nights, I do not disturb the servants at all hours to see to it. Hardly fair. Now, sit. You're shaking." Gideon ripped the quilt from the bed and wrapped it around her. "I know you said you don't want to discuss it, but you must trust someone, Liv. It might as well be me."

"I *want* to trust you, but it is difficult to trust anyone fully," she murmured.

"I understand more than you know. But let us give it a go, as we have already revealed so much to each other."

Gideon sat before her but not so close as to crowd her.

"When I traveled to see the nuns, they told me that Chellenham was known to them. You see, they contacted him after my mother's death. The duke, then a marquess, sent his man of business to handle the transaction with the childless vicar and his wife."

"And your childhood?"

"Not as terrible as yours by any stretch. My adopted father was stern and pious, but he was not cruel—until he abandoned me. Sometimes he showed affection, but it wasn't often. He could be preachy, and he ran a strict household, but I was never abused or subjected to violence." Olivia revealed shakily. "I loved him; he was my father."

"And yet, he abandoned you, as you said. I cannot imagine how you felt and how that scarred you."

"More so than being attacked," she whispered. "On some levels. Do you see why it is hard to trust? As to Chellenham, I made inquiries and soon learned he was a man I wanted no acquaintance with. Promise me you will not tell him."

"I loathe the duke. You are better off. I promise I will never tell him."

Olivia exhaled. "Thank you. And his son? The marquess?"

And what about Brookton? "I will not tell him at this time, but I think you should consider approaching him in the near future."

Olivia's eyes widened. "How can you say that?"

"I have known Brookton a while now, and he is not the cruel reprobate his father is. He is your half-brother, Liv. As far as I am aware, the science is not there to prove it. But you need only look at him to know."

"I can't. I won't." She pulled the quilt tighter about her.

"Be at ease. There is no need to inform Brookton—now. Tell me you were not serious about leaving the city."

"It's one way to ensure I never run into these men."

"What if I say I don't want you to depart, temporarily or permanently?" Gideon replied softly. Shocking to discover that her departure would tear him in two and create a wound that would never heal. Being vulnerable was not an emotion he thought he would ever experience again, but here it is. "I can protect you. You need never see anyone you do not wish to," Gideon suggested.

"You're friends and in the same club as the marquess. Besides, I can look after myself. I do not need anyone." Olivia raised her chin in defiance.

"What about Pan? You needed him and still do. He protects you and keeps you safe. You have your defensive cocoon here. You rarely venture outside because your attack affected you more than you realize. I can offer the same sort of security, more so. You need never fear anything or anyone ever again."

"Fear? I am not a victim," Olivia snapped.

"Oh? We both have vulnerabilities. You know it," Gideon replied firmly. "And we are victims of our past. Admit it."

"What do you want from me? We've shared kisses and embraces—and physical intimacies. What else do you want?" she whispered.

"All I know is I have never felt this way before. I have not initiated sex because of what has happened to you—the violation. I did not want to rush you; I wanted us to know each other better. Yes, blast it all, to have some sort of courtship. Perhaps that was the wrong tack to take. I am willing to fight for what is between us. Are you?"

"I'm so weary of fighting."

"This could be our one chance at more. A chance at that dreaded L-word many are reluctant to speak of. We are not getting any younger."

Olivia blinked at him as if having difficulty comprehending what he was saying. "You are not speaking of—love? Surely not?"

"Loving, living, learning to trust, lust—all of it. Why not?"

"You—and me?" she scoffed.

"Don't dismiss it, Liv. You will break both our hearts. And contrary to what we previously believed, we *do* have hearts."

Her look softened. "Oh, Gideon."

Impulsively, he jumped to his feet and stood before her. He was already dangling out on a limb; he might as well go all in. "I ask you to come with me. I swear you will not be my possession but my partner in all things. We will share it all, Liv. Life, joys, sorrows, desire, companionship, respect, trust, and perhaps more." He held out his hand. "Take it, Liv. Take my hand and come away with me, now. Tonight. This very moment."

Their gazes met. The cold indifference Gideon had seen in her eyes when they first met was no longer there. There was a warmth, a decided regard, but it was hard to ascertain if further sentiments resided within her.

Endless moments ticked by. With a shuddering breath, Gideon closed his eyes. Olivia was going to say no and dismiss his heartfelt plea.

For the first time in his life, he laid open his heart, exposed his long-buried vulnerabilities, and it bloody well hurt.

Fingertips brushed by his palm.

Gideon's eyes snapped open.

Olivia's small hand enfolded his. His long fingers closed over her hand, and he gently squeezed in return.

She gave him a wobbly but warm smile. "Share it all, Gideon."

Chapter 10

OLIVIA TOOK GIDEON'S hand and followed him to his residence on Hyde Park Corner. A man she had only met a few weeks before and, in all places, a brothel. One night passed since she made that hasty decision. Olivia reached for the pot and poured tea into her cup.

Perhaps she'd made a grave mistake.

Taking a sip, she looked about the plush parlor. The room spoke of class and money, something Gideon had in abundance from what she could ascertain. It was decorated with a Rococo and Elizabethan mix, not that she was an expert. What little she knew, she had learned from books in her vicar father's extensive library.

Olivia's thoughts drifted to the absent Duke of Watford. Gideon had made such a heartfelt declaration, and the emotionally spoken words breached Olivia's protective walls.

She had taken his hand, acting on a reckless impulse. Then, he dumped her at his home and departed for points unknown. He mumbled that he had something to see to. And that he would return as soon as possible. She had not seen him since.

Gideon's staff was attentive and saw to her every need. So much for his emotional plea that they share everything. Even now, she could recollect every fervent word.

"I ask you to come with me. I swear you will not be my possession but my partner in all things. We will share it all, Liv." He had held out his hand. *"Take it, Liv. Take my hand and come away with me, now. Tonight. This very moment."*

Olivia set the cup on the saucer and placed them on the table. A wave of frustrating annoyance roiled through her. Somewhere along the line, she had turned into a romantic fool. She should leave.

And go where exactly?

James would welcome her back. She frowned, for she owed her dear friend an explanation, far more detailed than the scribbled note she'd left in her room. James had taken her off the street, where her father had abandoned her. He gave her a roof over her head, protection, and friendship.

And she returned it by running off with a spontaneous yet thoroughly tempting duke?

Gideon's butler, Hobson, entered the parlor and bowed. "Is there anything else you require, Miss Durham?"

"Yes, the whereabouts of the duke would do for a start!" she snapped. Hobson did not even flinch at her sharp tone. Olivia exhaled. "Forgive my temper. Do you know where he is?"

"His Grace rarely tells me of his comings and goings, miss. He instructed me to see to your every need and that he would return soon. He did not give me an exact date or time."

A terrible thought struck her.

Good heavens, he hadn't gone to Chellenham and Brookton? Not after he had promised not to tell the devil duke? Those peers stuck together and covered for each other, did they not? It was a horrible thought, especially after he had been supportive and kind since she blurted out her dark secret.

Olivia took another fortifying breath to calm her irritation—and her worry. "Please bring me a pen, ink, and stationery. I will want a letter delivered. Is there someone who can see it done?"

"Robert, the footman, will happily deliver whatever you wish. I can show you to the study where you might be more comfortable composing your missive."

"No, I will do it here. Thank you."

Hobson gave a stiff bow and left the room.

She had to speak to James right away.

GIDEON HAD SPENT THE night at The Rakes of St. Regent's Park club location, drinking copious amounts of alcohol while he brooded. Gideon rarely drank copious amounts, usually the occasional glass of scotch, and that was about it. He stared into the contents of his whiskey glass. His head swam, his thoughts muddled, and he didn't like the sensation.

The Rakes kept a few rooms for emergencies or clandestine meetings. He must have looked imposing and thunderous as Tolwood had departed almost immediately after he had arrived at the club the day before.

Impulsive behavior was not something Gideon could lay claim to—until he met a golden-haired beauty with haunting blue eyes. She had captured his attention and empty heart; they shared so much, giving, taking—and trusting. He had brought her to his town house in Mayfair and did not know what to do next.

So, he escaped.

Coward.

His cold, indifferent heart made up the essence of Lord Craven, the nickname he despised. The name spoke to his sexual cravings, not for its meaning of possessing a timorous nature. But for once, he lived up to the true gist of the word.

His selfish, sexual appetites fueled his existence these past several years. As long as he received pleasure in his debauched adventures, he did not give a hang for anyone else.

Yes, he was a miserable excuse for a human. A complete cad. Until Olivia, who, it turned out, was as deeply unhappy as him.

Gideon took a swallow and let the single malt burn down his throat. The alcohol hit his empty stomach in a fiery, raw blast of heat. His weary eyes cracked open as he wondered if she was still at Hyde Park Corner. Perhaps she'd left, and he wouldn't blame Olivia if she had.

Sighing wearily, Gideon emptied the glass and set it on the table. The liquid courage was not working. He would have to dig deep and find it without the inducement of alcohol. Locating this elusive courage should be smooth, considering his haughtiness and self-confidence in most situations. Liv had thrown out the window all previous actions and behaviors.

The door swung open, and Christian Bamford, the Duke of Allenby, Asher Colborne, Baron Wenlock, and Damon Cranston, the Marquess of Brookton, strode into the room.

Oh, God. *Brookton.*

Gideon thought back to last autumn, just before the delivery shook their club to its foundations. They were all sitting around the table, and the subject of illegitimate children came up, and Brookton gave a decided, fierce opinion on the matter. Not like him at all.

"Yes, children. Avoid at all costs. If it does happen, however, never deny the child. Never refer to them as a mistake. Or a by-blow, God, I loathe that term. A child should not be shunted about, lost in the morass of society, or tossed aside like rubbish. This child will be of your blood and deserves care and acknowledgment. At the most, love and acceptance.

I'm extremely cautious in my carnal dealings. My father, the duke, not so much. There are at least three siblings of mine out there in the world, borne from three different women of various classes. I've tried to find them."

Three siblings?

Was Olivia part of that three or part of the dozen or so others Brookton had alluded to? But a more interesting question: why was Brookton looking for these people? One thing Gideon would do here and now is banish thinking of illegitimate children as by-blows. Brookton was right. It was a loathsome term.

"Tolwood was correct. Watford is drinking himself to oblivion," Christian said to the other men. Then he turned and gave Gideon an arch of his eyebrow. "One of my footmen brought food and strong coffee, and William will bring it up directly."

"All of you, leave me alone," Gideon growled.

As usual, his fellow rakes ignored him and sat at the table.

"This is playing out almost exactly like my situation. Brooding and drinking over a woman. It is a woman, is it not, Gideon?" Asher asked, his voice soft with empathy.

He could be the cold, ruthless bastard he had always been and dismiss the overture. But Olivia had changed *everything*.

"Is this the part where you order us to leave so you can wallow some more? No woman is worth such bother and attention," Brookton said, sarcasm lacing his voice.

Many times through the years, Gideon had wanted to plow his fist into that handsome face and silence Brookton's sardonic tone forever. He wanted to do it as recently as a couple of days ago. But that would require an emotional response, so Gideon had never bothered to do it earlier.

However, now was not that time.

Gideon shot out of his chair and gave Brookton a glancing blow across the cheek. A scuffle ensued, with Asher holding Brookton back while Christian held Gideon.

"Easy, lads," Christian yelled. "Perhaps we should have set up a boxing ring here instead of card tables."

"Maybe we should have," Gideon ground out. He made another lunge toward Brookton, who growled in return.

"Enough," Christian said firmly.

Brookton broke from Asher's grip. "You are not the leader any longer, Christian." He dabbed at the few drops of blood accumulated on the corners of his lips. "That is the best you can do, old man?" he scoffed.

"I was aiming for your nose. Give me another chance. I will get it right this time," Gideon snarled in response.

"Let's have another drink," Asher suggested. "Gideon?"

"Why not? Release me, Allenby. I am calm enough."

Already this heated exchange had rattled him. An emotional outburst—how not like him. At. All. Seated once again and with fresh drinks, the men all looked at him as if waiting for an explanation. Brookton's lips curved into a slight sneer. Gideon honestly did not know what to say.

He wished Bran were here, but his friend had recently departed to Canada with his new wife and stepson. He would be gone for two years; Gideon could hardly confess his feelings. And what of the rest of this group of men?

"Whether you believe it or not, we *are* your friends," Christian said as if reading his mind. "Inasmuch as you try to stay above the fray, emotionless and detached, we care about you. That is why we are here. Tolwood told us you were in dire straits, and we did not hesitate to give our support."

"He didn't come with you?" Gideon asked as he sipped his scotch.

"He's always been a little afraid of you," Asher interjected. "And a little in awe."

Brookton rolled his eyes. "Jesus. Well, don't include me in that pathetic group."

Gideon shot him a warning look, then took another sip of alcohol. Asher had refilled his glass. His whiskey-soaked brain struggled to sort through his churning emotions.

To hell with it. He pushed the glass away. "Damon, I'm sorry I hit you," Gideon began.

"Damon? You have never called me by my given name. Why now?"

Why? Because he felt empathy toward the man for the first time. "Did you come here to offer friendship or stick the knife in, knowing my misery?" Gideon said, aiming the question squarely at Damon.

Damon shifted uncomfortably. "Since you apologized, let's say friendship."

"Then friendship it is, to all of you. I appreciate you coming here."

"Is that all you want, Gideon?" Damon asked.

"I want so many things," Gideon said in a low voice. "I want my empty life to cease being so bloody barren. I want to give a damn about something—or someone. Having just turned forty, I assumed it would never happen. Believing my heart was dead and buried, I continued with my hollow life, always reaching for the next meaningless encounter. Until—her."

"Ah," Christian said. "*Her*. I believe Asher and I know of what you speak."

"Tell us about—her," Asher encouraged.

"Feelings I have never felt before bubbled to the surface in those first few intense hours with her. I want to protect and care for her. Perhaps I want to love her, though I am incapable."

"Yes, you *are* capable, Gideon. Even you, the most jaded rake among us. Well, outside of Damon," Christian smiled.

Damon snorted.

William entered carrying a large tray of sandwiches and coffee with accompanying dishes and utensils. Christian handed him a few coins after the footman arranged the items on the table.

"Thank you, William. There is a pub on the next street, have a pint and a bite of lunch."

William took the money. "Thank you, Your Grace."

Once the footman departed, Christian poured black coffee into an enamel mug and handed it to Gideon. "Drink and eat. Look, I had all our favorites made. Beefsteak, cheese and onion, and ham and egg. Eat, Gideon, and tell us more."

"I met her a few weeks ago. A golden-haired angel who is even more damaged than I am."

"You are speaking of the kitten with the riding crop, are you not?" Damon asked.

Gideon growled, ready to pounce on Damon once again. "Watch how you speak of her, or I will rip your head from your body."

"First my bollocks, now my head. Easy, old man. I meant no disrespect. Gideon and I ran into each other at that new club, The Velvet Vine and Tackle. He was waiting on a woman, one who specializes in birching. To be certain, she is a cold beauty but a prostitute? How low does a man have to sink to consider a woman barely a notch or two from the streets?"

Asher snarled. "Watch it, Damon, or I will pummel you after Gideon."

Right. Asher's new wife had a tragic and dubious history, though Gideon and the rest did not know all the particulars. And he certainly wasn't going to reveal Olivia's past—or his own. That was a private pact between them only.

"I am only stating what judgment society will pass on such a union," Damon said. "Again, I mean no disrespect."

"He's not wrong," Gideon murmured. "It *is* what society will say. Not that I give a good damn about it. Do you give a damn, Christian? Or you, Asher? Bran left the country to protect his love from all talk and speculation. Perhaps the idea has merit."

"No," Christian said firmly. "I don't give a damn at all. I know what is said, that I married beneath me to a woman who has her own business and continues to work at it even after our marriage. I've joined her in that venture, and we revel in it—and our love. Hang the rest."

Asher nodded. "Yes, exactly. I completely agree."

"I held out my hand to her and asked her to come with me," Gideon said as he sipped the hot coffee. "I stated that we would share it all. And to my absolute shock, she took my hand. Now, she is at my town house—at least, I assume she is still there—because I fled as soon as I brought her there. I do *not* know what to do next. What I did was impulsive. Not like me at all."

"Gideon, I did the same thing once I brought Chastity to my place. As I said, I came here to drink and brood," Asher interjected.

"I can attest to that," Damon added.

"Yes, and you nearly were given a beating for your crass remarks," Asher replied sarcastically.

"But I also listened to your problems and suggested The Galway Agency for your various inquiries. Gideon, perhaps you should do the same. What do you know of this woman? One you have known all of a few weeks? Trust doesn't build that quickly, or anything else for that matter," Damon stated resolutely.

"And how would you know?" Gideon retorted.

But wait—an investigative agency. It was something to consider, but for what? His gaze swung back to Damon. To prove the blood ties between Olivia and the duke? How could that even be achieved?

Not that she wanted it done. In fact, she had been adamant.

"Regardless, staying here is not an option," Christian said, interrupting his thoughts. "Go home, my friend, and talk to—what is her name?"

"Olivia. Liv."

"Talk to Olivia. She has affected you like no one before. That alone is worth exploring, regardless of her background and occupation. Who bloody well cares what society thinks? Take it from me—and Asher. And Brandon, for that matter. When you find someone who speaks to your very heart and soul, it is *everything*." Christian pushed the plate of sandwiches toward him. "Now, eat. Then, go home. Face your fears and your future."

Grateful for the advice and, damn it, the friendship, he took a wedge of a cheese and onion sandwich and bit into it.

Face your fears.

Yes, it was about time he did.

In Gideon's past, no one had ever offered support and affection. Could he take a chance with a woman he had just met?

It may be time to try.

Enough wallowing in self-doubt and pity. The first order of business, sober up.

Next, back to Hyde Park Corner and talk to Liv—if she hadn't fled.

Chapter 11

OLIVIA SAT IN THE QUIET parlor for several hours. The clock ticked the minutes away from its perch on the fireplace mantel. Sitting next to her on the table was the letter she'd written to James. The footman hadn't delivered it, and Olivia doubted sending it.

The anger she'd felt earlier that morning had turned into crushing disappointment. Her opinion of men was decidedly low before. The one time she tossed common sense to the wind and took a chance on a man, he'd let her down.

The door slammed, and men's voices filled the front hall. Her heart stuttered in her chest.

Gideon?

She wrapped her hopeful thoughts with anticipation of seeing him again.

Pathetic woman.

Olivia placed her hands in her lap and fought to keep her face impassive.

Gideon stepped into the room, his gaze intense. He slammed the door behind him. A sharp breath caught in her throat. The duke looked wild and beautiful and appeared not to be in total control as his obsidian eyes glittered with all manner of emotions. Did she glimpse regret, desire, and doubt?

Her gaze roamed over his six-foot-one-inch length. His suit coat was unbuttoned, and his neckcloth askew. Dark whiskers were visible on his impossibly handsome face. The wind had tossed his raven black hair, or his hand had roved through his locks.

Gideon strode toward her and dropped to his knees in front of her. "Forgive me?" his deep voice quivered.

Under closer scrutiny, she could see his eyes were bloodshot with visible dark circles. He had not slept, and he'd been drinking—the odor of stale cigar smoke and strong spirits mixed with his alluring scent.

Olivia cupped his face. The rough feel of his whiskers tickled her fingers. "Where did you go? Why did you leave me?" she asked, her voice gentle.

He leaned into her touch. "I went to my club on Albany Street. I had no idea what to do, and I needed time to think—and drink."

"Why?" she asked softly.

"There are so many things I want."

Her thumbs stroked his cheeks. "Like what?"

He met her inquiring gaze. "I want to throw your legs over my shoulders, spread you wide, and lick and taste you until you scream. But most of all, I want to make passionate love to you. Kiss and caress every inch of your skin. Hold you in my arms all night. Long, slow, agonizing strokes until we can no longer bear them. How could I ask this of you? Your past precludes any possibility of sex."

Olivia sighed. "Gideon. Two disgusting men violated me. My father abandoned me and left me in the streets without coin or a roof over my head. I survived. I came with you because I trust you as much as I am able to trust. I can't explain why. We only just met, but I do. You said we would share it all. Please, let us try."

He stood. The kiss he gave Olivia was poignant but also untamed and passionate.

Olivia gasped as he scooped her up in his arms. "Gideon!"

"Hush, sweet. Get the door, will you? Can you reach?"

Olivia leaned down and turned the handle. Gideon stepped into the hall and headed toward the stairs.

"Hobson! We are not to be disturbed!"

They laughed with pure joy as Gideon rushed up the stairs. He brought her into a large room bespoke of the man who slept in it. The elegantly ornamented bedroom consisted of dark wood walls and green and gold draperies and bedding.

He lowered her, then Gideon turned the gaslights on, and soft but bright illumination filled the room. He then removed his coat, waistcoat, and shirt. Olivia walked toward him, laying her hand flat against his chest, then she trailed her fingers over his shoulder but stopped when her finger came across raised bumps. Curious, she followed the line over his shoulder and shoulder blade. Why hadn't Olivia seen these before? Well, because she had never seen him bare-chested in a well-lit room.

"What is this?" she asked softly. Olivia had a suspicion, and it was too terrible to contemplate.

"Cigar burns. Whinstone did it various times during my childhood; they are elsewhere on my body. Reminders of the abuse I endured. A reminder that I bore the disfigurement and didn't give him the satisfaction of crying out. But that only made him angrier, you see. So, I learned to muster tears for his amusement."

Olivia embraced him. "Damn your awful stepfather. And your mother for allowing it."

"Like you, I survived," he murmured. "It may have made me stronger, but it also made me an unfeeling sod. I felt sorry for myself, which turned me hard, and bitter. And entirely selfish."

She stepped back and looked up at him, her eyes swimming with empathic tears. "I know exactly of what you speak, for I did the same."

Gideon caressed her flushed cheek. "Then let us banish those people forever."

A single tear ran down her cheek. "Yes. Banish."

He gently brushed away the tear with the pad of his thumb. "Good. I want to make love to you. Because you are attracted to me as I am to you."

Gideon leaned in and whispered in her ear. "You are wet for me. I would lay coin on it. We will not have sex if you do not wish it. But let me worship you. Say the word if you wish me to stop, and I will. Could you put your trust in me as I have in you? Give and take, Liv."

She did not answer right away.

"We take this one day at a time," Gideon urged, his words coming out in a rush. "Revel in the emotions sparking between us. Say yes. And make me the happiest of men."

His heartfelt and passionate words had seized her breath. She laid her hand flat over his heart; it thumped quickly like hers—hot desire shot through her veins.

Olivia took his hand from her cheek, raised it to her lips, and kissed it.

"Give and take—one day at a time. Very well, Gideon. I will try."

He slid the small jacket from her shoulders, then kissed the bare skin tenderly.

"The duke I observed at The Velvet did this to his duchess," Gideon murmured.

"Did he?" she replied shakily. "And what else did he do?"

"He kissed her all over," Gideon whispered as he backed her toward his bed. "Reverently, as if she were the most precious person in his entire world."

Slowly and with care, he undressed her, layer by layer, kissing every part of her skin that became exposed.

"And you are precious to me," he added.

His emotionally charged words arrowed straight to her heart, giving it a decided jolt.

Then he stopped, looking into her eyes.

"What is it?" Olivia asked.

"I am looking for any sign of anxiety or trepidation. I see none."

"That is correct, Your Grace. But look deeper, and you will see much more. Such as desire—and trust. As I said, as much trust as I can muster. Whatever I have, it is all for you."

Gideon unfastened his trousers, then pushed them down and kicked them aside. His naked body was a visual feast of masculine perfection and carved lean muscles.

Beautiful.

There was no other word to describe him. In their brief relationship, Olivia innately understood that Gideon was not perfect. But underneath his cold exterior, she knew a man of deep feeling resided.

They both carried a lot of hurt and rejection. And vast buried damage.

Gideon reached for her hands and placed them above his heart. With the tips of her fingers, Olivia explored him through the light dusting of black, curly hair over to his nipples. She caressed them into firm peaks and then leaned in to suckle them. A low, rumbling growl left Gideon's chest. His large hand clasped the back of her head, holding her in place.

Heavens, he's enjoying it.

How would it feel to have him do the same to her? Her insides dipped at the thought.

Gideon suddenly cupped her face and tilted her head to look at him. His intense gaze sent her heart fluttering. His dark eyes sparkled and shone like a black flame dancing in the irises. Their gazes locked. How did she ever think this man was cold and indifferent?

"I cannot believe this is happening to me," Gideon whispered. "After all these years."

Before she could ask what, he captured her mouth. His kiss devastated her. Gideon plunged deep, tasting, licking, and swirling every inch of her mouth.

He moaned. So did Olivia.

He was undoubtedly skilled for a man who claimed he had never kissed during his assignations. After several minutes, Gideon ended the kiss. His fingers roamed through her hair. Grabbing a fistful, he gently pulled her head back so she had no choice but to stare up at him.

"No one is welcome in what we share," he said vehemently. "I am at heart a selfish man, greedy even. I have never felt like this before. I want to possess you, claim you—love you in a way I did not think I could. I will never share. Never."

"I agree," she whispered. Gideon's fervent words sent a thrill of desire through her.

Love? Is it possible?

He kissed her again, hard and brief, then moved behind her and slowly removed her corset, laying hot, insistent kisses on every inch of exposed skin.

His large hands traversed her naked body, leaving a sizzling flame in its wake.

"No one has ever brought me to such a state. Only you, Liv."

His words.

There was such feeling and emotion in his husky voice.

They lay on the bed, Gideon rising above her. He then thoroughly explored her body with hands, lips, and teeth. Cupping her breasts, Gideon lowered his head and suckled a nipple, and it pebbled under his lips and hardened into a sensitive nub. Flicking his tongue, Olivia writhed and moaned in response. His free hand teased her curls.

"God, you are so gloriously wet. As I surmised."

He caressed all around her feminine core, stroking with care and tenderness, then inserted two fingers, thrusting slowly.

"Do you want me to stop? Is what I am doing too much like—like—"

"My assault? It's all right, Gideon. I know it is *you* touching me. I will let you know if it becomes overwhelming."

In his leisurely explorations, he found her nub. The sucking at her breast and stroking of her clit were all done in perfect rhythm. Such finesse. Olivia's eyes widened in wonderment. She had never felt like this—as if she were to fly above the clouds.

"Look at me, Liv. I want to see your face when you come."

His strokes increased, and so did her groans of desire. Her back arched off the bed, but she kept her gaze locked with his.

"Oh!" Olivia cried out as her inner muscles clutched his fingers. Her body shuddered and shook with her release.

Gideon removed his hand and gathered her close to his heart, smoothing her hair. After several minutes, he lay back on the bed and pulled her next to him, her head on his shoulder. Olivia cuddled in close and laid her hand flat over his heart.

"I didn't know it could be like that."

"Neither did I," he said. "Giving you pleasure was entirely satisfying."

"Oh, I could sleep now," she murmured, burrowing closer to his heat.

"Then sleep, Liv. I want to take this further. But when you are ready."

"And how do you want to take this further?" she asked sleepily.

"I want to thrust my aching cock inside you until I am completely spent. I want you to ride me, take your pleasure, and kiss me senselessly. I want to lick and kiss you here," Gideon cupped his hand between her legs. "And make you come again."

"Oh," she whimpered, moving against his hand. "I want all that too. Forget sleep. Thrust until spent. Now, Gideon."

He sat upright, opened his night table drawer, and retrieved an envelope.

"A condom. Safety first in all things."

Rising to his knees, he affixed it to his erect shaft, then climbed over her again. "I am afraid this will be quick; I want you too much to go slow. Those long agonizing strokes will come later."

He entered her slowly, taking his time, allowing her to grow used to his filling and stretching her. What a fascinating sensation, but much too tight. Olivia bit her lower lip, and he momentarily ceased.

"Have I hurt you?" he asked worriedly.

"Only a little. Give me more."

He groaned at that statement and did precisely that, sinking deep inside her. Now fully seated, he started to move. The pace quickened, and Olivia wrapped her legs around him, urging him on. Tilting her hips, his cock made direct contact with her sensitive nub.

"Oh, yes, there!" she cried out.

He pounded her now, and Olivia reveled in it. The headboard banged against the wall and no doubt the servants could hear.

What did it matter?

She was climbing, ready to become airborne again. Her peak slammed her hard; her nails dug into Gideon's back as her breath came in short puffs, ending with a moan.

Gideon was not far behind her; he groaned with a few more thrusts and started shaking above her.

They stayed joined, holding each other close until their breathing started to slow. Then Gideon lay flat and pulled her into his embrace.

Olivia stroked his whiskered cheek. "As far as the trust, Gideon. I will try. If I do hesitate, please know it is not you."

She wanted so much more from life than taking revenge on depraved strangers at a brothel. Her girlish dreams contained images of a handsome prince on a noble steed, riding to her door to carry her away. She banished those fanciful and hopeful images years ago. When Olivia turned to the one man in her life for support—her father—he rejected her. Implied the attack was the result of her wanton ways. And her disobedience by venturing onto London's streets against his wishes.

But she would not think of the man who raised her tonight.

Gideon took her hand and kissed the palm. "We will fight this together. One day at a time. Damn it all, Liv; we can face and fight anything and everyone. Now, we sleep. And when we awake, we have the rest of the night."

And what about the rest of their lives?

Chapter 12

GIDEON AWOKE AND GLANCED at the clock. They had slept close to an hour.

Warmth, heat, comfort, and contentment. Home.

Like none, he'd ever known. He experienced all that with Olivia.

Gideon wished to stay here forever—connected and joined. This lovemaking had him utterly undone.

Olivia murmured and cuddled in closer, still partly asleep. Quietly he moved away from her and tore off the used condom. Gideon had promised her long, slow, agonizing strokes.

Washing quickly, he brought over a warm cloth and rubbed it along Olivia's silky skin.

"Oh," she murmured. "That feels nice."

When finished, he reached for another condom.

"More?" she questioned.

"Oh, so much more."

Once inside her, Olivia groaned with every measured thrust. These last years, filled with meaningless, desolate encounters, broke apart and faded from his memory.

They all meant nothing. While this—meant *everything*.

Yes, he had mulled over this thought before, but so what? He would no doubt think about it again because it was true. Moisture gathered in his eyes, and he blinked back the sting of intense emotion that threatened to overtake him again.

Olivia raised her hips and met his languorous movements. "Gideon."

Her voice was full of awe, and Gideon understood how she felt.

He watched as another glorious climax seized Olivia. Her eyes widened, and her cries of passion clutched his heart. Many minutes passed as he concentrated on bringing her to another release.

Gideon could now tell when her desire attained its peak. He leaned in to capture her lips; his tongue thrusts matched the steady slide of his cock.

Liv whimpered and enthusiastically met every movement.

Gideon's orgasm intertwined with hers. Wave after wave of sensual sensations wracked him. Olivia's arms and legs wrapped around him tightly, shaking and shuddering. He threw his head back and cried out from the intensity of it.

Still holding each other, his ragged breathing gave way to exhausted sleep.

OLIVIA WATCHED GIDEON sleep for a long time.

He must be exhausted.

She gently pulled the quilt over him, and Gideon did not flinch. Impossibly long lashes feathered his flushed cheeks. His sensual lips parted slightly as his even breathing indicated a deep sleep. Unshaven and disheveled, he looked like a fallen angel.

Olivia looked about the room. Considering the size of this bedroom, he must have a separate bathing area. She stood and reached for his shirt and slipped it on.

On the walls were gilded framed oil paintings of battles fought long ago. Medieval knights in epic combat, sailing frigates fighting stormy seas, and red-coated soldiers lined up with muskets on a wide, barren field.

Next to the brown leather settee was a sideboard with two crystal decanters and glasses. On the opposite wall were two doors. She padded to one, opened it, and peered in—a walk-in wardrobe. Olivia crossed the threshold and smiled at the racks of suits, waistcoats, shirts, and coats lining both sides of the narrow space. The shelf above held many hats of different sizes and colors.

She headed toward the suits, lifted a sleeve to her nose, and inhaled.

Pure Gideon.

A faint whiff of his cologne mixed with his spicy scent. She rubbed the rough wool against her cheek to immerse herself in his potent aroma. Olivia turned and opened one of the many small drawers and discovered gloves of every kind made of chamois and leather. Another drawer held neckcloths and cravats of all colors and types.

Heavens, there was enough clothing here to dress five men. Well, he was a duke, after all. She turned and left the dressing room, softly closing the door behind her. Upon opening the door next to it, she gasped.

His private bath was stunning and thoroughly modern. The tips of Olivia's fingers brushed across the top of the large porcelain claw-foot tub, which was big enough for two. Hand-painted tiles with scenes of stately gardens adorned the walls. On the opposite wall was a large window with elaborate stained glass, a pattern similar to the garden design of the wall tiles.

A copper gas heater was attached to the conduits coming through the wall, as was the nearby ornate marble washbasin. The intricate etchings of the commode matched the marble basin, and it had a mahogany seat—such luxury.

She would run Gideon a warm bath. The pipes rattled and shook, startling her. A puff of gas came out of the taps, making her cough. Sticking her hand under the faucet, Olivia adjusted the faucets until an even mixture of hot and cold water came forth.

Next to the basin were several items on a wooden tray: a bottle of Taylor's Lime Aftershave, a straight razor, sandalwood shaving soap, and a brush. Also on the tray was a container of tooth powder and a bottle of Creed's cologne next to it.

Olivia unscrewed the cap and inhaled.

Gideon, in every way.

She could smell cloves, bergamot, and a hint of citrus, lemon perhaps? Sauntering over to the bath, she added a few drops of the scent to the water. Olivia leaned against the edge of the tub and relived the past hour. She had no idea that sex could be so all-consuming and compelling.

Her fingers absently ran through the rising water. Brought back from her pleasant thoughts of a naked Gideon above her and thrusting deep, she turned off the taps, laid the bottle of cologne on the counter, and headed to the bedroom.

Gideon's eyes fluttered open.

"Gideon, wake up. I've run you a bath. Come."

"I must be dreaming. An angel is whispering in my ear."

She laughed lightly.

"I could sleep for hours," he yawned, "But I'm glad you woke me."

He yawned again, stretched, and stood. Then he glanced down, as did Olivia. He was hard as a pike. She grinned and shook her head in amusement as he looked back at her.

Olivia held out her hand, and he took it. Then she led him toward the bathroom. He climbed into the tub and lowered himself. Since his legs were so long, he had to bend them slightly at the knee.

Olivia picked up the sponge and his soap and sat on the edge of the large tub. She lathered his body using a slow circular motion, beginning at his neck and across his shoulders.

Dipping the sponge in the water, Olivia then squeezed it, and rivulets of warm water trailed down his muscular chest. She leaned forward to wash his back, brushing her breasts by his cheek. A ragged moan tore from his throat.

"I picked a good time to give my valet, Jergens, the week off. You are doing an admirable job as his replacement," he murmured seductively.

Olivia laughed. "I'm glad you are pleased, Your Grace."

After dropping the sponge in the water, she soaped his hair and massaged his scalp. Gideon leaned his head back and sighed.

"No one had ever done this for me before besides a few servants. This sort of familiarity is entirely new to me and welcome." Gideon sighed contentedly.

His words filled her with joy because she felt the same.

Such intimacy. Not only lovemaking but spending time together.

"I've never brought a woman to my residence before," he continued. "I've never brought anyone to my private place."

"Then I am honored. I mean that."

Olivia stood and collected the pitcher from the counter. Filling it with warm water from the taps, she rinsed his hair, running her fingers through it while slowly washing the soap away.

Once Olivia set the empty pitcher on the floor, she headed toward the counter and busied herself. Glancing back at Gideon, she found his intense gaze was firm on her. Liv smiled and set the tray aside. She removed his shirt and stood before him, naked. Olivia stepped into the tub and straddled him, her knees resting on either side of his hips.

"I thank providence for ordering the extra-large bathtub," Gideon murmured seductively.

Olivia laughed as she reached for the shaving whisk and soap cup. After swishing the brush in the water, she lathered his face.

A dollop of soap dripped onto his upper lip. Liv reached out with her finger and swirled it away. Her finger lingered, roving over his lips. A husky moan escaped from him.

Olivia passed him the straight razor and held a round mirror before him.

"You do not want to shave me?" Gideon asked.

"I do not know how to. You would trust me with a razor?" Olivia teased.

He captured her gaze. "I trust you with my very soul."

Her lower lip trembled with emotion. "Oh, Gideon."

Silence filled the bathroom. The scraping of the razor over his heavy whiskers and the occasional splash of water were the only sounds. Once finished shaving, Gideon laid the razor on the tray and sponged off the excess soap. He reached for the mirror and laid it next to the shaver.

"Do you know how astoundingly handsome you are?" Olivia said as she stroked his freshly shaved cheek. "I especially like your nose." Her finger traced the length of it. "Long and sharp, but it fits your features perfectly. Very aristocratic."

"Do you know how intoxicating you are, Liv? Do you know how much I want you—again?"

Olivia glanced downward. His prominent erection was not hard to miss. "I have an inkling," she laughed.

"Sit here, ride me."

"Truly?"

"Yes, here is where trust comes into things. I swear that I have been careful in all my previous dealings. I will not come inside you. I want you to take your pleasure, and when I am close, I will tell you so you can rise off of me. Do you agree? If not, you can fetch a condom from the bedroom."

Olivia traced his lips with the tip of her finger. "I would prefer it if you wore the French letter or condom. It is not so much a lack of trust in you—"

"It's all right, Liv. Go and fetch one."

Nodding, she rose and climbed out of the tub. After locating the envelope on Gideon's bedside table, she returned.

Gideon clasped his cock. "Put it on. I'll help."

Once the condom was affixed, Olivia grasped his shoulders and lowered herself until he was inside her.

Laying his hands on her hips, Gideon moved her back and forth in a rocking motion.

"Oh! Oh, yes," she moaned.

He moved her hips faster while lifting his own, thrusting deep. Olivia met his movements and leaned forward so her sensitive nub could rub against him. He leaned in and suckled on her breast. It didn't take long, Olivia cried out, and her nails scored his shoulders.

"Do it; come for me again," Gideon demanded.

Could she?

It appeared so, for Olivia rode him again to another earth-shattering peak. Gideon swore, and she cupped his cheeks and kissed him fiercely as his body jerked with his release.

Gideon had introduced her to a sensual and private world where only the two of them resided. He stroked her arm as he held her close.

Nothing else mattered. The past forgotten, if only momentarily. Would there ever come a time when Olivia could banish it permanently?

She couldn't think of that now or what may lay in the future. That would come soon enough with the breaking dawn. All Olivia wanted was to stay here, in his arms.

Perhaps—forever.

And that had her petrified right down to her toes.

Chapter 13

THE FOLLOWING DAY AT breakfast, Olivia joined him wearing the same gold and brown gown she had worn to the tearoom. Gideon stood as soon as she entered the room, then dismissed the footmen.

"Allow me to fetch you breakfast. We worked up quite the appetite last night, and I made certain the staff laid out a spread of assorted breakfast foods," he suggested.

He pulled out her chair, and she sat, giving him another of her sunny smiles. "Then wait on me by all means," she purred, sending frissons of desire along his spine.

All Olivia had to do was beam at him, and he was gone.

Gideon strode to the side table and lifted the lids on the silver chafing dishes. "There are scrambled eggs with chives, or poached eggs, bacon, or country sausage, crumpets, or cheese turnovers," he took the lid off the last receptacle. "Oh, and look. Poached salmon."

"Salmon, my favorite. You requested it just for me?"

"Yes. I did."

"Would it be terrible if I said a little of everything?"

Gideon laughed. "Not at all. A little of everything, it is."

He gave her a teasing smile and placed the heaping plate in front of her. "Eat it all like a good girl."

"Are you commanding me, Your Grace?" she teased.

"You? Never."

Gideon could not believe his behavior. Who was this man flitting about the room, serving food, and teasing light-heartedly?

A smitten fool, that's what.

What the hell? He rejoiced in the sensation.

After collecting his breakfast repast, Gideon sat at the opposite end of the table. They ate quietly, then Olivia placed her utensils across her plate.

"I know we said last night we were taking this a day at a time, but blast it; I need to know *something* of the future. Am I your mistress? Am I to be a paid employee of Your Grace?"

Gideon's blood ran cold. "Money. Is that why you're here?" he asked warily.

"No, you daft man. How can you say such a thing? Is this an affair of the heart, then? I have to know where I stand." She threw her napkin on the table in exasperation.

"Yes, it most definitely *is* an affair of the heart. Mine is fully engaged, I assure you. I thought I made that clear last night,"

Olivia sighed. "You did, most thoroughly. But a woman must hear the words and experience the proof. My heart is engaged, too. Most definitely. So, where is this heading?"

Here was the opportunity to place a time limit on their affair. A brief sojourn into bliss, then return to his disconsolate and debauched life? How could he return to it after being in her arms and inside her? Part of her. Joined.

"We spend time together, get to know each other more, and make love day and night. Why can't we have it all, Liv?"

"Oh, you make it sound so easy," she said wistfully. "You never fully explained why you left me that first night."

"Simply put, I was terrified. By the intense emotions, the prospect of having someone in my home, and my impulsiveness. Scared stiff by how much I want you. It overwhelmed me. And, in the past, when overwhelmed, I ran and hid. I am heartily sorry, Liv. Old habits and all that. I'm working on it."

And that was quite the confession.

"I understand more than you know. Please, in the future, promise we will tell each other when things become too much to handle," Olivia affirmed in a soft voice.

"I promise," he murmured. At least, he would make an attempt.

Olivia nodded and took a mouthful of egg and chives.

"Come with me to Foxmont, my country seat," Gideon blurted.

"Is it in Watford, in Hertfordshire? No, I would have heard of your title since I lived further north in Kettering."

"No, it isn't in Watford, even though that is the name of the dukedom. Foxmont is outside the small village of Fobbing in Essex. About thirty miles east as the crow flies, a little over an hour by train. The place is private, and we would be away from prying eyes." Gideon sipped his tea. "I haven't been there in ages, though my steward has kept the place running efficiently, or so I assume. There is one snag, however."

Olivia buttered her cheese turnover. "What?"

"Whinstone is in residence, and I must go personally to see him off the property. While there, I will instruct the staff to prepare for our arrival and remove every last stain and trace of my miserable duke stepfather."

Olivia chewed her turnover thoughtfully and swallowed. "I thought you hated the man? Why allow him to stay?"

"Out of sight, out of mind. I reasoned if the duke were thirty miles away on a country estate, I wouldn't have to see him, talk to him, or deal with him in any way. So far, it's worked. I haven't seen him in months, and I am sure that is where he tucked away his mistress."

Gideon told her all about his mother coming to see him and why.

"Oh, my. That *is* a complication. What will you do?"

"Speak to Whinstone, see what he wants. I will make his immediate departure part of any pact with him. If I were truly heartless, I would have cut him and my mother off long ago."

"Then why didn't you?" Olivia asked.

"I suppose I am not as callous as I believed. But I will only be pushed so far. And I'm at the breaking point with these two leeches."

"After how they treated and abused you, you still pay their bills."

"Well, only a few sporadic accounts. The debts that could not wait for the quarterly payments, gambling, and the like. Giving them what they wanted to keep them at bay, giving me some peace. My late father instilled a sense of duty in me since I learned to walk, and some of it stuck—obligations to the dukedom and all that rubbish. My father left Mother a tidy sum, which she and Whinstone have lived off these past years."

Gideon snorted. "My late father was shrewd, doling out the money in increments. If he had given it to her in one lump sum, it would have been gone decades ago."

Speaking this aloud, it was clear he should have refused to pay incidentals and the like, but he owed it to his father's honor and memory to keep at least a minimum of obligation. How strange that he never used that particular honor criterion in his own dissipated dealings.

You arrogant bastard.

"When will you leave for Essex?" Olivia asked, pulling him from his self-reflection.

"Day after tomorrow. Stay here, Liv. Relax. Read. Sleep. Take tea in the afternoons. And I will return as soon as I can."

"I will," she stated, reaching for a crumpet. "And I will think it over. Going to stay with you at Foxmont."

Gideon raised an eyebrow. "Minx. Think it over?"

"What can you tell me about it?"

He finished his eggs, all while crafting a reply. "Honestly, I haven't been there much since my father died. While he was alive? I have pleasant memories of a well-situated Georgian brick manor house surrounded by sweet chestnut trees and ash and sycamore. The gardens are lush with wildflowers and shrubs, like bilberry and holly. Very pretty in the autumn." He gave her a teasing smile. "Did you know the Romans introduced the sweet chestnut tree to Britain? Not only for the nuts they ground to make flour but for timber."

Olivia laughed. "No, I didn't know that."

"You will think on Foxmont while I'm gone?"

She sobered. "Yes, on that and much more."

The air between them crackled with life.

"After breakfast, let us take a walk," Gideon suggested. "There is a dressmaker not far from here who has a few gowns you can buy for the trip. If you decide to join me, that is. I do have an appointment later this afternoon." He told her of his newfound work with certain members of the House of Lords and a select few Members of Parliament.

"Oh!" Olivia exclaimed. "I think that is brilliant. I am so proud of you for taking your responsibility seriously. Well done."

That praise, the warmth, and admiration in her voice were music to his ears. Tremain Hornsby was right: love *can* make one examine one's soul.

And hell, he *was* falling in love.

It beggared all belief.

He would work twice as hard at the parliamentary causes in order to bask in her approval.

"Your words mean the world to me, Liv. You have no idea."

"Take as long as is necessary this afternoon. There are so many people in need."

"Yes, there is. But as soon as I return, it is off to bed. We will have supper served on trays between the bouts of lovemaking."

Olivia blushed prettily. "And I will ride you again?"

He closed his eyes, remembering the night she did that very thing. Gideon moaned. "Yes, for all its worth."

Gideon, at last, now understood what Christian, Asher, and Brandon had discovered. Now that he had experienced it, he never wanted to let it go.

Ever.

GIDEON SETTLED INTO his first-class coach, his overnight bag placed at his feet by the porter. The trip to Foxmont would give him enough time to gather his thoughts. The whistle blew, and the train lurched forward, expelling a burst of steam.

He had not faced his stepfather in some months. The prospect did not appeal. The man stood nearly six and a half feet tall, and Gideon always felt small in his presence. The four inches difference in stature only constituted part of the reason. His stepfather was cold, authoritative, dismissive, indifferent, and had been as far back as Gideon could remember.

After all, Gideon had learned it from somewhere. His stepfather's eyes could freeze you where you stood with their piercing ice-blue gaze. He would look down his long, hawk nose, pursing his thin lips, and spew his long list of how Gideon had disappointed him.

What had he not mentioned to Olivia?

Gideon was seriously contemplating marriage. To her. Right away or as soon as he could make such arrangements. Which meant he wanted them to spend most of their time at Foxmont, except when he needed to come to London for his parliamentary commitments. Which meant Whinstone had to leave. Immediately, if not sooner.

Gideon sat back in his seat and closed his eyes. Last night exceeded all his expectations, and the experience was so intimate it stilled his heart to recall it.

Olivia had unlocked his heart and let warmth and affection flood in for the first time in his lonely life. They shared a healthy passion, which made the prospect of marriage satisfying. If the past two nights were any indication, there were many more exciting explorations. But what he felt was beyond the carnal.

Already he missed Olivia, the feel of her soft body next to his.

Last night was one of the best nights of sleep of his life. She gave him comfort and surcease to all the gloomy thoughts of self-loathing and lonesomeness that often rattled about in his brain.

The constant ache in his chest, the excitement at seeing her, proved his point. Gideon derived great enjoyment just speaking with her. This morning, sharing breakfast and conversation with her again had such a domestic intimacy that he yearned for more.

He wanted to do everything for her.

This *must* be love.

The impossible had happened.

Gideon had fallen entirely and profoundly in love. No one had ever stirred these feelings in him before; he recognized and welcomed the love.

Olivia's strength and vulnerability stirred such a maelstrom of emotions in him.

He supposed—or at least hoped—she felt the same.

Gideon soon drifted off into a peaceful sleep.

Chapter 14

ANNOYED, GIDEON WAITED in Foxmont's primary library as if he were a guest when it was his country estate by birthright. He paced and then sat in the leather wing chair facing the fireplace. The room was plain and cold, with few furnishings or decorative items.

It was not as Gideon remembered it.

Whinstone certainly made himself at home, the miserable cretin.

Well, that will cease.

The door opened at last, and his stepfather strode in, removing his gloves. The duke had been out riding, the crop still tucked under his arm, his tall boots splashed with mud. The man looked no older except with a few more wrinkles, perhaps. The severe lines carved around his mouth were a little deeper. He still had the broad-shouldered but lithe look of his younger years. But then, Whinstone was only eighteen years older than Gideon.

"What do I owe this pleasure, Watford?" Whinstone ground out.

Such a warm greeting from the man who had been his stepfather for thirty years, Gideon thought sarcastically, but he expected no less. The duke walked to the sideboard, threw his gloves and crop down on the table, and poured himself a brandy. He did not offer Gideon anything.

"Well? Speak, boy, why are you here? Get one of your whores pregnant? Did you beat one of the lads you bugger to a bloody pulp and need my help to hush it up? Do not look so indignant. I know where your cock has been. 'Lord Craven.' You disgust me."

Gideon tightened his fists, willing his anger back.

Damn him to hell.

Whinstone knew referring to him as "boy" would cause a reaction. Nor would Gideon answer to the scurrilous and fallacious gossip, for none of it was true.

"I have come to inform you I intend to move here, so you are to vacate this manor house forthwith. I asked Mother to give you notice but thought it best to do it in person. Your free ride is at an end," he said through clenched teeth.

"Why? I don't remember you showing any interest in staying here. There must be a reason."

"I intend to marry in the near future."

"Intend to marry? Will you, indeed? Done sowing those oats, I take it? About time you set aside your debauched ways and set up your nursery."

Gideon watched his stepfather pace about sipping his brandy. What hypocrisy. If this were in medieval times, he could imagine sitting in the castle keep while his stepfather skinned and butchered a dead stag while they spoke.

"I will give you a list of a few suitable names, young women of good breeding," Whinstone continued in that cold, arrogant way. "You will choose one, marry her, get her pregnant with an heir and a spare; then you may continue your depraved and corrupt way of life. It is no matter to me, but the line must be secured. I promised your mother I would assist in seeing it done. You are forty, after all. It is well past time."

"The line must be secured? When did you ever care about such things?" Gideon scoffed.

"I have concluded that nothing else matters *except* the title. Nothing will be remembered, not our achievements, exploits, not even the name: nothing but the title. When we are dead and buried, nothing continues—*but* the title. Especially for a duke and the requirement to ensure the line."

Again, what naked hypocrisy from a man who had done nothing to secure his own line. Could it be his pregnant mistress had brought these thoughts to the forefront?

Not that Gideon cared one way or the other.

"I have a woman in mind, so your list is useless. She is a vicar's daughter, not that it is any of your business."

Gideon inwardly admonished himself for revealing that bit of information. In fact, he shouldn't have mentioned the marriage at all. Damn the miserable memories and the damage it had inflicted—which resulted in the loosening of his tongue.

The duke barked a cynical laugh. "Does she have any idea what you have done these past years? How you've wallowed in the gutter?"

"I have told her of my past, and she has told me of hers. We are moving beyond it."

"What dissolute history could a vicar's daughter have? Come now; you did not meet this young lady at a vicarage. She is one of your whores, is she not?" The duke's eyes narrowed suspiciously.

"She is not a wh—"

His stepfather held up his hand. "Enough. You will not follow through on this lunacy. You have one of the richest dukedoms in the realm, and you think to sully the family with an alliance with a damned slut? Your mother will be mortified at the news. If you like how this woman sucks your cock, keep her on as a mistress. But marry and see to your heirs."

"It is no one's business whom I choose, and it is most especially not yours—or my mother's," Gideon replied in a calm but deadly tone.

The duke slammed the snifter on the table. "Even if you could veil her sordid past, a vicar's daughter? Perhaps she could marry a schoolmaster, but not a duke!" his stepfather thundered. "Fuck her and have done with her. But you will *not* marry her."

Gideon's fury broke through. He stood and faced his stepfather toe-to-toe.

"You have no say in my life, not for years. You must pack your measly possessions and leave Foxmont in three days. Where you go, I care not. See Mother for a handout as you usually do."

Whinstone gave him an oily grin. "Your mother sent a message informing me of your conversation with her. If you want me gone, you will pay my specific price. It is 1898, and the laws have changed regarding divorce. I wish you to convince your mother to remove the hooks she planted in me these last decades and release me."

Gideon laughed. "What? You could have divorced her years ago when the laws changed."

"Well, doing so was not to my monetary advantage then. Besides, I am fifty-eight, and I need an heir."

And there it was. This talk of ensuring the line had nothing to do with Gideon but Whinstone's selfish needs.

"Speaking of setting up a nursery, Mother told me of your request regarding the poor woman you impregnated." Gideon crossed his arms. "You want to marry your mistress and make the child legitimate, and that is why you had Mother approach me. *That* is your true motivation."

Whinstone shrugged. "Annabella is a baronet's daughter, and I'll wager, a good breeder. If the child is not a boy, I will keep going until I get one. I've put this off long enough. I will require a generous settlement in the divorce if you wish for me to keep quiet about the more sordid aspects of my marriage to your mother. Think of the public scandal."

"I don't take kindly to threats," Gideon hissed dangerously.

The duke picked up his gloves and crop. "Think over what I said, and we will continue this conversation over dinner. Did you bring your valet?"

"No, Jergens is not with me."

"I will have one of my footmen attend to you."

Turning on his heel, Whinstone marched from the room.

My footmen?

Yes, the man was entirely too comfortable here. He was acting as if this was his estate. It was past time for him to go. Gideon growled, his insides in knots as always in dealing with his stepfather. Because part of him would always be that vulnerable, lonely boy that Whinstone had preyed upon.

And Gideon would ensure that part of him would stay well hidden in the future.

Chapter 15

GIDEON IMPATIENTLY waited, tapping his fingers on the table. Since his childhood, no one ate until Whinstone deemed to make an appearance.

His stepfather strolled in dressed for dinner in his black evening coat, silver waistcoat, and crisp, snowy cravat with a diamond stickpin glittering in the cloth. The duke had golden-brown hair threaded with gray and a sharply angled face. No doubt the bastard was starting to feel his age, and it explained the urgency in seeing to his heir.

The footmen jumped to attention and served the soup.

Gideon stared into the bowl. God, he hated Minestrone. His stepfather had kept his eating habits the same for the past several years.

Whinstone reached into his side pocket and pushed a meticulously folded piece of stationery toward him. "I have taken the liberty of writing down a few names of suitable women for you to consider."

Gideon glanced at the paper and then looked away. "Stop trying to control me. Those days have long passed."

The spoon halted halfway to the duke's mouth. "As you said. The naughty daughter of a vicar. However, this list will serve in case circumstances change. As I said earlier, assist me with what I want, and I will return the favor."

"And do what, exactly?"

"Get me the divorce and a settlement, and I will be gone from your life forever. And your mother's. I am thoroughly sick of the screeching, controlling harpy."

"I take it you never loved my mother, then?" Gideon asked sarcastically.

He knew the answer; he just wanted his stepfather to admit it.

"No. I never even liked the duchess. But twice a week for seven years, I went to her bed and performed my duty. She finally got pregnant, only to have the temerity to have two miscarriages during that time. One was far along enough to be fully formed. A son. I never forgave her for that."

"As if she did it on purpose. You always were a cold bastard and never loved anyone," Gideon barked.

The duke's frosty eyes narrowed in obvious annoyance. "Love. Stuff and nonsense and the fiction of drunken poets. You are a fine one to talk. You know nothing of what love is, either. It is duty and survival. That is all."

Gideon shook his head in disbelief. "If I know nothing of love, it is thanks to you and my mother. I would hazard a guess you've never had a tender feeling in your life. Not even lust, I'll wager."

"I feel lust. Unlike you, I am discreet in my affairs. I do not rut everything that moves or breathes. No scandal will land at my door. Can you say the same, boy?"

Gideon pushed the soup bowl away. "I just turned forty, and I am hardly a boy. Call me that again, and I will beat you bloody as you so richly deserve."

Whinstone grunted in response. The footmen hurried over to remove Gideon's bowl and brought platters of sole to the table. Jesus, he hated this type of fish as well. Knowing his stepfather, he no doubt had these foods served, knowing that Gideon detested them. Gideon picked up the smallest slice with the serving utensils.

"How long have you known this—vicar's daughter?" his stepfather sneered.

"Long enough."

The duke's booming and humorless laugh filled the cavernous dining room. "You are a fool. That is not love; you are cunny-struck."

"And how would you know?"

"I know. I married at twenty-two because of lust and was a widower by twenty-four. My first wife is decaying in the ground with her infant," the duke replied dismissively.

"You were married before my mother? Why didn't you mention it?" Gideon couldn't believe this.

The duke slurped his soup. Then he hesitated and responded with a chilly coldness, "She isn't worth remembering."

Fury boiled in his veins. Good God, the man was even more of a monster than he had initially believed.

Gideon dropped his fork and knife in contempt. "I do not want that life for me. I crave more. I want to love."

"Ha!" his stepfather barked. "Now I know you have gone mad. As I said, it's stuff and nonsense. You've caught a fever, and it will pass soon enough. Now, enough of this. What of the proposal I have laid before you?"

"I will approach Mother about the divorce. In the meantime, you are to vacate Foxmont in three days."

Whinstone reached for a roll and tore it in half. "Let's make it three weeks. I need time to make arrangements, which will also give you time to secure your mother's agreement. In writing, legal like. As for the settlement, I will require sixty thousand pounds."

Gideon started coughing and took a drink to wash down the horrible-tasting fish.

Sufficiently recovered, he shook his head. "You have overplayed your hand, Whinstone. For that price, you can keep Foxmont, and damn you and your bastard spawn."

"I don't want this damned drafty place. I will file for divorce and drag the case through the courts. Call upon the newspapers and tabloids and give them salacious personal details, some true, some fake, but it will be enough to sully your name and your clinging, aging mother's."

Whinstone's piggy eyes narrowed further. "I will also tell them of your slut. I will find out what brothel she came from, as I have eyes and ears all over the East End."

Gideon was out of his chair before he could blink. This time, alcohol did not slow down his reaction time as it had with Damon. He caught his stepfather square in the face. Bone cracked, and Whinstone screamed in pain. How long had Gideon waited to do this to his abuser?

It was tempting to continue to thrash him until he was a bloody pulp beneath his fists, but Gideon shook out his hand and returned to his seat. He would be no better than Whinstone if he did as he wished.

"You miserable cretin, you hit me!" his stepfather whined.

"I'll do worse if you do not stop caterwauling." Gideon turned to the footmen. "Leave us."

The young men needed no further instruction as they hurried from the room and closed the door. No doubt this exchange will be the tattle below stairs.

Whinstone held a cloth napkin to his nose as he tilted his head back to stem the bleeding.

"As I said, you have overplayed your hand," Gideon said, his voice calm. "To hell with you and my mother. Drag the family name through the mud. I could not care less. Nor do I care if you get a divorce and marry your mistress. That has nothing to do with me. So, I will *not* be approaching my mother on that particular subject. When I leave in the morning, I will stop by the village to arrange with the parish constable to physically remove you in three days."

"You cannot do that," Whinstone snapped.

"I can. There is no written contract between us, nor are you paying me rent. You are a squatter, and the authorities will treat you as such. If you have any further need for money, that is between you and my mother, as I will no longer be funding your vices. You had better hope the baronet's daughter comes with a settlement because once you divorce my mother, the spigot is off permanently." Gideon pushed the plate of sole from him and stood. "Goodnight. And fuck you."

As Gideon strode from the room, Whinstone's torrent of colorful obscenities followed him up the stairs.

One of the first things he would do was fire the entire staff here at Foxmont. Gideon recognized no one save Henderson, the butler. Was Mrs. Peterson still here as a cook?

He had no time to investigate the matter. The sooner he was away from here, the better.

Chapman, his steward, had told him there was a substantial turnover in staff over the past couple of years, as many did not want to serve Whinstone in any way. There was a minimum of servants on the payroll, and the place showed neglect.

That neglect was all on Gideon's shoulders. It was far easier to tuck Whinstone away out of sight. Yet more proof of Gideon's selfish nature. He never thought of the staff, some of which had been at Foxmont for decades. Chapman assisted some in finding other positions, but the rest?

Blast it all.

The only positive note to this visit is he had finally stood up to that odious toad. The bonds of cruelty and abuse that had had such a hold on him for decades were finally breaking apart.

And it was well past time to right all other wrongs.

SANFORD WATCHED HIS stepson leave the room with his chin held high.

Insolent pup, with whom does he think he is dealing?

The duke marched to the wall and pressed the bell, still holding the bloody cloth to his nose. When the butler entered, he demanded, "Send for the doctor, then bring Jonas to me at once. Is he on the premises?"

"He is, Your Grace."

The burly ex-convict, Jonas Bisby, would be the man to carry out this particular work for him.

"Well then, just don't stand there, you addle-pated old fool; get on with it!" he roared at the butler. Henderson disappeared, and Whinstone marched over to the decanters and poured a whiskey.

Watford was always an infuriating little pustule. But, oh, how he had fun bullying and beating the little bastard until he shot up to a little over six feet in height when he was sixteen. After that, Sanford kept the abuse verbal only.

There was a delicious sort of gratification to watch the boy, then, as a young man, struggle to hide his fear, then later, his disgust and loathing. Sanford fed on that hate for years, and it almost made up for putting up with his annoying lady wife.

Almost.

To know he had inflicted permanent damage on Watford was gratifying, indeed. But how dare Watford lay a hand on him.

Oh, he will pay for that transgression.

Jonas lumbered into the library. He touched his forelock. "Aye, Your Grace."

"There is a train leaving at nine this evening. You are to travel to London post haste to my stepson's 34 Hyde Park Corner residence. You are to evict the slut in place by any means necessary and dump her in Whitechapel, where she belongs. Inform her if she dares to contact my stepson again, you will cut off her pretty tits and slit her throat for good measure."

"You know for sure she's there, Your Grace?"

"Not completely, but I know my stepson. If he believes himself in love, then he has the woman with him. He's a needy little bastard."

Sanford paused. "Tell her that it was Watford that gave this order, and he wants nothing to do with her and has had his fill. Take someone with you, someone who can keep his mouth shut. And do not rouse the duke's servants, be as quiet as possible, understand?"

"If you wish, Your Grace, we can slit her throat for real. Whores are always turning up dead in Whitechapel, sure as brass."

Sanford seriously contemplated the suggestion. Then he gave a nonchalant shrug. "No. We will be civilized in this instance and give her a warning. But make sure she understands the consequences. My stepson travels to London in the morning, so all traces of her must be erased from his residence before then, understand?"

Jonas touched his forelock. "Leave it with me, Your Grace."

Tossing aside the bloody cloth, Sanford reached into his side pocket and pulled out a small roll of pound notes. He peeled off a couple and handed them to Jonas.

"You and your man will have to stay the night in London but return on the first train in the morning. I'll pay you the rest when you finish the job. Once you are back, we will rent wagons and load them with whatever we can carry. My stepson wants me gone from the premises? Then we will help ourselves to whatever is valuable in this wretched pile of bricks."

"Aye, Your Grace." Jonas departed.

With a smug smile, Sanford poured a generous snifter of brandy.

"Is he gone?"

Sanford didn't turn to acknowledge the reedy female voice. It was his current mistress, Annabella. She could be a blubbering, clinging thing, but he would tolerate her—as long as she carried his child.

He swirled the brandy in the snifter. The prospect of marriage did not appeal, but his child *must* be legitimate.

His *son*.

And by God, his son would be everything Watford was not. Strong, formidable, resolute. Whatever other descriptive words fit, Sanford would ensure it if he had to beat the boy—the best way to toughen him up.

With a sort of twisted admiration, he was impressed by how Watford had stood up to him. He toughened up at last.

It took long enough.

Sanford chuckled as he picked up a napkin and held it to his broken and still bleeding nose. Yes, all those beatings finally made a man out of Watford. He had finally struck back after all these years.

"Sanford, what happened, are you injured?" Annabella asked tentatively.

"Go back to bed. In your own room. I don't need nursing; the doctor is coming directly."

"But, I—"

He turned to face her, his face no doubt looking as thunderous as he felt.

"I said leave me!" he roared.

Annabella visibly winced and hurried from the room. Sanford didn't care; he had more important matters to consider.

Evict him, will he?

He would make certain Watford paid the price.

Chapter 16

OLIVIA DECIDED TO SLEEP in Gideon's bed. His scent gave her comfort in his absence. Already she missed him, and he had barely been gone twenty-four hours. She snuggled closer into the pillow and inhaled. A pleasant ache throbbed between her legs. Last night, they had made love many times, and again that morning. Indeed, she had no idea sex could be so—enjoyable.

Soul-stirring—so heartbreakingly intense.

Gideon concealed his emotions much the way she did. But when they were alone together, the walls around their hearts disintegrated. Olivia had seen the change in him.

She'd heard gossip about his cold disregard for people in the past. But now, he had joined a group of progressive men in Parliament to bring positive change to those less fortunate.

Oh, how it revealed the well-hidden good man that had resided inside him all these years. When Gideon looked at her, the ice in his dark eyes melted. His smile radiated as glorious as an early sunrise.

Two people resided inside him: Gideon, the compassionate man, passionate lover, and the overbearing haughty Duke of Watford. Make that *three* men living within him. There was also the damaged and scarred boy. Perhaps that was what she feared most, that the other two would take over, and Gideon would cease to exist.

As far as the future, and in what capacity she would be with him, and for how long, was not something Olivia wanted to contemplate today; she was too deliriously happy.

And there was no denying she was falling in love with Gideon.

There.

Olivia admitted her feelings to herself at last. Satisfied she had resolved her internal issues, she drifted into a deep sleep.

The door to the bedroom burst open, and two brawny men entered, closing it quietly behind them. One held a lit lantern, and the other carried a large knife.

"Not a peep, princess. Or I'll gut the first person that bursts through that door, understand?"

Cold fear gripped her tight. Holding the blankets up to her chin, she nodded.

"Look at her, all cozy-like in the master's bed. I'll bet it's soft, and I'll bet *you're* soft." The taller man grinned; yellow teeth were visible in the shadows from the illuminated light.

Not again. *Two men.*

The memory of her brutal attack flickered through her mind. She would not survive another violation.

"Where are your things? Speak up! We haven't got all bleeding night," Yellow Teeth demanded.

"Room down the hall," she croaked.

The other man grabbed her arm roughly and pulled her from the bed so suddenly that she fell to the floor. "Here now, keep it quiet. It's past eleven, and we don't want no disturbance. No harm to the staff if possible."

"Right," replied the other man. "He didn't say nothin' about no harm to her, though."

Who was this 'he' they spoke about? Olivia's insides knotted, her mind racing in all directions.

Yellow Teeth grabbed her arm and brought her roughly to her feet. "Listen to me. The Duke of Watford wants you gone from his home and bed, and you're never to return nor contact him." He laid the knife across her cleavage, and the cold blade pushed against the top of her breasts. "If you do, I'll cut off these pretty titties of yours and slit your throat for good measure. Understand?"

No. Gideon would *not* do this. She refused to believe it.

Olivia must have been shaking her head because Yellow Teeth continued, "His nibs said he got everything he wanted from you. He's had his fill. You know the duke never stays with a woman more than a night or two. Don't tell me you believed his soft lies. Women. You're all so bleeding stupid."

The other man cackled evilly, his gaze fixed on her bosom. Nausea churned her insides. A flicker of doubt ignited, and it began to pick at her. Could Gideon be behind this? What did she know of him, really?

Her mind raced, trying to go over their short time together. Was everything they said to each other and what they shared physically all counterfeit on the duke's end? Was she stupid and gullible? The doubt started to spread through her like a virus.

Yellow Teeth pushed her toward Wool Trousers.

"The room down the hall, get her gear, and let's hit the cobbles before the staff stirs."

Wool Trousers took the knife, passed the lantern to the other, and held the blade at her throat as he pushed her toward the door.

"Open it and keep quiet. Show me the room." He came up behind her and rubbed his groin against her backside. "Blimey, but you're a lush one."

"Never mind that you, bastard," Yellow Teeth hissed. "Just hurry up."

The tea and biscuits she had before bedtime churned in her stomach. Her trembling hand reached for the handle and turned it. The door squeaked open, and one of the men pushed her out into the hall. The place was deathly silent; no doubt the staff had already gone to bed.

Olivia's legs felt like rubber, but she trod toward the guest room.

Once inside, Wool Trousers whispered his foul breath into her ear. "Gather up everythin' you own. We're leavin'."

"I have to change—"

"Bollocks to that. What you wearin' is enough. Hurry up, or I'll give you a clout."

He could not be serious; she only wore a thin cotton nightgown. She would freeze.

Stay calm.

Olivia blinked back hot tears as she grabbed her carpetbag. She hadn't brought much to Gideon's home. Once they settled their plans, she intended to return to The Velvet to gather the rest of her belongings.

Olivia stuffed her few pieces of clothing into the bag along with her toiletries. Her hands shook. Her memory returned to the thirty gold sovereigns Gideon had offered her that first night. She could use the money now. Her savings were still in James's safe, and Olivia hadn't had the chance to collect them. Leaving the money there could be the wisest thing she had done. At least there would be a small amount of coin to see her through.

Depending on what these disgusting, ugly men would do—to her. Olivia glanced frantically about the room, looking for anything she could use as a weapon. Then what, hit her attackers? Raise a ruckus? They would harm the staff; she knew it deep in the chilled marrow of her bones.

Wool Trousers pulled her from the room toward Yellow Teeth, who waited in the hall. They were down the stairs and out the rear entrance before she could blink, and the men shoved Olivia into a small carriage. Yellow Teeth climbed in with her while Wool Trousers sat behind the horses and snapped the reins. The horses' hooves pounded on the cobbles.

"Gideon is not behind this."

Olivia's mind swirled in confusion. Whether she made the declaration to convince herself or make the point to Yellow Teeth, she was unsure. One moment she was convinced Gideon had nothing to do with this abduction; the next, she cursed his callous dismissal of her.

"What do you know of His Grace? He's a spoiled, pampered aristo who uses up people and spits them out," Yellow Teeth snarled. "They all do it."

"Please, let me go." Her voice shook. Cold, raw fear gripped her.

"We're taking you to Whitechapel to be among your own. Now, shut your gob. You're lucky I didn't let *him* in here with you. He'd have you bent over the seat, quick as brass."

This kidnapping could not be happening. Even though Olivia kept repeating in her mind that Gideon could not be behind this, the sliver of doubt grew, and its brutal tentacles curled about her heart.

If he did, then that layer of trust that had built between them had just been smashed to bits.

Along with her heart.

Before she knew it, Olivia was dragged from the carriage and into a dark alley. She tried to get her bearings but could not ascertain her exact location. Whitechapel, to be sure, but what street was anyone's guess? She could hear laughter, raised voices, and bawdy singing. Could she be near a pub? If so, then she could be anywhere.

Blinking, Olivia tried to make out any nearby buildings and chimney stacks when Yellow Teeth's meaty fist pounded her midsection. Her blurred vision could make out Wool Trousers standing nearby, cackling while he rubbed his crotch.

Another punch sent her reeling, and she sprawled on the wet, grimy cobbles.

The spring late-night air was cold and damp, and the odor of rotting rubbish wafted from nearby overflowing bins. A boot slammed Olivia's ribs, and Olivia cried out in agonizing pain. Her carpet bag hit her in the chest, and she fell to the ground. Olivia grabbed it as a shipwreck victim clung to debris to keep from drowning in the cold ocean.

"Here, she's softened up. Bend her over the crate there," Wool Trousers hissed.

"We haven't time for this—"

"Bugger that. A couple of quick thrusts, then you have a go."

Olivia's insides twisted in disgust.

No.

Her head spun, and her vision was hazy and doubled. Wool Trousers lumbered toward her. Olivia frantically looked about for anything she could use to bludgeon them, and all she had was the bag.

That would have to do.

Wool Trousers wrenched her to her feet and spun her around. With all her strength, she swung the bag in a roundhouse blow, knocking the wretched man in the head.

He staggered, then fell to one knee, cursing all the while.

Olivia didn't hesitate; she thrust her leg out, hoping to disable him by kicking him in his man parts. Instead, the blow landed in his chest area. Wool Trousers cried out, and she gave him another swat with her carpetbag.

But it wasn't enough to debilitate him.

The man scrambled to his feet and grabbed her arms. Olivia struggled the best she could, kicking and flailing. But he was too strong.

"Enough of this," Yellow Teeth hissed. "We've got to go—"

"Here! What are you two doing?" a woman's voice rang out. "There's a copper round the corner. I'll whistle for him, yeah?"

The men backed away, and Olivia fell to the ground, her shaky legs unable to hold her weight.

Five women were standing at the head of the alley. Olivia could not keep the bile down, and she vomited. A black fog covered her, but she fought it. She could not fall unconscious, not now.

Fight.

"It's just a bunch of bleedin' back-alley Sallys. Feck off, the lot of ya!" Wool Trousers yelled.

A woman with red hair stepped out in front. Lifting her skirt, she whipped out a large knife from her garter. "No, *you* feck off and all. I meant it about the copper. Leave now, and I won't call for him, yeah? I am handy with a blade; I will carve you off in bits."

The men cursed, and Olivia heard their boots pounding away on the cobbles. The sound grew fainter until she made out the jingle of the harness as the carriage departed.

The red-haired woman kneeled and cradled her close. "Bleedin' hell, but they worked you over."

Another woman glanced down at her. "Ain't never seen her before. What street does she work, I wonder? One of the Old Nichol's Gang prossies, maybe."

"Give over, Cath! She's in her nightdress. Here, help me. Can you stand, love?" The red-haired woman asked.

It took Olivia a few seconds to realize the woman addressed the question to her. She tried to speak, but her lip was swollen and split.

"C-c-c-can you take me to The Velvet Vine and Tackle?" she managed to say.

The other woman snorted. "I knew it. She's the same as us."

They helped her stand, and she wobbled, so the redhead grasped her arm tightly.

"Not the same as us. The Velvet is a posh place. Classier than the alleys, at any rate. It's only a few streets over. I'll take her. You lot get back out there as we've shillings to earn. Stay close together, as I taught you. Pass me her bag, Cath."

The walk toward the brothel was laborious and slow, as Olivia could hardly stand.

"Chin up, love," the woman soothed. "We're almost there. It's lucky we came along. We have to look out for each other, sure as shite." The woman had a slight Irish accent and smelled of beer and rose-scented soap. Although tall and attractive, her clothes were shabby.

"Thank you. Please, what's your name?" Olivia rasped.

"My name's Mary O'Toole. Come down to the Ten Bells when you're feeling better, and we'll share a bowl of stew and a mug of ale. I'm there every day for lunch. What do you say, love?"

Olivia nodded.

Finally, they arrived. The woman banged on the door, and the small window slid open.

"It's Olivia. Get Pan. Hurry." Olivia managed to croak.

The blackness she fought so hard to keep back overcame her at last.

Chapter 17

GIDEON CAUGHT THE EARLY train back to London. Be damned if he would stay in his stepfather's presence a moment longer.

Their final words were acrimonious and bitter, as usual, with the duke's closing pronouncement that he would not suffer a whore as Gideon's wife. Gideon, in reply, told his stepfather to go straight to hell—a tender parting.

Gideon should never have mentioned Olivia the way he did, let alone his possible plans for marriage. All it had accomplished was giving his stepfather fuel for his vitriol. He knew better.

Dealing with Whinstone fermented old resentments and laid the damage bare. Well, at least he got a long-overdue punch out of the way. Physical altercations never solved anything, but it was damned satisfying at the moment.

Gideon adjusted the ruby cufflinks on his shirt, then sat his hat on the seat next to him. The English countryside whizzed by his window, but it could not pass quickly enough.

He ached for Olivia.

Standing up to Whinstone and declaring his feelings cemented them further into his weary soul. He *loved* Olivia and should have told her while she lay in his arms the night before. His stomach grumbled as he had to forgo breakfast. The desire to be out of his stepfather's presence—and be back in Olivia's—spurred his actions.

Marriage.

Somewhere in the dark recesses of his mind, at some point, he knew he would have to marry. If he hadn't met Olivia, perhaps he would have taken the duke's folded piece of paper and coolly chosen a random name.

Traditional marriage was out of the question. Damn it all if Gideon would wait weeks for banns to be read and months for a standard betrothal. He did not need the permission of Olivia's adoptive father, as she was well past the age of consent.

How surprising that they both had fractured relationships with their respective so-called father figures. Having a title caused a lot of past sins to be washed away. Like the sin of "marrying beneath you."

Gideon hated society and its judgmental ways. He should take a page from Christian's book. And Asher as well. Marry the woman you love, stand proudly beside her, and hang everyone else. It will be a new century in two years; would all this society falderal even matter? Gideon supposed he would have to show respect for the institution if he and Olivia were to have children.

Children.

One thing he would make damned sure of, he would *never* be like his stepfather. Or like Olivia's adoptive father. Gideon would show affection and understanding towards their children and freely give his love and support. Share everything.

And never, *ever* strike them, no matter what.

In the murky recesses of his blackened soul, he knew he could effortlessly become a man like his cold, unsympathetic stepfather. He had been that man for more years than he cared to count, and he would have to fight it for the rest of his days.

With Olivia at his side, the battle—and the war—would be easily won. Already she was his touchstone to humanity.

Gideon sat back in his seat and gazed at the scenery. A sense of calm settled inside him. For once, a bleak future did not yawn before him. Satisfied that he had resolved any possible problems, he lowered his head and dozed.

HE HAD A FEW QUICK stops before Gideon returned to his town house and Olivia. He wanted to buy Olivia some flowers. And speaking of amends, he decided to see his Aunt Mirella, as her house was on the way.

She greeted him more warmly than he deserved, for it had been ages since he had seen her. How many times had he wished Mirella were his mother instead?

"Dear Gideon, what do I owe this pleasure?" she gushed happily.

"First, I apologize for not coming sooner for a visit and not asking you personally to take Mother in. I should have done it instead of sending my steward, Mr. Chapman." He handed her a bouquet of daisies and other wildflowers. "For you."

"Oh, how wonderful. Mary, put these in water and bring us tea, please."

The maid took the flowers and departed, leaving them alone.

"There is no need for apologies, Gideon."

"There is."

They exchanged small talk until the maid returned with the tray, then left them alone again.

Aunt Mirella poured him a cup of tea and passed it to him. "A duke has many duties; I understand why you did not come before now."

Gideon scoffed. "Many duties? Not really. You do realize what you will be taking on regarding my mother?"

His aunt nodded. "Portia is two years older. Even as a child, she was a selfish being. But here's the thing, try as she might; Portia never could intimidate me. Besides, Portia is my sister; I care for her despite her flaws. She won't come easily."

Gideon crossed his legs and sipped his tea. "No. But she will have no choice as I am stopping the rent on her residence."

"About time, my dear Gideon. Portia should be paying her way. Perhaps she will think twice the next time Whinstone comes hat in hand for money."

Aunt Mirella sighed. "You know, I begged Portia to allow you to come live with me after her marriage to that despicable man. She considered it. But Whinstone put an end to that proposition."

And Gideon knew why. The duke wanted him around to bully and beat for his amusement. But he would not tell his aunt that sordid story. Not today.

"I wish that she had allowed it," he murmured.

Her brows furrowed. "Perhaps I should have been more forceful."

"Do not concern yourself. I do have one question. My mother recently stated that my father had a mistress. Is that true?"

"Would it matter if he had? Would it change your opinion of him?" his aunt asked.

"No, I suppose not. I don't have that many memories. I was ten when my father died, and he wasn't around much near the end."

"Your father loved your mother—at first. I believe that, in her way, she loved him. The early years of their marriage were happy, and your mother's demeanor was essentially kind—for a time. Even she could not keep up the pretense for long. By the fourth year, they were apart more than they were together."

Aunt Mirella frowned. "Your father did not have a long-term mistress. He told me he had two brief dalliances after they separated. I don't know how to say this."

She fished a handkerchief from her sleeve and dabbed her eyes. "Your father and I grew close during his last two and a half years. It was before I met my late husband. Oh, drat it all. We had a brief affair, and there was even talk of a future. But then he fell ill. Cancer of the stomach. Then, he was gone so quickly. Oh, I shouldn't be telling you this. I still carry the guilt to this day. I betrayed my sister. And you."

Well. You could knock Gideon over with a feather.

There was no use in mentioning how he was neglected and abused as a child. Why heap more guilt on his poor aunt? Another sign he had changed. Gideon wouldn't have cared about his aunt's feelings in the not-so-recent past.

"A future, Aunt?" he asked softly. "A man cannot marry his sister-in-law. It is in the Marriage Act. Even if my parents had managed to obtain a divorce."

She sniffled and wiped her nose. "I know. It would have been a clandestine affair carried out in the shadows. Deep down, we knew there was no future. Your father may have known he wasn't well and didn't tell anyone, even when we were involved. Perhaps he wanted a bit of happiness."

Aunt Mirella tucked the handkerchief under her sleeve. "It was your father that suggested I take you in. I adored you and thought I would always have a piece of William with me. Why am I telling you this? Perhaps to explain why I owe my sister—your mother—more than I can say. And you. I mourned William and stayed away those first months after your father died because I would have betrayed my true feelings."

She took his hand. "Then, when she married Whinstone, I was angry. Shocked. How could she insult your father's memory like that? I stayed away for even longer, which was selfish of me."

Gideon squeezed his aunt's hand. "It appears we are a selfish lot down the line. Do not worry, Aunt. I hold nothing against you or my father. I am pleased you found a little happiness together, however brief. I'm glad you told me."

She beamed at him. "You are a dear boy. Well, hardly a boy anymore. A dear, sweet man, then."

Gideon laughed, patted her hand, then released it. "I assure you, Aunt, I am none of those. Let us move on to a pleasanter subject. I've met someone." He gave his aunt the bare minimum of facts for now.

Her face lit up. "I am so happy for you, my dear."

"Eventually, I intend to split my time between London and Foxmont. Extricating Whinstone, however, is another hurdle to overcome, and I have to see that Mr. Chapman makes the arrangements."

"Is your steward here in London?"

"Yes, he has rooms not far from my residence."

"Allow me to send one of my footmen to collect him. Then you can meet here, in privacy. And you can relax, have more tea and biscuits, and keep me company."

It would delay reuniting with Olivia, but it was best to get things in motion.

"Very well."

"I want to hear more about Olivia. When will I meet her?"

Gideon smiled. "Very soon."

BERNARD CHAPMAN ARRIVED thirty minutes later, and the two men moved to Aunt Mirella's library. He bade Chapman sit in front of the desk while Gideon sat behind it.

"There are going to be some changes, Chapman. You best have your notebook at the ready. Do you need a pen and ink?"

"No, Your Grace, I have a pencil here." The man reached into his side pocket and retrieved his notebook and pencil. "Please, continue."

"First, you must notify the landlord of my mother's residence. Our lease will terminate at the end of this month. My mother will be moving in here, with my aunt. Make the arrangements. I doubt she has more than a few trunks."

Chapman was writing furiously. "And her account at Miklewhite's Grocery?"

"Close it and any other accounts. I am no longer paying for incidentals. If the duchess comes to you with any outstanding bills, you will *not* pay them."

"Understood, Your Grace."

"Next is Foxmont. In the future, I will be dividing my time with London. I have already given Whinstone notice to vacate the premises, and I saw the local constable before I left this morning to ensure he would follow through on the eviction. The man did not seem overly keen to kick a duke out of a manor house, so I may require other options. What do you suggest?"

Chapman, a man Gideon hired about eleven years ago, wasn't much older than himself. He was of medium height with thinning hair and spectacles. Chapman certainly looked the part of a steward.

Chapman stopped writing and pursed his lips. "I know this is none of my concern, Your Grace, but I am pleased you're kicking the duke to the cobbles, as it were. A thoroughly unpleasant human to deal with."

"An understatement, to be certain. I am sorry you have dealt with Whinstone these past years, and I shall see to it you have a bonus."

"I must confess, Your Grace, because I loathed dealing with the duke, I avoided any visits to Foxmont. It was not well done of me. I paid the bills and hired staff when needed, but I should have had a more hands-on approach. I do apologize."

"Well, I also neglected my duties concerning Foxmont. We can share the blame and make the necessary corrections when my stepfather is gone. Whinstone claims I have no right to evict him; is that correct?"

Chapman shook his head. "There is no written agreement between you. However, he could claim ownership since he lived there for three years. The laws regarding land ownership and squatting are muddled, but you are a duke, and there is a legal title in your name. If he kicks up a fuss, this could become a protracted case. You will ultimately win, I am certain, but the case could be in the courts for years. In the meantime, Your Grace, it is feasible a judge could allow him to stay there until the case resolves."

"Damn it all," Gideon mumbled. "Whinstone doesn't have any money of his own. Do you know anything about his dukedom?"

"Nothing, Your Grace. Perhaps we could hire an investigator, and we also could hire men to accompany me to Foxmont, where I can personally oversee his eviction."

Investigator.

The Galway Agency. Why not, indeed? Not only was one of the owners married to Christian, but Asher also used them.

"Contact The Galway Agency as soon as possible. The office is on Cleveland Street, 148 or 149, I cannot remember. We will send one of Aunt Mirella's footmen. Have one of them come here right away. If they are available, we will coordinate with them to see to his eviction."

Chapman stood and went into the hallway to locate a footman.

Meanwhile, Gideon's mind pinged in all directions.

At last, he was putting his life in order, dealing with things he had long procrastinated over, like his mother and stepfather. He brought clarity and purpose to his role in the House of Lords. The most relevant point on the agenda, however, was Olivia.

Did she love him enough to consider sharing what remained of his life?

He was getting ahead of himself. But organizing his life before offering for Olivia's hand was best.

OLIVIA OPENED HER EYES to find James sitting by her bedside. She could open her swollen eye slightly and gazed about, taking in her surroundings. She was back in her old room. Relief ran through her, and tears spilled down her cheeks.

James took her hand. "There now, Olivia, my dear. No need for tears. You are safe."

"Mary?"

"The woman who brought you? I gave her a pound for her trouble and thanked her on your behalf. It's morning now. Near noon actually. You slept all night. The doctor examined you while you were unconscious, and there were no broken bones. Your ribs might bruise, but you should be up and around by tomorrow."

"My face?"

"Not as bad as it looked last night. Bruising around the eye, your lip split and a little swollen."

Olivia pushed herself into an upright position. Sore, but it could have been so much worse. "I am such a fool," she whispered.

"Olivia, you are not the first to toss caution to the wind and embrace a chance at love. Now, what on earth happened? Mary says there were two men in an alley."

Olivia pulled the quilt tighter around her body and shivered. "They burst into the bedroom at eleven o'clock last night. They dragged me out and tossed me in an alley here in Whitechapel. They said they acted on behalf of the Duke of Watford and that he had his fill of me, and I was not to contact him in the future." She fought back the tears, "He is done with me."

James took her hand and squeezed. He did not speak, but Olivia could see the sympathy and pity in his eyes. She exhaled.

"My dear friend. As I told you before, peers care nothing for deeper emotions. I know firsthand. Years ago, I struck up a friendship with a boy at school. We were fifteen, curious, and what usually can transpire at those all-boys schools happened between us. It carried on and off through university. Yes, I come from a well-off family. Anyway, once adults, the emotions deepened. I imagined myself in love with him. One night as he held me in his arms, he told me he loved me, too."

"Oh, James." Olivia knew with clear clarity that this tale had no happy ending.

"We were in his family's library when his father walked in. He caught us in a heated embrace. Did the viscount have an attack of apoplexy? No, not at all. It seems he had guessed at his son's sexual preference. He said to Charles: 'If this man is who you want, I will arrange it so you can be together. He can be your steward, live with you. You can have a life together. However, I will be cutting your allowance to a mere pittance. I will sell all unentailed properties and leave you with nothing but the title. You will no longer be part of this family.'"

Olivia's eyes widened. "What happened next?"

"The viscount said to Charles: 'Or you can take up your responsibility and duty as my heir and agree to an arranged marriage with a suitable young lady. Then all will be restored to you. You can never see this young man again. You must be safely married and have an heir. If you wish to dally with other men, have it. But not before.'"

James frowned. "I looked to Charles, waiting for him to declare his love for me, that he would give up everything to be with me. Alas, he did not."

"He walked away?"

"Literally. Charles said I was to leave and never contact him again. Then he turned on his heel and departed. My heart smashed to bits. The viscount acted sympathetic enough but ultimately showed me the door with one last parting thought: that duty outweighed everything, including the first blush of love. You must also come to terms with it, Olivia."

Perhaps, but it stung all the same.

"I am sorry that happened to you," she said sympathetically. "And yes, I will have to come to terms with it. But until then, can one of the boys escort me to the Ten Bells?"

"Dearest, you should stay abed."

Olivia pulled her hand from his and swung her legs over the side of the bed. "I'm fine. I have someone to see. Would you consider giving Mary O'Toole employment and your protection? I owe her so much. I shudder to think about what would have occurred had she and her friends not stepped in. I must see her and talk with her."

"Of course. But I must protest. You've had a terrible experience—"

She laid her hand on James's cheek. "My dear friend. I have lived through worse. I survived. I will survive this."

Though her words sounded determined to her own ears, inside, her heart smashed to bits, too. In the clear light of day, she remained convinced the Duke of Watford had instigated her abduction and attack.

So be it.

She would never make the mistake of falling for or trusting any man again.

Chapter 18

BARELY AN HOUR LATER, Althea and Eleanora Galway stood in Aunt Mirella's library. The sisters looked formidable, with clear-eyed intelligence and confidence wafting off them both.

"Your Grace," Eleanora nodded.

"Your Grace," Gideon replied. "Watford is fine, or even better; please call me Gideon. I thank you both for your promptness. My steward, Mr. Chapman, will attend our meeting and take notes."

Miss Althea took out her notebook, and they sat in the chairs provided by another of his aunt's footmen.

"Thank you, Gideon. And you may call us by our first names as well. Christian speaks highly of you, and I would like to think of you as part of our circle of friends."

"I am humbled," Gideon murmured. "And grateful for the offer of friendship. I accept it gladly."

"Good," Eleanora nodded. "Now, what can we do for you?"

"My stepfather is the Duke of Whinstone. I need any information you can gather on the man as swiftly as possible. Presently, he is at my country seat in Essex. I've given him notice to vacate in three days. His dukedom is impoverished and has been as long as I have known him. As far as I know, he has no money or property. I need to know the particulars. The gossip. Anything of his dealings. He has been adept at playing his cards close to the vest."

"We may need Allenby's assistance, Sister," Althea murmured.

"Would you object to Christian joining this investigation?" Eleanora asked.

"Not at all. As you say, Christian is a friend."

How surprising. Because a few weeks ago, Gideon would not have referred to Christian as such.

"Would you like immediate surveillance on Whinstone?" Althea asked. "We can send along a couple of associates within the hour, and they will report his movements, any visitors, and other comings and goings. We can also take photographs of anyone around the place and any suspicious activity."

Gideon's eyebrow arched. "And how is that possible? The photographs, I mean."

"Well," Althea enthused. "We have acquired an American Eastman-Kodak folding pocket camera with celluloid roll film. Thanks to Christian. They sell out as soon as they arrive, so we were lucky to snag one. We have our associates act as amateur photographers, and *violá*; we have pictures of places and people for our varied investigations."

Gideon was suitably impressed. "I had no idea about a pocket camera. Fascinating."

"A recent invention. And Archie Fitzgerald, one of our associates, has learned to develop photographic films. We have set up a darkroom, as it is called, for that very thing." Althea smiled. "Oh, you must come by someday to see the setup and the camera."

"I will, Althea. Thank you."

"We will start our inquiries immediately," Eleanora assured him. "Where can we contact you?"

He gave his address and any relatable information, like the location of Foxmont, and Whinstone's mistress, Annabella, a baronet's daughter.

"Essex, that is about an hour by train?" Eleanora asked as Althea scribbled.

"Yes."

"We will have to arrange overnight accommodations for Archie; make a note, Althea," Eleanora instructed.

Althea mentioned the fee, which would include the investigation and incidentals such as accommodations, train fare, film cost, meals, and whatnot. No matter the final bill, Gideon could well afford it. Practically speaking, he should have investigated his stepfather long before now.

After this meeting, it was home to Olivia. At last.

Gideon couldn't wait.

GIDEON ENTERED THE town house calling Olivia's name. He'd stopped at a street vendor before visiting Aunt Mirella's and bought flowers for his aunt and Olivia. He had chosen red roses for Olivia as the seller informed him that red roses spoke of a declaration of love.

What did he know of such things?

He had never courted or wooed a woman before. He dropped his overnight bag in the front hall and headed toward the stairs.

"Your Pardon, Your Grace, but Miss Durham is not here."

Gideon turned to face Hobson. "What do you mean? She went out?"

"No, Your Grace. When the staff rose early this morning, we found Miss Durham had left and taken her belongings. I assume it was after the house was abed. The rooms upstairs remain undisturbed. I thought you would want to see them."

Hobson reached in his side pocket. "I found this in the parlor, for a Mr. James Sidle in Whitechapel. She wrote it three days ago but never had it delivered."

Gideon snatched the letter from Hobson's gloved hand and thrust the roses toward him. He slipped the note into his pocket and took the stairs two at a time.

He entered his room first. His bed looked to be in shambles as if someone had slept there. He stalked down the hall and kicked open the guestroom door. He pulled open the wardrobe—and nothing. The bed was not slept in, so Olivia had been in his. Then what possessed her to leave in the middle of the night?

A stab of pain shot through his heart. Sitting on the edge of the bed, he reached in his pocket for the note and tore it open.

Addressed to James Sidle.

He unfolded the note and read:

JAMES, I SIT HERE ONE day after leaving, and my anger has turned to bitter disappointment. You must think me foolhardy to go off with a man I barely knew.

But I did.

I cannot explain the reasons, except I felt I had met my soul mate. We are so much alike that it is frightening. I sensed in him so much that was wrong with myself.

We are broken things. Together, we make a whole being. Gideon hides behind a cold, icy mask, but I have felt his heart beat.

I was prepared to give him everything, but he abandoned me. He dropped me at his residence and left for parts unknown. I am giving him until this evening to return; if he does not, please allow me to return to The Velvet. Please send back your reply as soon as you get this. I promise never to permit my heart to lead me astray again.

Your dearest friend,

Olivia

WE ARE BROKEN THINGS.

Gideon crumpled the letter in his fist.

They *were* very much alike. The soul mate description did indeed fit. He had an austere upbringing, absent of love and affection, as was her past to a point, in a much different way.

Gideon smoothed the letter and reread it. Olivia had yet to mail it. Why? Because he had returned that night?

Putting aside his hurt pride, the fact that she had slept in his bed, then left in the middle of the night made no sense whatsoever.

It was patently obvious where she went: The Velvet Vine and Tackle.

Gideon ran into the hall. "Hobson! Get me a Hansom cab! Now!"

OLIVIA STROLLED INTO the Ten Bells on Commercial Street, and Gordon, one of the lads from The Velvet, stayed on her heels. At one o'clock in the afternoon, the place was quite lively. She had never been here or any other pub, for that matter.

The walls were adorned with blue and white floral tiling and dark wood trim. The tiled mural on the far wall was the decorative centerpiece—a weaver in his shop, plying his wares from an era long ago.

She scanned the busy pub, and Mary's red hair caught her eye. She went to the table where Mary sat with four other women. They might have been the same women in the alley last night, but the darkness had made it difficult to tell.

"Well, look at you, up and about. How are you feeling, love?" Mary asked.

"Better, thank you. Is there somewhere we can talk?"

Mary stood, took her elbow, and steered her toward a small table in the corner. A man walked up to them with a bar towel tossed over his shoulders. Gordon stood off to the side, keeping watch.

"What will it be? You have to order something or push off."

"Steady on, Mike," Mary said.

"Beef stew and bread for us and those ladies over at that table. Give them whatever they wish to drink." Olivia reached into her reticule and laid a handful of shillings on the table. "We'll have bitter. And be quick about it."

The man touched his forelock and moved off. Olivia could hear him snort and mutter derisively under his breath. "Right. Serve the *ladies.* In a pig's eye."

"I didn't think to see you so soon, love."

Olivia smoothed her skirt. She wore a gray wool gown. Though she had a few fancier ones, they weren't suitable for sitting in a pub.

"I am not one to lie about. I feel better, and makeup helped hide some of the uglier bruises."

"Who were those shites, anyway?" Mary asked.

"Hired by an aristocrat to throw me out like yesterday's rubbish."

Mary sat back and nodded knowingly. "Got tired of you, did he? Bloody cheek. Those high in the instep lordlings can do as they like. Believe me, I know."

"You were involved with one?"

"Worse. One of those aristos is my father; my story is not new."

Olivia nodded. No, it certainly wasn't a new story. She did not want to speak of Gideon as the hurt was still too raw. His cold rejection stung, and the wound festered and would not likely heal anytime soon.

The man returned with glass mugs of bitter. Sitting them on the table, he headed back to the bar.

Mary picked up the mug and took a long swallow. "Ah, it's good, that is. Thanks, love; I enjoy a mug of cold beer, maybe a wee bit too much. Your man gave me two pounds. More than generous. Should keep us set up in decent rooms for a month at least."

Olivia smiled. James had said a pound. Of course, he gave Mary more than one pound; it spoke of his generous nature.

"That's why I am here, Mary. Pan is very kind and protective of his people. He said I could offer you a job. You'll have your own room—a private place. He shares the profits and does not force you to do anything you don't wish. It will be safe, a warm bed. Three hot meals a day."

She clutched Mary's arm. "The streets are not safe. Why ply your wares in a cold, dark alley when you can do the same under a safe roof? Pan keeps bully-boys to protect us." She inclined her head toward Gordon. "Say you'll come back with me, Mary."

Mary lowered her head as if looking for guidance in the foam of the glass of beer. She glanced back up. "I thank you and Pan for the offer, but that kind of place is not for me, love. I worked at a posh place in the West End some time back. No, I'll go on as I have been. Besides, I can't abandon my girls. They need me."

Mary smiled wanly and drank down a few more swallows of the bitter. "The Ripper is gone these ten years; the streets are not so bad."

"And who is to say that another murderer will take his place? And what of the gangs? It's too dangerous."

Olivia sighed as the man returned with the stew and bread. She couldn't force Mary to return with her, and perhaps her motives were selfish to a degree. Olivia had hoped the woman would return with her so she would have a female friend, as she had never befriended anyone else except for James.

Life was hard for a woman alone.

It could have been her sitting at that table with the other women. If James hadn't found her, she knew she would have been selling herself in alleys for a few coins.

Mary patted her hand with firm reassurance. "There now, love. Get that worried look off your face. I'll be fine."

"The offer is open anytime. Just ask for Pan, and say Olivia gave the okay." Olivia picked up her spoon and took a bite of the thick stew.

"Very well, I'll think about it, love. I mean it, I will."

She hoped all would be fine, for Mary's sake.

Meanwhile, Olivia had her own life to sort out.

A small part of her still couldn't believe Gideon was behind this, not after all they had shared, physically and otherwise, and not after what they had revealed about their pasts. But the cynical, hardened part of her whispered incessantly that he is a duke, a selfish peer who does as he pleases and one that uses people—chews them up and spits them out.

Olivia was not going to resume her Mistress Birch routine. That much she had concluded. Perhaps with James's assistance, she could find a position in the country somewhere. Do wealthy widows still have companions, or was that from another age altogether?

What to do?

Stay strong, remain calm, and take charge of her life. No more hiding, no more avoiding the future.

And if that future did not include Gideon, then so be it.

Chapter 19

GIDEON POUNDED ON THE door, yelling obscenities until finally, the peep window slid open and blue eyes stared back at him.

"Lord Craven. We are not open for business until three o'clock. Come back then."

He recognized Pan's smooth, dulcet tone.

"Sidle, Stop calling me by that ridiculous moniker. Open this door, or I swear I will smash it down. Olivia!"

"Calm yourself, Your Grace. She is not here. Olivia is running an errand." He opened the door, and Gideon tried to push past, but two gigantic men stopped him. "Do not make a scene. We will talk here. She doesn't wish to see you. And why should I allow it? Explain to me; convince me that you deserve another chance."

"Explain what?" Gideon snapped. "My feelings for Olivia are not your business, and I don't care that she considers you a friend."

"I consider her far more than that; she is like a sister. And if she asks for my protection, I will give it. Why should I encourage Olivia to talk to you?"

Gideon exhaled, trying to gain control. "When I departed for Essex, we were fine. All was well. Now I come home to find her gone with no explanation? I want to talk to her and ask her what happened."

"You know nothing of why she left?"

"No!" More calmly, Gideon said, "We kissed goodbye. Olivia slept in my bed last night, and the servants stated she was in high spirits when she had tea and biscuits before retiring. None of this makes sense."

"Then return tomorrow morning at ten, and I will encourage Olivia to meet with you. The two of you need to talk. About your feelings, most of all. Now, will you leave peacefully?"

Gideon took a step closer. "Very well. I will go for now. But I will be back tomorrow morning, and you *will* allow me to see her. Or I swear I will bring a battering ram and gain entry that way."

"My," Pan tittered. "Such passion. Tomorrow morning, then."

The door slammed in his face.

Gideon stepped back. Dare he go around the rear of the property toward the residence? He knew his way in, considering he had been here with Olivia. But the outside door was locked; blast it all. Olivia had used a key to gain entry.

Frustrated and at a complete loss as to what had ensued, Gideon stood by the side of the building, mulling over his next move. If Olivia were indeed out on an errand, she would return here at some point. He could wait, approach her, and demand to speak to her.

That was the old Gideon. Be damned if he would force her to see him. His mouth quirked. But isn't that what he had just done? Pound on the door and demand that he gain access?

Emotion had carried him away, and that strange impulsivity had reared its head again. Best to be civilized about this and return tomorrow morning.

OLIVIA RETURNED TO The Velvet an hour later. She almost expected Gideon to be waiting by the door, but he was not. Olivia wasn't sure if she should be disappointed or relieved.

James operated his business as a nocturnal venture. During the day, the staff cleaned The Velvet stem to stern. Everyone pitched in by changing linens and scrubbing the floors and walls. James gave them their own rooms, fed them, and shared in the profit; it was not too much to ask everyone to keep the place spotless and running smoothly.

Olivia started to climb the stairs to do her part when James called her into his study. A tea tray sat on the table, and he motioned for her to sit and then poured.

"Mary O'Toole was not interested in the offer, I take it?" he asked.

James handed her the cup and saucer and took a seat opposite. He served her favorite, orange pekoe. Taking a sip, she glanced at James over the rim. His delicate beauty sent many male and female hearts fluttering, but she had never seen him with either gender.

He had told her once that "my gate swings both ways. In this cold world, it behooves one to take love where you can find it." Yet, he had prevaricated when she asked him if he had ever been in love. Now she knew the whole story. If anyone understood about being involved with an aristocrat, it was James.

"No. Mary did not want to leave her girls. But I told her to think it over, and she said she would. And if she changes her mind, to ask for you at my behest."

James tsked. "Pity, that. She is quite attractive and could have made a pretty penny here. Perhaps she will think it over. Well, onward." James sipped his tea. "Dearest, brace yourself. The duke was here not thirty minutes ago."

Her heart tumbled in her chest. How dare the duke show up after having his thugs toss her in an alley? The damned cheek of the man. So arrogant. But on the other hand, why show up here if he initiated her removal?

"Whatever for?" Olivia sniffed. "I am out of his life as he wished."

"Do you love him?"

"Yes. No. How can I? After what the duke has done to me? We've barely known each other for a few weeks, and even at that, he abandoned me!" The cup rattled on the saucer, so she placed them back on the tray.

"Perhaps he had reasons," James ventured, watching her closely.

She folded her arms and huffed. "Why would I love such an unfeeling man?"

James set his cup on the table. "Come now, Olivia. You are spouting nonsense. Shall I tell you how I know? I will admit the man is a fine specimen. But the emptiness in his alluring dark eyes drew my attention from our first meeting, and I observed heart-wrenching loneliness. Remember? I told you this."

James paused. "The man who confronted me at the door was the farthest thing from that cold, indifferent man. His eyes were alive and animated. Full of concern and worry. And love." James smiled. "And anger. It seems he has quite a temper."

Confusion rolled through her. "But those men said—"

"When he returns in the morning, see him and have it out. Trust your feelings. Trust *him*. I must say he created quite a scene. Watford was very loud, profane, and insistent. He threatened to return tomorrow morning with a battering ram if needs must. I have to say. It was all rather medieval and arousing."

Olivia snickered. James could always make her laugh in the direst of circumstances.

"I told the duke you were running an errand and not to be disturbed," James continued. "I also assured him that you would see him tomorrow. I know that was presumptive on my part. I *am* sorry. I mentioned nothing of your abduction. He appeared truly puzzled as to why you left. Talk to him, Olivia, and judge for yourself. If you do not have it out with him, you will regret it for the rest of your days. Believe me. I know."

She sobered. What could she say? Her pride throbbed with the pain of rejection. Yet, why show up here and create a scene if he had her forcibly removed from his premises? Why tell James he knew nothing concerning her departure?

Grudgingly, Olivia agreed. She would have him forcibly removed if the haughty duke did not offer a suitable explanation.

GIDEON HAD NO SLEEP. His emotions whirled about him furiously all night. Never in his life had he lost control as he did at The Velvet yesterday afternoon. The crowd gathering on the sidewalk kept him from breaking the door down as he bellowed and swore at Pan and his hired bullyboys.

He pulled on his leather gloves. Well, as strong as he claimed to be, he doubted he could have made a dent in the thick oak door at any rate, which elucidated his threats of bringing a battering ram. The note he received last evening claiming that Olivia would give him a brief audience was the only reason the weapon was not strapped to the carriage's roof.

Gideon exhaled, trying to calm his raging temper. He had no idea what to expect. His plan consisted of convincing Olivia to pack her belongings and return with him—permanently. The task may be daunting, and he had to remain in control.

Giving instructions for the coachman to wait, he knocked on the door.

Once allowed to enter, Gideon was shown to a room similar to his study. A multitude of bookshelves lined the walls. Books of science, philosophy, and fiction crammed the shelves. He wandered over to glance at a few of the titles. It must be this Sidle's private area.

Gideon removed his hat and his gloves and unbuttoned his greatcoat. He tossed his gloves in the hat and threw them to the settee. He could use a damned drink; however, there were no decanters in the room.

The door opened, and Olivia glided in, head held high. She wore a plain gray gown, her hair tied in a severe knot. She appeared pale and drawn. But that was not all.

His fists clenched. So much for staying calm and collected. "Who hit you? He will cease to draw breath!" he roared.

Though Olivia tried to hide the bruising with makeup, it was apparent someone had battered her lovely face. Her slightly swollen lip sported a jagged cut in the plumpness.

She halted, her eyes blinking rapidly. "You act surprised? You ordered this abduction and beating!" she cried.

Gideon pointed to the man standing at the entrance with his arms folded. "Get out!"

"He stays. As protection," Liv sniffed.

The words, at last, began to sink in through his fury at seeing someone had harmed her.

Abduction and beating?

The rage rushed out of him in a whoosh.

"I do not know what you are talking about," he began, his voice calmer. "I came home yesterday to find you gone. Do you honestly believe I would have you seen from the premises in such a way? You think me an animal?"

Perhaps Gideon was an animal, for he wanted to rip someone to shreds. Anyone. And that son of a bitch hovering at the door just may suit. A growl escaped his throat.

"Your Grace, are you telling me you had nothing to do with me being pulled out of your bed, told to pack in haste, and dumped into a dirty alley in Whitechapel where I was beaten and threatened?"

Good Christ, no wonder she thought him a base beast. After what had happened to her in the past, she thought he would instigate such an action. Her accusation tore at his heart. The heart that only came to life the moment he had met her.

Gideon took two tentative steps toward her, and she backed up, fear flickering ever so briefly on her face. "Liv, I swear, I had nothing to do with what happened to you. I came home yesterday with roses and plans for our future. Why would you think I would do such a thing?"

Olivia rubbed her forehead. She turned toward the man. "Gordon, leave us. I'll ring if I need you."

The man gave a quick nod, stepped out into the hallway, and closed the door behind him.

Olivia staggered to the large wing chair and sat down, shock showing across her features.

"I-I don't understand. Those men told me you wanted me gone and had your fill. That you did not want to see me ever again," she whispered.

Gideon dragged the matching chair across the carpet until it stood opposite hers, and he sat. "You believed them?"

"Not at first. With each blow, those men convinced me otherwise. If a group of women hadn't entered the alley, I would have been raped, and I would not have survived it."

Gideon leaned forward. "May I take your hands?" he asked.

Olivia nodded.

Clasping them gently, he said, "I swear I had nothing to do with it. I would never hurt you. My God, Liv. If you cannot accept my trust, how can you ever accept my love?"

A few stray tears rolled down her bruised cheek. "I did not *want* to believe it. But as I told you more than once, my trust has been battered. Perhaps beyond repair."

His insides roiled with a multitude of emotions. Gideon raised her trembling hands to his lips and kissed them passionately. "I never should have left you. Forgive me. I pledge I will never leave your side again."

"Oh, Gideon," she sobbed.

He yearned to take her in his arms. Carry her out of here. Protect and love her always.

"I should have told you the other night while you lay in my arms. I am in love with you, Liv. Love: complete and utter passionate devotion."

He kissed her hands again. "Never have I felt this way. It's vexing and confusing. Trust me, know I will never see you harmed again. I will slay whoever threatens you. Know this."

Olivia nodded. "I love you, too. I am sorry that I doubted you."

His heart dipped clear to the floor. Kissing Olivia's hands one last time, he laid them gently on Olivia's lap and sat back in his chair. As much as he wished to pull her into his arms and hold her close, they had more to discuss.

"Thank you for the declaration of love and the apology. Now, let us puzzle this out. Besides us, who knew you were staying at the town house?" Gideon asked.

Olivia frowned. "Well, James. I left him that brief note. It was not him, though."

That smarted. Olivia quickly deemed Sidle innocent yet believed he had instigated her abduction. A stab of regret and disappointment moved through him.

"Did someone here at the club read the note before Sidle could? Someone who harbors some grudge or dislike of you?"

Olivia's brows furrowed. "No, not that I am aware. We all get along unless I'm more oblivious and naïve than I originally thought."

"My house staff was aware," Gideon said. Then he paused, going over his conversation with his wretched stepfather.

Did he let it slip that Olivia was with him? No, he hadn't revealed anything to Whinstone. But that didn't mean he didn't guess at it or contacted one of the Hyde Park Corner servants.

The realization that the duke would set such a horrible plan in motion slammed him. The man had a long reach and was vindictive enough to see it done.

"I've hired The Galway Investigative Agency. My friend, Christian Bamford, Duke of Allenby, is married to one of the owners, Eleanora. She and her sister, Althea, have taken the case."

"Women running a detective agency? I think that is wonderful. Wait—what case?"

Gideon held nothing back. He told Olivia of his meeting with his stepfather—leaving off the horrible names Whinstone called Olivia—his aunt and the agency.

"My," she stated, "You have been busy. Why are you doing all this?"

"My life—until I met you—was a loveless wasteland. I didn't care for anything or anyone. I was a loathsome human; let's face facts."

Olivia shook her head. "That is what you outwardly project, but deep down and hidden away was—and is—a decent man, you know this. Or you wouldn't be making these changes to your life. Reconciling with your aunt, joining progressive causes, and cutting those who have harmed you from your life. It shows a strength of character and purpose."

Gideon raised an eyebrow. "If you believe all this, why did you readily accept the word of a couple of street thugs?"

Olivia exhaled. "As I said, my first reaction was *not* to believe it. But it isn't easy to take root when trust has been ripped from you. Again, I am truly sorry. We are both damaged in our ways, which makes any relationship between us problematic. As you said, how can there be love without trust?"

"And how can there be trust if there is no love? We do love each other. Despite all the odds and all that damage, we have fallen in love. Anything is possible, Liv. I believe it to the very marrow of my bones. We are halfway there; we need only commit to each other to allow the trust to take root and grow. And it will. You have to give us a chance."

He never spoke with such emotional fervor before, but he meant every word. "Ultimately," Gideon continued. "I want us to consider marriage."

Olivia's jaw dropped open. "You wish to marry—me?"

She sounded so disbelieving.

"I see no reason to delay. As I said, we love each other," Gideon replied matter-of-factly. "It's one of the reasons I am kicking Whinstone to the cobbles. I want to make Foxmont *our* home, our main base of operations, as it were."

He gave her a warm smile, but she still looked stunned.

"I did not expect marriage," she whispered. "Perhaps a long-term, mutually pleasurable affair, but marriage? I'm completely shocked."

Gideon's mouth quirked in amusement. "Yes, I see that you are."

"But we have known each other barely a few weeks—"

"Yet, we are soul mates. Broken things that together make a complete being."

Her face flushed. "You read my letter."

"I did. I was frantic to find out why you left and where you might have gone. Forgive me for invading your privacy." He stood and held out his hand. "Take my hand and come away with me, now."

Chapter 20

OLIVIA STARED AT THE large, masculine hand held out toward her. He had long, elegant fingers; his touch was potent and dizzying. How could she have thought that Gideon was behind her late-night abduction?

Looking into his glittering, onyx-colored eyes, she knew the truth. This man loved her and would never, ever hurt her.

God, she was a fool. Because of her past, she thought the absolute worst of the man she claimed to love. Without hesitating, she slipped her hand into his.

He squeezed it and pulled her up to stand before him. He let go of her hand, and those magical fingers gently roved over her face.

"Are you in pain? What did those cretins do to you?" he asked, concern in his voice.

She could not help but lean into his warmth and comforting embrace. "James called in a physician. No broken bones, and I will heal. A few punches and kicks. It could have been so much worse."

Olivia could see the purple rage Gideon fought to tamp down. He leaned in and kissed her nose.

"I told my stepfather I had met a vicar's daughter, that I had plans of a future together, and he was to leave. How imprudent of me. I wonder now if he was behind your attack?"

Olivia gasped, pulled back, and stared at Gideon. "Oh, that would be awful. Is he capable?"

"Whinstone is a cold bastard. I would not put this attack beyond his scope, even though I never mentioned any names. He gave me a list of so-called suitable women, and I refused. I also rejected his monetary demands of a divorce settlement from my mother. That also could have fueled his revenge. How to prove it?"

"He called me names, didn't he? He guessed at my vocation."

"I told him he was mistaken. I punched him in the face and broke his nose, I believe."

Olivia's hand covered her mouth in shock. That could anger the duke enough to seek retribution. But so swiftly? Well, with the trains, a trip to London was feasible.

Olivia's mind was in a whirl. Then, she realized something. "You stood up to your abuser."

Gideon nodded. "For the first time in my life. I should have done it long before, and it was damned satisfying. All I want now is him out of my—our—home, then out of our lives, and I do not want to think of him any longer."

"It will get around that I am a prostitute," she whispered.

"You worked at a brothel, nothing more. Even if you were a prossie, I don't bloody well care. You are *mine*. We belong together. We mend each other. You know that we do."

She nodded. "Yes, I know it. What happens next, Gideon?"

"You, my love, will pack everything you wish to bring, and you and your trunk are coming home with me. Then, if you are able, I will make love to you all night or as long as you can tolerate my attention."

"Truly, Gideon. We've only known each other for barely a month. Despite my momentary lack of faith, how can we trust and love each other so thoroughly? Most people will think us mad. This isn't normal. This sort of whirlwind love affair only happens in fairy stories."

He kissed her forehead affectionately. "Good. I don't want normal. If our life together resembles a fairy story or one of those outrageous penny novels, all the better."

Olivia stood on the tips of her toes and kissed him. Gideon groaned and took the kiss deeper. When she flinched, he stepped back.

"Sorry, love." His thumb brushed by her cut lip. "Someone will pay for this; I vow it."

Olivia hugged him tightly. The faint scent of sandalwood soap filled her nostrils: comfort, warmth, and solid strength.

That was Gideon.

He had given her everything without question, especially his heart, soul, trust, and love, yet she had doubted him. Pain laced through her.

"Gideon, please try to understand. It is not so much that I didn't trust *you*. I did not trust my feelings. I eventually accepted the explanation that you tossed me aside; because isn't that what men do? At least the ones I allowed myself to love. Yes, I lumped you in with my miserable vicar father, and I was wrong to do so."

"Liv—"

"No, let me continue. I accepted the blow of your supposed rejection so I could move on. I was beginning to doubt that I could ever love with my whole heart. Could I ever trust a man not to hurt me again?"

She let out a shaky breath. "If there is any man I wish to love and trust with my entire being, it is you, Gideon. The hole in my heart left by my father and my attackers—past and present—will mend. *You* will be the healer, and the damage to my trust will be restored—only with you."

"God, I love you."

Gideon swept her up into a devastatingly passionate yet gentle kiss. How long it went on, Olivia had no idea. He laid soft kisses on her forehead once again.

"My love, my mother and stepfather are no better; in fact, they are worse," he said in a quiet, solemn voice. "The cold, indifferent Lord Craven you met that first night became molded in ice over the years, and I knew no other way."

Gideon caressed her cheek. "You see, I refer to myself as the Duke of Pain in my more maudlin moments. Pain from my father dying too young and my mother never loving me or showing me affection. Pain at the verbal and physical beatings my stepfather subjected me to that my mother sanctioned. I did not feel anything but pain—until *you*. Whinstone married my mother for position and money—not love. I'll be damned if I will live my life like that. I knew nothing of love—until *you*."

A lump formed in her throat.

His words. The Duke of Pain.

Oh, her heart broke for him at that confession of what he had endured.

Olivia clasped his hand and kissed it. "We truly are broken, are we not?"

Gideon kissed the top of her head. "Not anymore. Not as long as we are together."

"Take me home," she whispered, tears filling her eyes.

HE PACED THE FLOOR, recalling his conversation with Olivia on the carriage ride home. She told him the men who had abducted her were rough-looking and speaking, just the type his stepfather kept around. Louts and bullies to a fault. He laughed when she told him about her names for them: "Yellow Teeth and Wool Trousers."

The situation itself, however, was far from humorous.

Gideon's blood still boiled that those hired men subjected Olivia to such patent cruelty. She had apologized for doubting him again, but he waved it off. While a part of him ached that she had believed the lies, however briefly, another part completely understood the reasons for her suspicions. It was time to forgive and embrace life fully.

When he arrived home, there was a note from The Galway Agency, saying their associate was already on-route to Essex to begin surveillance on Whinstone. Also, Christian was making inquiries on the Whinstone dukedom. So far, his friend had hit a brick wall as if there was a barrier of protection around it. Which meant there must be some scandal tucked away. The peerage certainly knew how to protect one another, even from each other.

But Gideon had more pressing matters to attend to.

Olivia.

He found her sitting in her adjoining room, at the dressing table, brushing her damp hair. She had just had a long relaxing bath and was wearing one of his dressing gowns.

"How was it?"

Olivia turned and gave him a warm smile. "The bath? Absolutely glorious. I sat in the water until my skin wrinkled." She lifted the collar of his dressing gown to her nose. "And being wrapped in your scent acts as a calming balm, to be certain."

He padded up behind her, reached for the brush, and gently ran it through her long, flowing locks. She leaned her head against his chest, and kitten-like mews of satisfaction left her throat with each glide.

"Oh, that feels nice," she purred.

"Love, I almost hate to bring this up since you are so relaxed. I wish us to move forward together. Put the past behind us. But there is one part of your past you must face."

Olivia sat up straight and stared at him in the reflection. "What do you mean?"

"Hear me out. It concerns Brookton."

He told her about Damon's statements about his father and the illegitimate children and about Damon's passionate speech regarding illegitimate children in general.

"He wishes to find any half-siblings. Although he acts like an arrogant sod, he is not like his father—not deep down where it counts.

He would respect your wishes about not telling Chellenham. What do you think?"

Olivia's brows knotted with concern. "I don't know what to think. I will consider it. But I am adamant about the duke not knowing."

"Understood."

"Why is he so keen on finding these half-siblings?"

"I do not know. You can ask Brookton if you decide to meet." Gideon continued to brush her hair gently. "Your hair is a crowning glory. God, how I want it draped across my thighs as you—"

She glanced at him in the mirror's reflection. "As I what?"

"Suck my cock. Make me come." He laughed at seeing her eyes go wide in the mirror. "I certainly changed the subject, didn't I? It appears I am, as rumor states—quite decadent and insatiable. Fathomless depths of stamina. But know this, only for you, Liv, and you alone."

Gideon laid the brush on the counter and rested his hands on her shoulders.

Olivia stood, took Gideon's hand, and led him into the bedroom. She pulled down his trousers until they hit the floor, and he kicked them aside.

"You are such a feast for the eyes," she murmured. "Lie down, and I will do as you wish. Or try to, as I've never done it before. I will spread my hair across your thighs, suck your c—"

Gideon pulled her tight against him and kissed her intensely, cutting off the rest of her sentence.

Sighing, Olivia tunneled her hands through his hair, grabbed a handful in her fist, and pulled him in for an even deeper kiss.

A low, husky rumble left the corner of his mouth. Then Gideon broke the kiss and lay on the bed.

Olivia dropped the dressing gown on the floor and climbed onto the bed, straddling his hips. She laid flat between his spread legs and grasped his shaft at the base, squeezing tight.

"Yes. Grip it tighter," Gideon growled.

First, she laid her long hair on either side of him, creating a blanket of blonde locks. Olivia gripped him again, squeezed, and slid her hand up and down his length.

"Tell me what you want me to do, Gideon. Instruct me. Guide me."

"God, you expect me to talk?" he laughed brokenly. "Take me deep. Lick, nibble, suck, do whatever you wish. Grip me at the root and guide it into your lush mouth."

Her mouth closed over the swollen head, and Gideon cried out, his head lifting off the pillow.

"Yes. Deeper."

Gideon gently grabbed a fistful of her hair and then guided her to a faster pace. His hips rose off the bed with each bob of her head.

"Jesus, I'm close—" He croaked. He pulled away from her, reached his peak, and cried out blissfully.

After he cleaned up, Gideon pulled her next to him so they were both lying on their sides. Olivia curled in next to his warmth.

"So much to explore," he whispered. "Together. I will do anything and everything you wish. I am yours. Deep down, your passion matches mine."

"Yes. Yes, it does, Gideon."

Moaning, Gideon reached between her legs and fingered her clit. "Anything, Liv. Share everything. Hold nothing back." He moved quicker; until they both were panting.

The intensity of Olivia's climax nearly tore him in two.

He enclosed her in his embrace. "I love you, Liv."

Never, ever had he felt so complete.

So loved. So *alive.*

Chapter 21

"YOU HAVE A CALLER, Your Grace," Hobson announced. "The Marquess of Brookton."

Olivia's eyes widened at the announcement.

"I didn't contact him. I have no idea why he is here. Shall I send him away?" Gideon asked.

They were eating a late breakfast. Isn't eleven in the morning a little early for callers? Olivia had no idea what the proper times were for such.

But *Brookton.*

She could run upstairs and stay hidden or confront this head-on.

"My love? I can see him in the library, and you can continue with your meal. What do you want me to do? Say the word."

Olivia laid her utensils across her plate. "No. Have him shown in here. We will speak to him. Alone."

"Hobson, show in the marquess, then give us privacy."

"At once, Your Grace." Hobson snapped his fingers, and the two footmen swiftly departed.

Brookton breezed into the room, rubbing his hands together. "Brilliant. Hobson said you were eating a late breakfast, and I am famished and—" He froze when he spotted Olivia. "And you are not alone."

"No," Gideon replied, giving her such a heart-rending look of love her heart skipped a beat. "I will never be alone again."

Brookton rolled his eyes. "God, not another one hit with Cupid's bow. This is becoming tedious."

"Afraid so. Help yourself to the food and take a seat. We both wish to speak to you."

Brookton shrugged and moved to the sideboard, filling his plate. He then sat next to Gideon.

"Why are you here?" Gideon asked as Brookton shoveled a forkful of eggs into his mouth. "You rarely stop by for a visit."

"I've never stopped by for a visit," Brookton murmured as he nibbled on a piece of bacon. "I've heard from Huxley. The absentee viscount has returned to London and wishes to see The Rakes. I told him that you and I and Tolwood are the only semi-original ones left—that he knows of. So, he wishes to see us both when convenient. He was not too keen to have Tolwood there. Poor bugger, always left out. Why we keep Tolwood around, I have no notion."

Brookton ran a piece of bread through the egg yolk and ate it. "Huxley wants to meet this afternoon, and I said I would ask you. Oh, also, I am planning a trip to Spain next month, and I may be gone for a few weeks. I need you to take over as leader temporarily."

Gideon's mouth quirked. "Not asking for much, are you? Since we meet monthly, I think we can bear your absence for a few weeks. I'm not interested in being a leader, not even temporarily."

Brookton cast a glance at Olivia. "Or a member at all, I take it?"

"That is a discussion for another time. We have something more important to deliberate with you. It is of the utmost confidence, and we will have your word that you will not repeat the conversation."

Brookton snorted. "What is this? What possible secret do you have to tell that involves your paramour? No disrespect meant, my dear lady."

Olivia could see fire come alive in Gideon's eyes. There would be fisticuffs if she didn't intervene.

"For your information," Olivia stated evenly. "I am not his mistress, nor am I a courtesan. I am Gideon's fiancée. We are to be married."

"Congratulations, I suppose? Is that the secret? I am not to repeat where you met. You have my word, and I shall keep those scandalous details to myself. At least, society would deem it a scandal, not I." Brookton turned his attention to his plate, eating more eggs and bacon, then buttered a cheese scone.

Gideon inclined his head toward Brookton as if encouraging her to continue.

"That is not what I—we—wanted to speak with you about," Olivia continued. "But we appreciate your discretion regarding how we met. No, I wish to discuss your wretched father and his illegitimate children. Gideon tells me you wish to find some of them. Why?"

Brookton slowly raised his head and pinned her with his intense blue-eyed stare. The exact shade of blue as her own eyes.

"Why? It's none of your concern—why."

The coldly spoken words made this more complicated than Olivia had imagined. Best to just put it out there.

Mustering her courage, she said, "I am your half-sister."

Brookton didn't move or change his expression. Then his gaze slid to Gideon. "What in hell is this?" he spat. "What did you tell her?"

Gideon explained about the nuns, the name her late mother spoke of, and how a vicar and his wife adopted her—even her abandonment in London.

Brookton turned as white as a sheet. "This cannot be true."

"My God, man. Look at her!" Gideon exclaimed. "It's like looking in a mirror. Olivia is your older half-sister. There is no mistaking the resemblance between you."

Brookton ran his fingers through his golden hair. "I've spoken to doctors and scientists. The European medical field is working on classifying blood types in people. One possible benefit from this? They may be able to determine if someone is blood-related. But the science is a couple of decades away, perhaps longer. In the meantime, there is no way to prove such scientifically."

His gaze slid to Olivia, and his expression softened. "There is only someone saying they *are* related. But Gideon is correct; the resemblance is there, and I cannot deny it."

"I never knew my mother as she died shortly after my birth," Olivia stated, her voice quiet and reflective. "The nuns contacted your father, and he did not deny knowing my mother, nor did he deny that I was his offspring. My mother and your father obviously had relations."

"Obviously," Brookton muttered.

"I spoke to Sister Rose two years ago, and she remembered my mother and the incident of my birth vividly. I can give you the name of the order as the location is north of here. But first, you must promise me not to tell your father. I don't want him to know, and I don't want to know *him*."

"How very wise of you. Stay clear of the man. I give you my word that I shall never tell him. Olivia, may I call you Olivia?" Brookton asked.

"Yes."

"Then you must call me Damon. I apologize for my past crass behavior toward you, and I have no excuse except that I can be a horrid human being. Shall we become acquainted? Could we be friends? At some point, will we think of each other as brother and sister? Can it be achieved?"

Olivia's eyes welled with tears as emotion threatened to overtake her. "I would like to try."

"Don't think I've made some miraculous change in personality," Damon said. "This news has profoundly affected me, and I need time to reflect on it. But as far as you are concerned, Olivia, I will curb my worst impulses."

"That is quite the concession," Gideon said sardonically. "And I am glad you apologized for your actions, especially at the park. Perhaps there is something worthwhile in that empty soul of yours."

"Oh, please. The fact that I made a lewd proposition toward a woman who turned out to be my half-sister has scarred me for life. And deservedly so. I apologize once again."

He sounded sincere. Olivia acknowledged his apology with a smile.

Hobson entered the room. "Miss Althea Galway to see you, Your Grace. She insists that it is urgent."

Damon stood so swiftly that he knocked over the chair. Yes, already she was thinking of him as Damon. His cheeks flushed at the mention of Miss Galway's name. How odd; was he acquainted with the lady detective?

"Show her in, Hobson," Gideon declared.

Damon threw his napkin on the table. "I have to go."

Hobson escorted Miss Galway into the room. She was attractive, with dark brown hair shot with gold. Her gaze locked with Damon's, and Olivia could swear crackles of electricity leaped between them. How curious, indeed.

If Damon was flustered before, he quickly gained control. He bowed slightly. "Miss Galway, we always seem to be running into each other. How long has it been? Several months at least."

"Several months hardly constitutes 'always running into each other.' If we are lucky several months more will pass before it happens again," Miss Galway retorted.

Oh, dear.

Perhaps Olivia was wrong about the sparks, for that was a direct hit if ever she had seen or heard one.

Damon mockingly laid his hand on his heart and staggered. "Ouch. Bullseye. You've got me, Miss Galway. A fatal shot to the heart."

Miss Galway frowned, but there was no mistaking the high color in her cheeks. "You don't have a heart," she murmured so low that Olivia was unsure what she said.

If Damon heard, he ignored it. He came around the table and faced Olivia, then took her hand. "I must dash. But I would like to come and visit before I leave for Spain, may I?"

"Yes. You may."

Damon faced her, lifted her hand to his lips, and kissed it. Then he peered over her hand to catch her gaze and mouthed, "sister."

One of those tears lingering in the corner of her eyes escaped and trickled down Olivia's cheek.

Damon stood upright. "Gideon. I will send word about the meeting with Huxley. When *are* you available?"

"Best make it late tomorrow morning. Yes, send word."

Damon gave a jaunty wave and turned to depart. But he stopped before Miss Galway and stood very close to her. Taking her gloved hand, he slowly lifted it toward his lips.

Miss Galway did not pull away or offer any verbal insults. Instead, she met his gaze boldly. There were those jolts of electricity again, and the air snapped and crackled. Damon lingered as if he were nibbling on her knuckles.

"Good afternoon, Miss Galway. Until we meet again, it may be sooner than you think."

And with that, Damon quit the room.

"Oh, that scoundrel," Miss Galway hissed crossly through clenched teeth. "I am sorry, Your Grace, if he is your friend. I should not be saying such."

Gideon stood, sauntered toward her, and offered his arm. She took it, and he escorted her to the table. "I understand completely. Brookton has that effect on people. And I said to please call me Gideon. And this is Olivia Durham, my fiancée. She will sit in on this meeting as she is well aware of the particulars. Can I fetch you something? A scone? Something more substantial?"

"Oh," Miss Galway seemed surprised at the fiancée reference, but she recovered quickly enough. She then glanced at the sideboard filled with silver chafing dishes. "It does look tempting."

"Please," Olivia smiled. "Have something. Would you care for tea, Althea? And do call me Olivia. I hope we can become better acquainted, for I am dying to hear about your investigative agency. I admire you and your sister for starting such a venture."

"Oh, thank you." Althea smiled. "And I would love a cup of tea. And Gideon, some bacon and toast, if you please. And perhaps cheese as well."

Althea took out her notebook once the food was served, and they were all settled in their seats. Then Olivia watched with fascination as Althea placed the sliced cheese and bacon between the toasted bread.

"My favorite sandwich." She bit into it, chewed, then swallowed. "Archie sent word from Essex. He has taken several photographs of the people in and around Foxmont. And reported activity about the place as if someone is fixing to move out."

"Well, that is good news," Gideon stated.

"Would you like to see the photographs immediately?" Althea asked.

Gideon looked at Olivia, and she nodded. How fascinating that they could already communicate without words. Gideon was silently asking permission to mention her abduction. And she agreed.

In telling the tale, Gideon also mentioned his suspicion regarding his stepfather.

Althea's eyes widened. "That is too awful to contemplate. We will recall Archie immediately so he can develop the film, and I have another associate I can send in his stead to continue the surveillance on Whinstone."

Althea turned her gaze to Olivia. "I am sorry that happened to you. Being pulled out of bed and abducted? You were not seriously harmed?"

Olivia pointed to her lip. "A few bruises and this. Thankfully, there was no physical violation, thanks to women coming to my aid."

"I am relieved to hear that." Althea took another bite of her bacon and cheese sandwich.

After she had eaten some of it, she continued. "Now to Whinstone's past. Christian immediately inquired and found a virtual cone of silence around the man. He did hear whispers that the present financial circumstances had more to do with Whinstone's father. Christian will get to the bottom of it. He has taken to investigating like a duck to water."

Gideon smiled. "Besides his happy marriage, Christian has a purpose in his life."

"Exactly," Althea said as she sipped her tea. "Perhaps we can put you on the payroll as well, Gideon. Think of it, duke detectives!"

Olivia and Gideon laughed. Then Gideon sobered. "I understand about finding purpose in one's life, and I believe I have found mine."

He explained about joining the group of progressives.

"That is indeed a worthy purpose," Althea nodded. "It is too bad certain other peers didn't pick up the progressive mantle."

"You mean, Brookton? He is a scoundrel, to be certain, but like all of us in The Rakes of St. Regent's Park, he is also a little lost. Lonely. Perhaps—damaged. I believe he will find his way eventually. What you need to know about him is that he is more bluster than anything."

Althea frowned as if contemplating what Gideon had said but remained silent. After finishing her sandwich, she dabbed the corner of her mouth with the napkin. "I had best set the wheels in motion and recall Archie. I will have the photographs ready for you to inspect late tomorrow afternoon. Will you both be in?"

"We will make certain that we are. Whomever you send to replace Archie, have them take care and stay well out of the way of Whinstone's bullies. They are capable of anything, and I do not want anyone else harmed."

"I will pass that on. What if we prove that Whinstone was behind this abduction? What recourse do you have?"

Gideon frowned as he stood to escort Althea to the door. "I don't have much recourse at all. When has a duke ever been prosecuted for such a crime? All he has to do is deny it. His bullies may take the fall, but Whinstone? Practically impossible."

"The justice system is not fair," Althea fumed.

"That it is not." He opened the door. "Did you come by carriage?"

"Hansom cab."

"Hobson," Gideon called to his butler. "See that Miss Galway is taken in my carriage wherever she wishes. And have the carriage at her disposal for the rest of the day."

"Right away, Your Grace," Hobson replied.

"How generous. Thank you, Your Grace." Althea smiled. "Goodbye, Miss Durham. How very nice to meet you."

Olivia smiled. "And you. We will have a tea tray ready for your visit."

"I look forward to it."

Gideon closed the door and headed toward her. Standing behind her, he placed his hands on her shoulders and kissed the top of her head. "What a damned muddle," he murmured.

Olivia laid her hand on top of his. "Is it true? We cannot accuse Whinstone?"

"Criminally? No. Well, I am not certain. He could feasibly get a trial in the House of Lords, judged by his fellow peers, but that is a farce. True justice is hardly ever meted out. They all stick together. I will consult my solicitor."

"Let's wait until we have definite proof first."

He nuzzled her neck. "Very wise."

Hobson entered. "I beg your pardon, Your Grace, but the Duchess of Whinstone wishes an immediate audience."

Gideon growled. "What is this, the revolving door at the Midland Grand Hotel?"

Revolving door?

Gideon must have read her mind because he leaned in and whispered, "I will take you to see it soon. Quite the invention." He kissed her cheek. "You don't have to stay and endure my mother's presence."

Olivia straightened her shoulders. "No. I have to meet her sooner or later. Best to have it done now."

Gideon's mother was as he had described. The older woman had an imperious, pretentious air. Her dark eyes, similar to Gideon's, were cold. Already, Olivia didn't like her, for the woman did not spare her son a warm glance or smile.

Before the duchess could speak, Olivia stood before Gideon as if protecting him. Which, in essence, is what she was doing.

"Your Grace. I am Olivia Durham. I'm engaged to your son. I wish I could say I was pleased to make your acquaintance, but I am not."

The duchess raised an eyebrow. "How dare you speak to me this way. Gideon! It is not to be borne. How dare you have your doxy address me."

Olivia squeezed Gideon's hand briefly before moving toward the duchess.

"I am his fiancée, not his doxy or any doxy at all. Gideon and I will be making a home together and, if we can, eventually have children. If you wish to be a part of our family's life, you must make amends. How you have treated your son—your only child—in the past and the present is abominable."

The duchess sputtered. "What lies has Gideon been spouting?"

"You enabled and supported his abuser. That is not something I can ever forget, let alone forgive. Whether Gideon does, is his decision. You have to earn my regard, and how it stands now, that may take years—if at all. You are a sorry excuse for a mother. A selfish woman who did not protect her child. How you can live with yourself, I do not know."

Olivia took another step closer. "But know this. I will protect Gideon with my last breath. I will give him all the love he deserves but never receives. I will show him respect and give him the kindness that was sadly lacking in his life all these years. Everything *you* never gave him."

What possessed her to speak to a duchess in such a manner? She turned to look at Gideon. He was not angry but looked at her with such aching love and tenderness her heart stuttered in her chest.

She had meant every word.

Chapter 22

GIDEON COULD NOT BE prouder of his beloved. When had anyone stood up for him? The inspirational words Olivia had spoken would remain forever etched on his heart.

And those comments had rendered his mother speechless. He made similar remarks to his mother through the years, but to have someone else say it? She stood, gaping, like a carp flopping on the pier.

"Why are you here, Mother? Speak your piece."

Her narrowed eyes shifted Gideon's way. "To tell you that I will be giving Sanford his divorce. His child must be legitimate. I need your assistance to get the case through the courts as swiftly as possible."

"You are giving him what he wants."

"Yes, I am."

Gideon shook his head. He shouldn't be surprised by this. "You are aware that all divorce cases are public? There will be reporters in court, and they will no doubt print the salacious details in the papers?"

"It will not reflect on me, as Sanford will take the blame. I am to call him out for cruelty and adultery."

"None of it is a lie," Gideon interjected. Whinstone must be desperate to make the child legitimate if he agreed to those terms. "And the monetary demands?"

"It is none of your business."

Gideon nodded. "You are correct. I do not care how you waste your money. Why tell me this?"

"As I said," his mother sniffed. "I need you to have the court hear the case immediately."

The last thing he wanted was to assist Whinstone in any way, but, as always, he would barter to turn it to his advantage.

"Then you will agree to move in with Aunt Mirella immediately, as I have already given notice on the town house. You have until the end of the month."

"But that is only a little over two weeks away."

"Then you had best get packing." Gideon strolled toward her, took her arm, and pulled her toward the door. "Time to go."

"Wait! You haven't addressed how that woman spoke to me!" she whined.

"I agree with Olivia's every word. And another thing, the accounts will be closed at the grocer and the apothecary. Buy your own goods in the future; as I said before, time to budget. And do not drop in unannounced again, Mother. Hobson! See the duchess off the premises." Gideon pushed her through the door and slammed it shut.

Olivia clapped her hands together. "Bravo. You handled that well."

He strode toward her and pulled her into his arms. "As did you. My God, the look on her face. She's never been spoken to like that before by someone other than family. Well done. And your words."

Gideon kissed her passionately, showing her how much her speech touched him.

Sighing blissfully, Olivia pulled back. "It's true, Gideon. We must protect each other and ensure that love, respect, kindness, and trust are the watchwords for our relationship. There will be times we disagree, perhaps vehemently. But as long as we keep our vows, we will come out on the other side. I know it."

Gideon took her hands. "Then let us vow here and now. We will not allow any outside influences to come between us. We will communicate fully and honestly. We will love and respect each other until the end of our days. We can accomplish anything. Never again will we be broken as long as we stand together. I am yours."

Olivia nodded. "And I am yours. Oh, Gideon, we can make this work. I know we can. You have my vow."

He held her close to his heart, believing they had that chance at happiness. But something nagged at the back of his mind. That there were still obstacles ahead.

But they would face it—together.

LATER THE FOLLOWING morning, Gideon and Damon arrived at Warren Cowley, Viscount Huxley's home. Gideon did not know what to expect, as the man had been absent on and off since last summer. Huxley placed himself in the Bevan-Standon Sanitorium, located in Hertfordshire. The sanitorium was started by Doctor Gethin Bevan and his daughter, Cristyn, now married to the Earl of Carnstone.

The private sanitorium specifically dealt with those suffering from addictions of all types.

Huxley's particular ailment? A form of sexual compulsion. The rest of the rakes had no idea how serious it had become until he up and announced he was cloistering himself away.

The butler showed them into the parlor, and Huxley stood to greet them. Gideon observed that Huxley looked far healthier than the drawn, thin ghost he had seen last autumn at a rakes' dinner.

"Leave us," Huxley said to the butler as he strode to the sideboard. "Can I offer you a drink, or is it too early? I can order a tea tray or coffee."

"No, thank you," Gideon replied.

"Nothing for me," Damon said. "I must say you look the picture of health. Are you cured of your particular malady?"

Huxley sat opposite them. "No one is ever truly cured of an addiction, whatever it may be. But I am coping well and ready to join the living—but not as a member of The Rakes. Those licentious days are behind me. Besides, I've met someone."

Damon scoffed. "Lord, not another one. Gideon here has fallen into that black hole. He's engaged, if you can imagine. To a charming woman. And yours?"

"I never said that someone is a woman."

Gideon and Damon were rendered speechless. They exchanged incredulous looks. Not that they frowned upon his pronouncement, but Huxley's sexual taste ran toward multiple women simultaneously. At least, it had.

"Why look so shocked, Brookton? You've been with men," Huxley stated matter-of-factly. "And so have I."

"Well, there's being with men during an orgy, a kiss and a caress here and there, then there is *being* with men," Damon replied. "I have not gone quite that far. Not that there is anything wrong with it. Blast it; it was all around us at school. You know I have always believed you gain enjoyment with whomever you can. Why are you telling us this?"

"Believe it or not, I consider you friends, regardless of what I said in the past. Christian came to see me before I left London. I said that we were *not* friends. Not for a long time. That we gravitated toward each other as children. 'What a privileged and carefree life we have all led. It's no wonder we became friends. The thread that held us together no longer exists.' They were bitter words I spoke. I hurt, and I lashed out. And I discovered that I need and want my friends in my life. I will be going to see Christian and Asher tonight for dinner. I will tell them the same thing."

Huxley crossed his legs. "So why am I telling you all this? I wanted to be upfront and honest. But obviously, I also must swear you to secrecy, considering the laws and such."

"Of course," Gideon replied. "Can you tell us who it is?"

"All I will say for now is that we met at the sanitorium. We still have to work out how to mesh our lives together. My close friend has not told his family anything, so we are taking this slow. I will be selling this place and moving permanently to Huxley Estate. I have had no presence in the House of Lords, so the members will not miss me. Besides, the House of Lords will matter less and less. Real power is in the House of Commons, anyway."

"There is still work to accomplish," Gideon stated. He then revealed about his joining Viscount Hawkestone's group. "There are MPs and Lords aplenty in Hornsby's small assembly. You have a seat, Warren. And one day, you will as well, Damon. You could both join the effort."

"I'll think about it," Damon replied absently. Which meant he wasn't interested.

"While I applaud your commitment, I am not in the right frame of mind to take up such a responsibility," Huxley said, his voice low. "I am still recovering and must advance my life in small increments. Resting at my country estate is a start."

"You know best, Warren," Gideon said.

"You've never called me by my first name before."

"No, I haven't. There have been many changes in my life as well," Gideon stated. "Accepting and acknowledging friendships is one. Keep us in your life, Warren, will you? I am glad to see you. And I'm pleased you are content and ready to move with your life."

Warren stood. "I am content. And so, it seems, are you, Gideon—quite a change in you. You've never been this open and accepting. I applaud the transformation." They shook hands. "And we *will* keep in contact."

Warren turned to Damon and held out his hand. "And I wish you all the best, Damon. And hope that someday your restless soul finds peace and happiness."

Damon rolled his eyes as he shook Warren's hand. "Oh, please. Spare me the homilies. I am fine just as I am."

As they departed and climbed into Gideon's carriage, Damon said, "So much for The Rakes of St. Regent's Park. You have all abandoned me."

Once seated, Gideon banged on the roof, and the carriage lurched forward.

"Come now, there are still members, and you can recruit new ones. You are now the elder statesman of the group. Well, you and Tolwood. Poor Merritt, is he still looking for a bride?"

"I suppose. I don't care. To be blunt, I never cared for Tolwood. Christian took pity on him and allowed him to join The Rakes. Don't forget: Tolwood is not a full-fledged member. I should cut him loose and be done with it."

Gideon chuckled. "Such compassion for your fellow man. Will you be coming back to my house?"

Damon shook his head. "Not today. I am still processing the shocking news about Olivia and our blood ties. As I said, I will see her before I depart for Spain." He pulled aside the curtain, staring outside. Damon's look turned wistful. "I always wanted a sister. I always wanted someone to love."

Gideon arched an eyebrow at the emotional confession. Damon was unaware that he had spoken that heartfelt comment aloud. Gideon would not acknowledge it.

There were more depths to Damon than he had initially believed.

ALTHEA GALWAY ARRIVED promptly at four o'clock with a young lad in tow.

Olivia smiled, "Welcome, please do take a seat."

"Thank you, Your Grace, Miss Durham. May I introduce Archie Fitzgerald? He is presently attending school while assisting us in our endeavors when he can."

Archie stood, cap in hand, looking from the tiered stand filled with sandwiches and treats back to Olivia and Gideon.

"Archie," Althea prompted.

"Right. Pleasant to make your acquaintance, Your Grace. Miss," he said, bowing slightly.

"Good. Now that formal introduction is out of the way, let's get right to it," Althea stated. "We can lay out the photographs here on the table." Althea retrieved them from a folder. They were large enough to make out minute details. Gideon and Olivia drew closer.

"This is quite an improvement over glass plates, I must say. You developed these yourself, Archie?"

"I did, Your Grace."

"Sometime soon, you must show me the process. I am completely fascinated," Gideon replied. He pointed to one of the photographs. "That is Whinstone, my stepfather."

"Yes," Archie nodded. "He was in charge, ordering everyone about. Wagons arrived last night, and I told my relief to let me know what they do with those wagons."

Olivia gasped, her hand flying to her mouth. She could feel the color draining from her face.

"It's him. Yellow Teeth, one of my attackers." She pointed to the photo, her hand shaking in alarm.

"Jonas Bisby, he's been with Whinstone for years, doing his dirty work." Gideon smashed his fist on the table, startling them all. He then strode toward the wall to push the buzzer.

"What are you doing?" Olivia called out.

"I am going to have Hobson call for a carriage, head to the station, take a train to Foxmont and thrash Whinstone to within an inch of his life!" he roared.

"No, wait. Don't," Olivia said firmly.

Gideon stopped in his tracks. "Why?"

Olivia started to pace. "We have to be smart about this. Beating him—while giving me some satisfaction—would only be a temporary solution. We have to devise a solid plan to see him ruined and out of our lives permanently."

"Olivia is correct," Althea added. "Why don't we all sit and discuss it in depth? Archie, tell His Grace what you observed."

They all took their seats, and Olivia poured the tea and passed around a plate of biscuits. But Gideon had her concerned. He was seething, ready to blow.

After Archie ate several sugar biscuits and washed them down with tea, he retrieved some of the photos and passed them around.

"See in that one, Your Grace? This Bisby bloke carried out what looks like several paintings. I couldn't follow him. But when he returned, he didn't have them. I think he sold them. I have suspicions about the wagons, and they mean to take some of the furnishings and valuables."

"Oh, the nerve of the man," Olivia fumed.

"I can still catch the train," Gideon interjected.

"I think it best that Archie catches the train and returns to his post," Althea said. "And have Billy stay with you. The local constable is supposed to see Whinstone off the premises tomorrow afternoon."

"And if he shows up, and the duke still leaves with wagonloads full of goods, then what?" Archie asked.

"Don't interfere," Gideon said. "Follow him. It's probably best if we catch him with the goods. Is that right, Althea?"

"Yes. Absolutely. I wouldn't count on this village constable. What's the nearest town or city? There is probably a police constabulary that covers the region."

Before Gideon could answer, Hobson entered the room. "Your Grace, His Grace, the Duke of Allenby wishes an audience."

Christian breezed past Hobson. "You can leave us alone, Hobson; thank you." After the butler closed the door, Christian said, "I've got the information on the Whinstone dukedom."

Chapter 23

"THERE WAS A TRIAL IN the House of Lords in '48, and they kept the proceedings completely secret," Christian began as he paced back and forth in front of them. "Concerning Whinstone's father, the then duke. Apparently, the old duke misappropriated funds in the tens of thousands of pounds. It concerned a charity school venture."

"Why am I not surprised?" Gideon scoffed. "Like father, like son."

"As you know, there is rarely a trial in the House of Lords," Christian continued. "But 1848 was a challenging year, the potato famine in Ireland, unrest and revolt across Europe, another cholera outbreak in London, and numerous workhouse scandals. The lords did not want to add a thieving duke stealing money from impoverished children. Think of the headlines. They decided he had to be punished, which is why the secret trial."

Christian took a seat next to Althea on the sofa. "He was found guilty, stripped of all property, including entailed, and they took all the money. He also lost his seat in the House of Lords. A bankrupt peer cannot sit, which is why the current Duke of Whinstone is not in the house."

"I don't understand. Why didn't the lords strip the old duke of the title?" Olivia asked.

"You need an Act of Parliament to do it. They didn't want this public. Also, the then Duke of Whinstone agreed to hand over all money. And property even entailed, which I don't believe is legal, was part of the covert agreement. The money included the amount he had stolen, and the Lords supposedly restored the amount to the charity schools. All this is in exchange for keeping the title. He testified that his son, Sanford, who was eight then, should be allowed to restore respectability to the title. The majority of the lords on the committee—agreed."

Gideon sneered. "We see how that worked out."

"Can the Queen strip the title from him?" Althea asked as she poured Christian a cup of tea and handed the cup and saucer to him.

"No, she can only do that for royal peerage titles. Besides, we would never get an audience with Queen Victoria, she is much in seclusion, and I hear her health is not the best," Christian replied. "We must deal with the lords. We should approach the Committee for Privileges and Conduct. I spoke to one of the members unofficially, who voted on the Whinstone dukedom fifty years ago."

"My, you didn't waste any time, Your Grace," Olivia marveled. "How old is this lord?"

"He was twenty-three at the time of the trial and now seventy-three. I mentioned that the current duke's son is guilty of multiple criminal acts and has not lived up to the agreement reached a half-century ago. That I believe that the dukedom should be eradicated from the peerage rolls permanently. Lord Haverstock agreed."

Olivia clapped her hands together. "Why, that's wonderful! Taking the dukedom would be a decided blow to the man."

Gideon frowned. "My love, it won't happen overnight. It will take several weeks, even months, to follow all the protocols to enact an Act of Parliament."

"Haverstock told me we may need a Royal Assent to make the process go smoother and more swiftly," Christian interjected. "He offered to assist with that if needed."

Gideon scratched his chin. "The Hornsbys are looked on favorably by the Queen; it's how Tremain acquired his viscountcy. Perhaps we could ask him, as well."

"All this will be a moot point if we do not catch the duke in a criminal act," Althea said.

"I will testify to his hired man abducting me," Olivia pronounced.

Gideon took her hand and kissed it. She was so brave. "That is a beginning. But if Whinstone is stripping Foxmont bare, that will be the sugar on the sponge cake, as it were."

Althea stood. "I am going with you, Archie. We must leave for Essex immediately."

Gideon released Olivia's hand and stood. "And I will be going as well. Christian?"

"I think it best I head back to Westminster and start the process with the conduct committee," Christian replied as he sipped his tea. "I will ask them to draft a notice of intent of Whinstone's trial in the House of Lords with the sole purpose of stripping his title."

"I think that is wise. Whinstone has no friends among the peerage. No one will stand up for him. None that I am aware of," Gideon said. "We'd best prepare for our journey, then."

"Well, I am not staying here alone," Olivia huffed. "If you leave me behind, I will follow you on a later train."

Gideon reached for her hand and brought her to her feet. "My love, why would I leave you? I said I would never be from your side. Partner in all things, remember?"

Oh, how she loved this man.

"A point we must remember is rarely are peers subject to full criminal prosecution," Gideon said gravely. "I am not saying it doesn't transpire. With murder, there is no getting around it. However, theft of goods? An abduction that he can claim he knew nothing about? It could be tricky. Justice is not always fair and favors the wealthy and titled."

Stark words, and hardly just indeed.

But Olivia understood how the world worked. At the very least, if they could get his title revoked, it would be some semblance of justice, a beginning.

She glanced at Gideon, talking with Allenby and Althea. Would it be enough for Gideon, for all those years of being beaten, mistreated, and unloved? Could he find enough peace with his past to move on?

If Gideon could do it, then so shall she.

WHEN THEY COLLECTED overnight cases and caught the train, they arrived in the town of Stanford-le-Hope a couple of hours later. Thankfully, it was still light. After renting a carriage, they were off to Foxmont. Olivia had to admit this was all rather exciting, pursuing a villain. And no mistake, Whinstone was a villain to his rotted core.

As they pulled onto the road leading to the estate, the driver slowed, and Olivia stared out the window at all the magnificent trees covered with late spring leaves. Then Foxmont came into view, and it took Olivia's breath away.

The setting sun showered the manor house in a heavenly twilight. It sat near a pristine lake. It had so many windows; how could it not help but catch the sun?

Gideon leaned in and whispered in her ear. "Do you like it?"

"I adore it," she answered, awe in her voice.

"Well, I should prepare you for the interior of the place. It shows years of neglect and needs plenty of attention."

They came up to the front doors, but no one greeted them. Didn't servants usually welcome the guests?

Gideon strode toward the front entrance and entered, calling out, "Henderson!"

But no one replied.

Gideon disappeared into the hall while Althea, Archie, and Olivia were assisted from the wagon by the driver. They followed Gideon through the door.

Already Olivia could observe the neglect that Gideon had spoken of. There wasn't a thing on the walls, no portraits, mirrors, or tapestries. They caught up to Gideon, who stood at the entrance of a room—that was all but empty.

The place was quiet; not a person anywhere. No wagons.

"Blast it to hell. Whinstone is gone," Gideon growled. He turned to face Althea. "And where is this Billy person? I thought he was keeping watch?"

"I do not understand." Althea headed back outside, looking around the front entrance area. She bent to pick something up and hurried toward them.

"A note! Billy tacked it to the door, which must have blown off in the breeze. Billy is following them. He borrowed one of the horses from your stables. Once they settle for the night, he will send word of where they are. They departed at noon," Althea concluded.

"They could have gone in any direction," Archie said. "And how is he going to send word? Here? Or at Cleveland Street?"

"You told Billy we were coming here, did you not?" Althea asked Archie.

"I said we'd be along directly, just not when," Archie replied.

"Archie, head to Fobbing. They have a telegraph office, and I saw it next to the pub," Althea commanded. "Send word to Eleanora to keep watch for a message from Billy. And to telegraph us if she hears anything. Take the carriage. And tell the telegraph office to deliver it here as soon as possible, no matter the hour. We will pay extra."

Olivia was suitably impressed at how Althea took charge.

"Right-o." Archie turned to depart.

"Wait," Gideon said. "I'm going with you. I know we stopped to ask about the Chief Constable of the Essex Constabulary when we first disembarked from the train, but I believe it is time to bring the man up to date. Stanford is three miles from Fobbing. After we send the telegram, we will seek out the chief." Then he huffed. "Noon," Gideon grumbled. "They have been on the road for hours."

"The wagons would not get far if laden with goods. Ten or twelve miles, if they are lucky?" Olivia said.

"If that. How did Whinstone ever think that he would get away with this? He intends to unload and sell the goods before anyone discovers them missing. But the servants would know of his crime. The servants!"

Gideon took off at a run, making it difficult for Olivia, Althea, and Archie to keep up. Down a narrow flight of backstairs, they located the servants in a large dining area, or what was probably called the servants' hall. There were five of them, gagged and tied to chairs.

Taking a small knife from the drawer, Gideon hurried toward the older man who had blood trickling down the side of his face.

"God above, Henderson!" Gideon shouted as he carefully cut the cloth gag. "What happened?"

"I am so sorry, Your Grace; we tried to stop him," the older man coughed. "I tried to fight them, but they overpowered us and brought us here. They said if we said a word, they would return and murder us in our beds."

Althea and Olivia followed Gideon's lead, taking small knives from the cutlery drawer to cut the gags and ropes.

"Who are they, Henderson?" Gideon asked as he removed the ropes.

"The duke, his mistress, that Bisby thug. Two other men showed up this morning. And three recently-hired servants. They never did any work, Your Grace. Conditions here were abominable. Two long-time servants quit last month. I sent word to Mr. Chapman, the steward, but he never came. He never answered my letter."

"I don't believe he received it," Gideon said, barely containing his anger. "Or I would have heard of it. Where are the three recently-hired servants?"

One of the women stood. "They did a runner, Your Grace, begging your pardon. Paid with stolen goods, I'll be bound."

Gideon turned toward the voice. "Mrs. Peterson. My deepest apologies. I swear to you all; I had no idea what was happening here. I did not take my responsibilities to this household seriously enough or toward those of you who worked diligently here for years. I allowed Whinstone to stay here because I wanted him out of my sight. But I never gave a thought to how he would treat you all. I cannot begin to make amends."

The staff said nothing but were eyeing Gideon warily. Olivia couldn't blame them.

"Is one of you the housekeeper?" Olivia asked.

"Excuse me," Gideon said. "This is Miss Olivia Durham, my fiancée. Next to her are Miss Althea Galway and Archie Fitzgerald of the Galway Investigative Agency. We had hoped to catch Whinstone in the act."

"Hello, Miss Galway," Mrs. Peterson said. "I am the cook. We've not had a housekeeper here for four years. Mr. Chapman hired a few, but they never stayed." The cook introduced the remaining staff.

"Do you know where Whinstone and his accomplices have gone?" Althea asked.

"No, Miss Galway," the butler replied, holding a cloth to his head. "I'm sorry."

"Do not be sorry, Henderson. I am going to fetch the police. Do you need a doctor for your injury?" Gideon asked.

"No, Your Grace. Mrs. Peterson can attend to me. It is not serious."

"I will return shortly. Come, Archie."

Gideon and Archie disappeared up the stairs.

Olivia turned to face the shaken staff. "You have all been through a horrible ordeal, not only this evening but the past couple of years Whinstone has been living here. Believe me when I tell you that the Duke of Watford is truly sorry that he put you through this. As he said, he allowed the duke to stay here to be rid of the horrid man. I do hope you will find it in your hearts to forgive."

Good Lord, she sounded like she was the duchess already.

"And find it in your hearts to stay," she continued. "The duke and I will be making Foxmont our home. There will be many changes, all good, I promise you. Now, has Whinstone absconded with the mattresses?"

"No, Miss Durham," Alice, the head housemaid, replied. "We will ensure rooms are ready for you and your guests."

"Thank you. And Mrs. Peterson, could you make a light meal for all of us, the staff included? A few sandwiches and cakes, I imagine. And, one last request, do not place His Grace in the room Whinstone stayed in."

The staff moved away to attend to their duties and Henderson's injury. Althea slipped her arm through Olivia's as they walked toward the stairs.

"Well done," Althea whispered. "You handled that like a hot knife through butter. You will make a fine duchess."

Olivia laughed lightly. "Perhaps it is in the blood after all."

Althea gave her a puzzled look as they headed to find a room with furniture.

She could hardly reveal she was the illegitimate daughter of a duke. But inside, Olivia was riddled with doubt despite her calmness and taking control of the situation.

How could she ever pull this off? A duchess?

But with Gideon by her side, Olivia could accomplish anything.

Chapter 24

IT WAS NEARLY THIRTY minutes past eight before they were heading toward Foxmont again. Inside the carriage, Archie was crowded on the seat with two formidable police officers while the Chief Constable, Edward Rainer, sat next to Gideon on the seat opposite.

"A bad business, in pursuit of a duke. And in the dark," Rainer mumbled.

He was an older man with a shock of white hair, with threads of black at the temples. He was tall with the bearing of an ex-military man.

"Peers commit crimes like anyone else," Gideon replied. "And if the world were truly just, they would be subject to the same punishment as other citizens."

"True enough, Your Grace," Rainer replied.

"The man has been my stepfather for thirty years. I know how he thinks. He probably calculated that I wouldn't care if he stole a few bits and bobs from a house I haven't lived in for decades. That I would let it slide as I would be glad to be rid of him," Gideon said gruffly. "Perhaps the old Watford would have ignored it. But not now. Especially after abducting the woman that I love. Beating and humiliating her. *That* I would never ignore, he must be punished."

"Quite right, Your Grace," Rainer agreed. "Abominable. Since that occurred in London, you must address that matter with the Met Police. But the thievery? The Essex Constabulary will handle it; never fear."

"It helps that we know where he is," Gideon held up the telegram.

They had stopped in Fobbing on the way back, and there was a telegram from Althea's sister, Eleanora. Billy had been in contact as promised. Whinstone was staying at an inn just east of South Benfleet.

"It's obvious he's heading toward the largest town in the county, Southend-on-Sea, to sell the goods," Gideon proclaimed.

"I concur, Your Grace. Are you acquainted with the Earl of Southen?" Rainer questioned.

Gideon's eyebrows knotted. "Not personally; why do you ask?"

"He is in an asylum, the verdict from the court. The sentence came from breaking in and assaulting a woman at a brothel in London last year. I bring it up to show there is some justice for wayward peers, even though it was hushed up in the papers."

"Good to know."

He had heard of an earl's removal from the House of Lords. Had it happened already? Must have, lunatics, cannot serve, as they say.

"Since Foxmont is on the way," Gideon said, changing the subject. "We will stop briefly to inform the ladies of our plan, show you the rooms Whinstone emptied, and hear the servants' version of what occurred."

Rainer nodded. "The stop must be brief, for the sooner we catch up to the duke, the better. I can acquire detailed information from the servants later, Your Grace."

They no sooner arrived, and Olivia ran to his arms. Gideon held her close to his heart and smoothed her hair. Blast it all; he didn't care if everyone, including the staff, watched their embrace.

"All is well. We have a location thanks to Billy and the Galway Agency." After kissing Olivia's forehead, Gideon made quick introductions.

Henderson mentioned the man who had struck him at Whinstone's behest. Then Gideon showed the chief the bare walls and the empty drawing room. Then the library.

“I’ve seen and heard enough for now,” Rainer stated. “We had best be on our way. Catch him before he escapes. We can take it from here, Your Grace.”

“Not a chance, Rainer. I am coming with you. Ladies, I would take you, but the carriage is full as it is,” Gideon said. “And we have to bring back Whinstone and his accomplices. I would leave Archie, but I need him to point out this Billy person. And we may need the extra hands.”

“In other words, male hands,” Olivia huffed, clearly disappointed.

“Yes, love. Strength is needed in this instance. I am sure Althea would concur.”

“Reluctantly. Yes. Go with the duke, Archie. And mind what he says,” Althea replied.

After the farewells, they were on the road toward South Benfleet.

Once past the town, they found the inn in question, The Anchor and Swan. Over to the side of the building, parked under a shelter, were two wagons covered with tarps. Gideon and one of the constables stealthily made their way to the wagons. Lifting the tarp, the constable held his lit bullseye lamp high so they could see.

Gideon recognized the furniture and wall hangings from the drawing and dining rooms. He turned toward the chief and nodded.

A young man stepped out of the shadows, and Archie moved to stand next to Gideon. “It’s Billy, Your Grace,” he whispered.

Gideon held out his hand to Billy. “Well done,” he said in a quiet voice.

The young man nodded, took his hand, and shook it.

What happened next could almost be farcical theater, or that is how Gideon recalled it later. After entering the inn, they questioned the innkeeper about what room the man who owned the wagons stayed in. The men started up the stairs. A woman—a decidedly pregnant one—screamed at the top of her lungs as soon as she spotted the uniformed constables.

The caterwauling was loud and shrill enough to shatter glass. A couple of men came out of a room into the upper hallway, and the police constables ran up the stairs to subdue them.

Whinstone peeked out the door next to the room the other men stayed in, and his gaze locked with Gideon's.

I have you, you miserable bastard.

Whinstone's eyes narrowed, giving Gideon that contemptuous look he had always shown him since he was a small boy. Then he slammed the door and locked it.

"I'll try to go in. You go to the rear to ensure the duke doesn't go out the window," Rainer instructed. "Belcher," he yelled to one of the constables. "The young lads can assist Williams with the accomplices. You go with the duke. And Williams!"

"Yes, sir?"

"Shut that woman up. Gag her if you must."

Gideon and Belcher tore out of the inn, and as they rounded the corner to enter the rear yard, Gideon halted, watching in shock, as Whinstone stood on a small balcony, then dropped. The duke landed on a horse, one he had at the ready for a quick escape.

And he *was* escaping.

Snapping the reins, Whinstone tore out of the rear yard. The despicable man was an expert horseman, better than Gideon could ever claim to be. But be damned if he would allow the man to disappear into the shadows.

No one would harm Olivia and get away with it. Not as long as Gideon drew breath.

"Belcher, can you ride?"

"I can, Your Grace."

"I'll fetch two horses from the stable. Keep the light on Whinstone."

"He's heading west, Your Grace. Back toward London," Belcher replied.

"I will follow that son of a bitch straight into the depths of hell," Gideon growled as he ran toward the stables.

A bit dramatic, perhaps, but it fit Gideon's mood.

Locating two horses from the wagons, Gideon hastily buckled on the reins and saddles he had found in the small barn before returning to Belcher. Already Whinstone had a five-minute head start.

Rainer hurried toward him. "He escaped?"

"Had a horse at the ready, jumped on him, and tore off down the main road," Gideon grumbled as he mounted the horse.

Rainer passed Belcher a revolver. "Here, lad. Use it if necessary. Shoot the horse out from under him if needs must. Do not let him get away. Be careful, both of you. We are heading back to Stanford with the suspects. When you catch the runaway duke, bring him along, tied to the saddle, if necessary."

Gideon nodded, then turned and galloped down the dark road with Belcher close behind. His bullseye lamp affixed to the saddle, cast a fragment of light for their pursuit.

And what would he do when he caught up to his loathsome stepfather? Beat him to a bloody pulp? Take the revolver from Belcher and shoot Whinstone between the eyes? String him up to become carrion for the ravens?

Gideon would love to do all three, but he couldn't. It wasn't the 17th century; more's the pity.

No, he had to be civilized about it all. Take him in for trial. Whatever it took. Seeing some semblance of justice would have to do. If there was no possible way to arrest and prosecute him for the abduction and assault, they could charge him with the stolen goods.

Gideon wanted to slam the door shut on this aspect of his life. The damage his stepfather and his mother wrought will always be with him—permanent scars, inside and out.

But it would no longer rule his life or his selfish actions.

On that, Gideon swore a vow.

From now on, he would live his life in peaceful contentment in the arms of the woman he loved fiercely. The woman he longed to kiss so passionately; he'd take her breath away.

For she had already taken his.

"HYAH!" SANFORD YELLED as he slapped the reins against the horse's neck.

The animal whinnied in response but did pick up the pace somewhat.

Blast Watford and his stubborn pride. And his persistent pursuit. How dare he bring coppers?

Face it, stealing the furniture and other bits was a reckless plan. Sanford directed Bisby to sell several paintings, and Sanford had the two hundred and thirty pounds safely tucked away in his money belt.

It was a gamble that Sanford lost. He thought his indolent stepson wouldn't care about Foxmont and its belongings. When has he ever shown any interest?

Over the past two years, Sanford had Bisby sell a painting here and a figurine there. The sales were enough to give him pocket money to buy a few extras like bottles of expensive brandy and scotch.

That miserable butler had noticed and written the steward more than once. But the local postmaster never delivered the letters for several months thanks to a monetary deal Bisby made on Sanford's direction.

Watford showing up unannounced at Foxmont had changed everything.

Thankfully, he was not there long enough to speak to the staff, but he had seen the neglect, the empty walls, and the shelves. Sanford knew his time of staying at the estate rent-free would soon come to an end.

Which is why he forged ahead with his reckless plan of stripping the place clean.

The horse was already laboring, for Watford had also neglected his stables. The horses were old, only suitable for pulling a wagon or a small carriage. This nag will never reach London at full gallop, not thirty miles.

What could he do? Steal a horse at a farm along the way? Sanford didn't even know if there were farms on the route.

But there were more horses at Foxmont. A fresh mount and continue on his way.

And do what, exactly?

He left Annabella, and his unborn child, behind. With the money in his belt, he could ride straight to London, catch a train to the coast and take a steamer to North America.

But what if the child was a boy? His heir. It was the only reason he tolerated Annabella's presence. As money was the only motivating factor, he accepted his lady wife's company.

Sanford would hand it to Christina, his duchess. She readily agreed to the divorce so he could marry and have his heir.

Perhaps she loved him, after all.

She had always claimed such through the years, but Sanford brushed sickening emotional declarations aside.

Regardless, it is not as if the unborn baby was his only progeny. He had other offspring and maybe more children he was not aware of. There was a daughter, what was her name, Clara? Cloe? No, Claudia, that was it. A pretty thing. Who knows where she was, and who cared? Regardless, his bloodline would carry on one way or another. Illegitimate, perhaps, but his descendants, nonetheless.

Sanford glanced behind him at the long stretch of the dark road. He could swear that off in the distance shone a single light.

Damn it; they were in pursuit. Sanford was sure of it.

Growling, he dug his heels into the horse's flanks, and the animal whinnied but went no faster. Yes, this nag would not last to London. He would stop at Foxmont. He would make them sorry if any of those damnable servants got in his way. Watford no doubt untied them.

When Sanford departed with his goods, he briefly considered torching the place.

A cruel smile curved about his lips. Perhaps he would do precisely that.

Chapter 25

OLIVIA AND ALTHEA SAT around the long table with the servants, partaking in a light meal. No one spoke. The staff was still recovering from their ordeal and wary of their presence.

"It must have been intolerable having Whinstone here. Why didn't you all leave?" Then Olivia flushed. "I am sorry. At times, I can be too direct. It's none of my business."

"Well, miss," Henderson replied. "We serve this house and the Watford dukedom. If the duke wanted Whinstone to stay here, who were we to gainsay his directive? I assure you that we did the absolute minimum for Whinstone."

Henderson cleared his throat. "The people you see in this room have been here for thirty years or more. Where would we go? The bigger houses are letting staff go, where would we find employment? I wish Mr. Chapman had come to inspect the doings here, but he never did. I did write, maybe I should have written the Duke of Watford directly, but it is not my place to do so. I wish now that I had."

"Well, we will do something about it now. From what I've seen, it is a beautiful manor house. Plenty of potential," she replied with a smile.

"Oh, that it does, miss. You and the duke will be happy here; I know it." Mrs. Peterson said as she sipped her tea.

A terrible crash and the agonizing whinnies of a horse interrupted their conversation.

Olivia stood. "Gideon?" Would he have returned already?

"No, miss," Henderson said. "His Grace would have come in through the front door. This is someone else."

"Is there a hunting rifle around?" Olivia whispered.

"Yes, miss. I will fetch it." Henderson hurried away.

Althea came to stand next to her. Reaching into her large reticle, she pulled out a revolver. "My Bull Dog. Compact with five barrels, loaded with .442 Webley ammunition. I am a dead shot."

"Althea, you are full of surprises. I love it. Keep it hidden for now."

Althea slipped it under her cape.

Henderson returned with a rifle, loading in cartridges as he headed toward Olivia.

"This is a hunting rifle for shooting game birds, but it hasn't been used in years. I believe it still works. Though I am not sure how to use it."

"Give it here," Olivia said. Not that she knew how to use it, but it may work as a deterrent.

"Look! The stable is on fire!" Alice called.

They all ran to join her at the window. Three horses ran from the burning structure, taking off in different directions. A man, outlined in flame, was holding onto the reins of another horse.

It was *not* Gideon.

The man looped the reins against the post, then picked up what appeared to be a torch. He lit it with the growing flames and threw it onto the jut-out roof by the back entrance. The wooden slats were soon on fire.

Olivia did not hesitate; she marched outside with the rifle in front of her.

"Wait, miss—"

Now outside, she could make out the features of the very tall man. She had seen his cold countenance in one of the photographs—Gideon's horrid stepfather.

Laying on the ground was a horse in distress; white foam oozed from his nose and mouth.

"It's Whinstone," Henderson said, coming to stand nearby.

Olivia raised her rifle. "Do not move, or I will shoot. It will be my pleasure to blow a hole in you. You certainly deserve it."

"You must be Watford's slut. I have my horse, allow me to escape, and nothing further needs to be done or said."

Olivia stood with Althea, as well as the servants. "I think not. You've caused enough damage. You will stay here and wait for the police."

"I think not," Whinstone replied drolly. "Be damned if I will take orders from a brothel whore."

The servants gasped.

"You will," Olivia yelled. "Move an inch, or I'll shoot."

Whinstone laughed; he threw back his head and laughed like a villain in a play. It was enough of a distraction that Althea could pull out her Bull Dog revolver and get off a shot. Whinstone dropped to the ground like a large sack of potatoes.

He howled in pain, holding his knee. "You shot me!"

"No, that was Miss Galway," Olivia replied. "I would have aimed for your blackened heart instead of your knee. We need rope to put out that fire before it spreads."

The cook and the butler hurried to fetch a rope while the maids grabbed the buckets by the trough and filled them with water.

Two horses galloped into the rear yard.

"Gideon!" Olivia dropped the rifle and ran to him as he dismounted.

He gathered her into his arms. "Are you hurt?"

"No. Whinstone set the stable on fire and was stealing another horse."

Gideon turned to glare at Whinstone, who was still yowling.

Henderson handed the policeman the rope, and the copper soon had Whinstone trussed like a turkey.

"You shot him?" Gideon asked.

"No, that was Althea."

Althea came to stand next to them. "Olivia didn't hesitate. She got the butler to fetch a rifle then she marched out to confront the intruder. I was her backup."

"Well done, all of you. Where are the stable boys?"

"They come four days a week, Your Grace. They do not live on the premises," Henderson replied.

"I see," Gideon replied. "Belcher, do you still have your pistol?" Gideon took it and headed toward the horse lying on the ground.

"Oh, no, Gideon. Is there nothing to be done?" Olivia asked.

"No, love. The poor horse is suffering. Turn away, all of you."

A shot rang out, and the tortured whinnies mercifully ended.

Gideon handed the gun back to the policeman. "Now the fire. We must stop it from spreading."

Gideon, the policeman, the staff, and Olivia and Althea, managed to halt the flames from doing further damage. Thankfully, there was no wind tonight. The stable would need rebuilding and the roof by the back entrance repaired, but it could have been worse. So much worse.

Gideon assisted Constable Belcher in slinging Whinstone over the saddle and lashing him to it.

Then Gideon came to Olivia, framing her face with his hands. "I have to accompany Belcher to the Stanford-le-Hope police station. I will return as soon as I can."

"I'm bleeding," Whinstone yelled. "I need a doctor!"

"With any luck, you will bleed out before we get to Stanford," Gideon yelled. "But you won't; more's the pity."

He turned to Olivia and said in a quieter tone, "I do not know how long I will be."

"I'll be here, waiting. However long it takes, Gideon."

He caressed her cheeks with the pads of his thumbs. "I don't deserve you." Then in a soft voice, only she could hear, "I love you with every fiber of my being."

Olivia's heart soared. "The same for me. To the depths of my soul."

Olivia watched as they rode away, her heart bursting with love.

Althea came up to stand next to her. "Well, that was decidedly romantic. The farewell, I mean. Sorry, didn't mean to overhear."

"I never thought I would *ever* fall in love," Olivia said wistfully. "And certainly not with a duke." She turned to face Althea. "What Whinstone said about me being a brothel wh—"

Althea slipped her arm through Olivia's. "My friend, we are friends, aren't we?" Olivia nodded. "I don't care a whit about your past, whatever it is. If many years from now, we are sipping tea by the fire on a rainy afternoon, and you feel compelled to reveal your past, I will be all attention. Until then, it's the present and future that take precedence."

Olivia patted her hand. "You are so right."

THE SUN PEEKED OVER the horizon, casting shadows through the windows of the Essex police station. Gideon had been there all night, giving his statement and waiting to hear the results of the questioning of Whinstone, his mistress, and the hired men.

Rainer called Gideon into the office around eight o'clock. "Have a seat, Your Grace. I told you there was no need to remain. I would have come to Foxmont later this morning."

"I wanted to stay. Well? What was said?"

Rainer referred to his notes. "The man, Jacob Bisby, has denied that the duke had any knowledge or involvement in the kidnapping and assault on Miss Durham. Unfortunately, that will be a case for the London court to decide. If you choose to bring charges."

Gideon frowned. "That doesn't sound promising."

"It will be hard to prove, Your Grace. The case will hinge on Miss Durham's testimony. To say that women have difficulty bringing assault charges against men is a regrettable reality in British justice."

Rainer tsked. "And that is not all. The prosecutors will tear her to shreds once Miss Durham stands in the docket. Every aspect of her life lay bare. Believe me, the duke's solicitors will leave no stone unturned and distort anything that favors their client."

Gideon remembered what the judge had told Olivia, how the woman victim is put on trial more than the perpetrator, and it angered him afresh.

"That will be Miss Durham's decision, but I will certainly relay everything you have said. And the theft of goods?"

"Ah, we will have more success there, Your Grace. He was caught red-handed, as it were. With the testimony of the servants and your own, I can foresee a conviction to be certain. The two men taken with Bisby deny any knowledge of the theft, declaring Bisby hired them to transport goods. They can be charged as accessories whether they knew it or not."

"And what is Bisby saying about the robbery?"

Rainer shook his head. "Dedicated to the duke to the end, though I do not know why. He claims that he had no awareness there was thievery afoot, claiming the same as the hired men. That will not hold up because the butler said Bisby struck him and tied him up in the servants' hall."

"And the woman? Whinstone's mistress?"

"The lady denies all knowledge, claiming the duke was under the impression he was entitled to the goods. Again, that will not hold up in court. Can you explain to me, Your Grace, how such a loathsome man such as the duke inspires such loyalty?"

"I wish I could. The past is full of such men. And I regret to say the future will also be full of them. Many are in positions of power. What is the lady's name?"

Rainer looked down at his papers. "Miss Annabella Day, daughter of Sir Simon Day, baronet. Should I contact him, Your Grace? I understand from Miss Day she is estranged from her family."

"I would contact him. I doubt he wants his daughter's name bandied about in public. Will she be sentenced?"

"I believe so. Miss Day will be having her baby in prison."

"Sorry to interrupt, Chief Constable, but the Duke of Allenby wishes to see you and the Duke of Watford," Belcher said, standing in the open doorway.

"Well, three dukes under my roof, that is one for the books, what? Show him in, Belcher, and make us all tea, if you will."

"And the prisoners, sir?" Belcher asked.

"Them as well. Let's be civilized about it," Rainer replied.

Rainer and Gideon stood as Christian breezed into the room. "Gentlemen. I caught the first train early this morning."

Christian sat next to Gideon in front of Rainer's desk while Gideon made introductions. Belcher brought in mugs of tea for the men, then departed, closing the door.

Christian reached into his side pocket. "I have it, the writ. There will be a trial in the House of Lords. The conduct committee members assured me the dukedom will be taken from Whinstone. I mentioned that he was under arrest for theft of goods, and that convinced them. He *is* under arrest?"

"He most assuredly is, Your Grace," Rainer replied. "He was caught with the goods and tried to escape. His Grace can fill you in on the details."

Rainer sipped his tea, then stood. "Meanwhile, Your Graces, if you will excuse me, I had best file formal charges and see that things get rolling, as it were. Will you be at Foxmont? I will send the information once we lay charges."

"And that is our cue to depart," Gideon stated. "Could you allow us to see Whinstone for a few moments? We want to inform him of the writ."

"Follow me, Your Graces."

Rainer led them into the rear of the police station, where there were six small cells, most taken up with Whinstone and his men. Miss Day must be elsewhere.

"Come to gloat?" Whinstone sneered, sitting on the bench toward the back of the windowless cell. His injured leg was wrapped and propped up on a stool. A doctor had attended him as soon as they arrived at the station. At least the dose of laudanum had quieted his yelling.

"We have," Gideon replied. "Tell him, Allenby."

Christian held up the scroll. "This is a writ for your upcoming trial in the House of Lords."

"I don't sit in the House of Lords. What do I care?" Whinstone snapped.

"This trial is to abolish the Whinstone dukedom for good. As soon as the Act of Parliament is ready, the committee will pass it, and you will no longer be a duke."

Whinstone was silent. Since the duke sat in the shadows, it was hard to ascertain his features. Then he began to laugh, a maniacal chortle to rival any fictional villain. Then he quieted. "You have your revenge at last."

"Yes," Gideon answered. "I will have you out of my life. A victory, indeed."

"We will see," Whinstone scoffed. "You were always an annoying, whining bastard. I couldn't stand you. I should have sent you away to school at the first opportunity to expel your bothersome presence. But having you within my reach to torment and torture made the marriage worth it. That's all you were and ever will be—a whipped puppy."

Gideon's fists clenched, and Christian must have seen the anger on his face, for he pulled him away.

"I had no idea that you endured such. I am sorry, though that sounds hollow after all these years," Christian murmured.

"I kept it inside, allowed it to fester. It was turning me into an unfeeling, selfish excuse of a man. Whinstone had his triumph. But not anymore."

"Good. Be done with Whinstone. Dismiss his foul words, don't allow them to take root ever again. You never need to see or speak with the man again."

Well, there was that. To never see or hear from Whinstone again? Perfect.

"Come to Foxmont. There is no need to rush back to London," Gideon urged.

"I brought an overnight bag, just in case. Come, I have a carriage outside. Let us be off to Foxmont."

And to Olivia. Gideon couldn't wait to hold her in his arms.

Chapter 26

OLIVIA WAS OUT THE door when she saw the carriage come up the drive. When Gideon stepped down from the conveyance, she was in his arms.

Everyone was talking at once as they headed into the front hall.

Henderson gave Gideon a slight bow. "Good to have you home, Your Grace."

"Yes, home," Gideon whispered. "How's your injury?" He pointed at the plaster on Henderson's temple.

"I am fine, Your Grace. The one thing Whinstone did not steal was the food. We cannot lay out breakfast in the dining room, for the wretched man took the table and chairs, but if you would join us in the servants' hall, we can eat immediately."

"We would be pleased to join you all," Gideon smiled.

As everyone turned to follow the butler, Gideon grasped her arm gently, startling her. He coaxed her into the drawing room and closed the door, leaning her against it.

"I have waited all night to do this," he murmured.

Gideon kissed her with such ardent passion it took Olivia's breath away. Breathless, she kissed him back with equal, if not greater, eagerness. Things were getting heated as he thrust against her, his hardness causing her insides to flutter.

Then, he stepped away, leaving her panting.

Gideon held out his hand. "I know we've played this scene before and more than once, but I ask you to share our lives. I swear you will be my partner in all things. We will share it all. Life, joys, sorrows, sex, companionship, respect, trust, and most of all—love. Take my hand, Liv. Take my heart, for I am giving it to you. If you consent, we will be married immediately—civil ceremony or in a small chapel, whatever you wish. I love you—quite desperately. My heart doesn't beat without you."

Tears glittered on Olivia's cheeks as she took a step toward him. She slipped her hand in his. "Gideon, my love. We share it all. Let us be married as soon as possible. I love you so very much."

TWO DAYS LATER, AT Foxmont.

"I DO SOLEMNLY DECLARE that I know not of any lawful impediment why I, Olivia Durham, may not be joined in matrimony to Gideon Michael Broyles, Duke of Watford. I promise to care for you above all others, to give you my love and friendship, support, and comfort, and to respect and cherish you throughout our lives together."

Gideon smiled at her, and she could see tears in his eyes. He slipped the gold band on her finger. "I give you this ring as a token of our love and marriage, as a symbol of all that we share. And in recognition of our life together. I promise to love and respect you. Helping our love grow, always listening, comforting, and supporting you, whatever our lives may bring."

Mr. Bledsoe, Stanford-le-Hope's County Registrar, announced, "Then I pronounce you man and wife."

Applause broke out in the near-empty drawing room as Gideon kissed her gently.

Standing up for them were Christian and Althea, who had stayed on for the ceremony. Archie and Billy had returned to London two days ago.

The staff had moved smaller tables into the dining room, along with mismatched chairs. They had collected the furniture from the attic.

But Olivia didn't mind at all. Everything was perfect.

Goodness, I'm the Duchess of Watford now.

Olivia had insisted that the staff attend the brief ceremony, for she was very fond of them already.

"The wedding breakfast is ready to be served," Henderson announced.

"Will you stay and partake, Mr. Bledsoe?" Gideon asked.

"How tempting, Your Grace, but I must return to the office. It is rare for me to make a house call. And at such short notice."

"We appreciate all you have done to accommodate us," Olivia said. "Henderson, fix Mr. Bledsoe a small hamper of food to take with him."

"Why, thank you, Your Grace. And my hearty congratulations."

Oh. Your Grace.

Olivia would have to get used to that. And the fact they were leaving straight after breakfast for London. They would spend their wedding night at the town house.

They had assured the Foxmont staff that Mr. Chapman would arrive early in the evening to stay for the foreseeable future. The steward will begin to hire more staff and oversee any repairs. Gideon asked his steward to sell every stick of furniture and fumigate the place.

Then they would begin their life together, furnishing Foxmont in their way and overseeing all improvements. Already it felt like home, for hadn't Olivia stood with a rifle to defend it? But more importantly, they were a couple, bearing scars within and without. They had buried the damage in the past, becoming unfeeling, bitter people.

Not anymore. Not ever again.

Gideon held out his hand, his eyes reflecting love and devotion.

Olivia came to him, slipping her hand in his.

Not ever again.

TWO MORE DAYS LATER:

Olivia cried as she reached her peak. She collapsed on Gideon, laying her head against his heaving chest. A moment later, he growled as his climax peaked. They were in each other's arms, recovering from their exertions, when a knock sounded at the door.

"Sorry to interrupt, Your Graces, but the Duchess of Whinstone and Mrs. Granholm says it is urgent," the butler said through the door.

Gideon groaned as he nuzzled her neck. "My mother and aunt. Why can't people leave us alone?"

"We should have stayed at Foxmont," Olivia smiled, kissing his forehead. "If it's urgent, we had best face it so we can move on."

"Serve them tea," Gideon called out. "And we will be down as soon as we can."

"Yes, Your Grace." Hobson moved from the door, and his footfalls continued down the stairs.

Gideon jumped up, pulled on his trousers, and slipped on his dressing gown, tying about his waist. "If they are going to come this early, they will greet me as they see me."

Olivia laughed. "Early? It's nearly eleven. I won't be a moment. I will have Alice assist me with a layer or two."

When Olivia entered her chamber through the adjoining door, Alice dutifully stood, waiting. "Hobson said you will need me, Your Grace."

"I do, indeed."

Alice had traveled with Olivia from Foxmont and was learning her duties as a lady's maid from the housekeeper, Mrs. Potter.

Not twenty minutes later, they descended the stairs. They entered the morning room to find Gideon's aunt and mother drinking tea. Gideon kissed his aunt's cheek but not his mother's. But the duchess didn't seem to care.

'What is so urgent?" Gideon asked.

"Tell him, Portia," Gideon's aunt said.

"I am leaving for New York next month," the duchess announced.

Gideon continued to look between his mother and aunt. "And?"

"Take a seat, Gideon," his aunt sighed, "And you too, Olivia, my dear. Your mother is leaving for good, and the divorce is *not* going through. In fact, when Whinstone, Ellingford, or whomever he is when released, he will meet your mother in New York."

"And what of the child? The baronet's daughter?" Olivia asked incredulously.

"What about her?" the duchess sniffed. "Sanford is having his dukedom taken away, so he no longer needs an heir. I heard Sir Simon forgave his daughter. When she gives birth in prison, they can see the babe adopted. Or not. It's no never mind to me."

The duchess spoke the words so coldly that they chilled Olivia's heart. My God, this icicle of a woman was Gideon's mother. No wonder his childhood had been a barren wasteland. Olivia's first instinct about the duchess had been correct.

Leave the country? It was the best thing that could happen to Gideon. All Olivia wanted was for him to be at peace.

GIDEON SHOOK HIS HEAD. None of this should shock him.

"As for me, I cannot stay in London or England," the duchess continued. "I have been a duchess three-quarters of my life. The humiliation is not to be borne. Already my friends are giving me the cut direct. I cannot stay here." His mother paused. "I could refer to myself as the dowager duchess of Watford."

Gideon frowned. "You gave up that title when you married Ellingford. Take it to court if you wish to contest it. I will see that it never happens."

"Cruel boy. Regardless, I cannot bear being alone. Your aunt will not accompany me, so I have decided to forgive Sanford. As I told you, I love him, still. We cannot help whom we love." The duchess met Olivia's gaze. "You know that more than anyone, Gideon."

"Olivia is more than Ellingford could ever hope to be, you too, for that matter. Make one more sly insult, and I will throw you out on your ear." Gideon spoke in a deadly tone.

The duchess sniffled.

"And no tears; they ceased affecting me for decades," Gideon continued. "You want to leave, then goodbye, Mother. You may have quite a wait for Ellingford."

"I have seen him in Essex and spoke with Sanford's solicitors. They will claim he wasn't in his right mind and was under extraordinary stress. His trial is in two weeks. He will still be a duke when the sentence is passed, so the judgment will not be harsh—two or three years, perhaps. Before I depart, I shall hire a companion, and I will need your assistance selling the last of my jewels."

"You honestly believe that when that bastard is released, and you send him money for a ticket, he will actually come to you?" Gideon scoffed.

The duchess looked up and met his gaze. "Yes. How else is he going to live? He has nothing, and he needs me. My jewels?"

"No, I will not assist you. That is on *you* to sell."

The duchess stood, smoothing her gown. "Then goodbye, it is. Mirella, I will await you in the carriage." Gideon's mother swept from the room with her chin held high.

"My God, they deserve each other," Gideon spat.

"Is that true? He may only get a few years?" Olivia asked.

"I have said all along the courts favor the rich and powerful, especially those with titles. It probably won't matter that Ellingford is about to lose the dukedom. The fact he still has it when sentenced could work to his advantage." Gideon took her hand and squeezed it. "The world is not fair, my love. And I fear it never will be."

"I do not mean to pry, Olivia," Aunt Mirella said quietly. "But have you decided if you will bring charges here in London? Concerning the abduction and assault?"

Olivia exhaled shakily. "We spoke with Gideon's solicitor, and he advised against it. He laid out what I would have to bear in stark terms. I cannot go to court or put us all through such a public spectacle. Especially now I am a duchess. It would be fodder for the newspapers. You must think less of me."

Mirella leaned forward and patted her knee. "Never, my dear. We have only known each other briefly, but I already adore you. It is a personal decision, and no one can or should make it for you."

"My solicitor said the crown prosecutor probably would not take up the case anyway," Gideon interjected. "'Not enough sufficient evidence,' especially since Jonas Bisby denies the duke had any notion of it. The second man involved is long gone."

Mirella stood. "Well, my dears, the best we can do is to move on from these terrible incidents and live to the fullest. And I know you will."

"Oh, I intend to see that Ellingford gets the maximum of whatever so-called justice is meted out. I intend to be loud about the theft case in court and out of it. But yes, we will move on."

Gideon stood and took her arm. "And you will be a large part of that full life, Aunt. Olivia and I discussed it. At some point, you may like to contemplate moving to Foxmont. The entire upper east wing would be yours. It is larger than your town house."

"I will consider it," she smiled warmly.

Olivia rose to her feet and took Mirella's other arm. "Please do. We could use a mother figure in our lives, seeing we were both deprived of such a warm presence."

They escorted Aunt Mirella to the door, and once she departed in the carriage, Henderson closed the door and left them alone in the front hallway.

"I received word that Brookton wishes an audience to congratulate us and no doubt wishes to know all about the doings. Name the day, and I will send out the invite. Unless you'd rather wait." Gideon said as he slipped his arm about her waist.

"No. I meant what I said. I want to get to know Damon. Perhaps if all goes well, he will also become a part of our extended family. Perhaps having a family will have a good effect on him."

Gideon laughed. "Never in my wildest dreams did I imagine Brookton as part of my family, but fate is strange, indeed."

Olivia turned and embraced him, laying her head against his chest. His steady heartbeat gave her warmth, comfort, and a sense of safety she had never felt before.

"I thank the fates," she whispered. "Or we would have never found each other."

"True," Gideon murmured. "I thank the fates, indeed."

Whatever the future would bring, they would face it together.

Olivia and Gideon had found love at last, and they would revel in it.

Epilogue

TEN YEARS LATER

Foxmont, Essex

Every summer for the past five years, Eleanora and Christian Bamford traveled to their country estate, Bamford Park, and hosted a summer party by inviting friends and family.

Gideon and Olivia happily packed to join their tight circle of friends and family for the festive event.

Coming with them would be their son, the heir apparent, nine-year-old Jonathan Gideon Broyles, and adopted daughter, Marie, age sixteen. They adopted Marie at age six through Damon, which was a long story.

But Olivia and Damon had grown close through the years, becoming brother and sister as they had hoped, and they had discovered more half-siblings and even became close to a few of them. It was a strange sort of patchwork quilt family with half-siblings, but they made it work. Damon's transformation from a sarcastic, unfeeling rake to a decent man of honor began in the early years of their first meeting and only intensified when he met his current wife. But that, again, was a long story.

As for the former Duke of Whinstone: Sanford Ellingford served three years for the theft. Upon his release, he joined Gideon's mother in New York.

Gideon had heard through his aunt—for he never wrote his mother, nor she, him—that the couple passed themselves off as a duke and duchess when in reality, they were not. Seven months after his arrest and sentencing, the House of Lords stripped the dukedom from Whinstone.

But that little detail hardly mattered to certain portions of New York society that allowed the couple access to the affluent. In turn, his mother and stepfather leeched off the more gullible members of that elite society. Typical, Gideon sneered when his aunt informed him.

But Gideon no longer cared about his mother and stepfather's schemes.

As for Whinstone's child, Sir Simon had taken Gideon aside shortly after the birth and confidentially revealed that he and his wife were adopting the baby boy, and he would be known as Simon Albert Day.

The baronet's daughter, Annabella, served one year and six months for her part in the theft. Sir Simon welcomed his daughter back into the family and moved away from London society and its judgment to Cornwall.

As for Gideon, his life was everything he had hoped for and more. It was rewarding in all aspects.

Everything he could ever hope for but had been convinced he would never experience.

He still worked with the progressive group within Parliament. Gideon also worked with Damon's cause.

The Rakes of St. Regent's Park was still a functioning association but with different priorities. The men within the group, and the women, had become his close friends. Gideon's life was all the richer from knowing them.

At fifty, he kept himself fit, for he had more living to do as yet.

And loving.

Over the years, his love for Olivia had only deepened—if that were possible. Their pasts soon faded—not completely gone—but they could cope thanks to a recommended doctor from the recently formed

Psychological Society of Britain. Talking about their trauma with a third party put much in perspective.

Gideon also referred the learned doctor to Brandon Knight, his close friend, and his wife, Angeline. Gideon was grateful when, as promised, Bran and his family returned to England after two years in Canada. The two families were together constantly, or as much as distance and obligations would allow.

Olivia sailed into his study with their Scotch sheepdog, Lady, on her heels.

Gideon immediately swept Olivia into his arms. "Looking forward to seeing your brother?" he asked as he nuzzled Olivia's neck.

"I am looking forward to seeing everyone. We've all been so busy of late. But a good busy."

"Yes, busy living and loving. I am so glad you took my hand and agreed to be my duchess." He laced her fingers through his. "Remember? 'Take my hand, Liv. Take my heart, for I am giving it to you.'"

"My heart doesn't beat without you."

Gideon laughed at her repeating his words back to him: declarations he made ten years ago but all the truer today.

Gideon had found peace, happiness, and, more importantly—love.

*** Look ahead for a sneak peek of book #5 in The Rakes of St. Regent's Park, *The Not So Perfect Duke* (Althea and Damon's story!) ***

Author's Note #2

The revolving door at the Midland Grand Hotel (now the St. Pancras Renaissance Hotel) was installed some months later in 1899, but I used a little artistic/historical license so it would fit my timeframe.

The classifying of blood by groups was first discovered in 1901 by Doctor Karl Landsteiner in Vienna. The first successful and safe blood transfusion was done in a New York hospital in 1907. However, it wasn't until the 1930s that it was discovered that human blood groups really did contain clues to one's parentage, particularly paternity. DNA paternity tests went mainstream in the 1990s.

All the trivia Gideon related in this story, like the first phone call held at Brown's Hotel, are accurate. (Yes! I researched it!)

My scenario of the old duke losing everything but the title is unlikely in real life but not improbable. It did need an Act of Parliament to strip a non-royal peer of his title in the late Victorian age. So, seeing this story is fiction, I went with the not-improbable scenario.

Characters mentioned or appearing in this story:

Tremain Hornsby. Check out his story in *The Vicar's Frozen Heart* (The Hornsby Brothers #2)

Harrison Hornsby. Check out his story in *The Marquess of Secrets* (The Hornsby Brothers #3)

Aidan Wollstonecraft. Check out his story in *Love with a Notorious Rake* (The Men of Wollstonecraft Hall #3)

Rory Kerrigan. Check out his story in *The Copper and the Madam* (Blind Cupid #3)

Author Biography

A multi-published author from the East Coast of Canada, Karyn Gerrard loves to write sensual historical and contemporary romances. Tortured heroes are an absolute must.

Karyn's been happily married for a long time to her own hero. His encouragement and loving support keep her moving forward.

To learn more about Karyn and her books, visit www.karyngerrard.com[1]

Also visit her on Facebook, Twitter, Pinterest, Instagram, and Bookbub.

"Looking for a swoon-worthy read? You can't go wrong with the lovely and emotional romances from Karyn Gerrard." ~**Vanessa Kelly, USA Today Bestselling author**

"Karyn Gerrard writes very enjoyable, richly textured historical romances." ~**Kate Pearce, New York Times and USA Today Bestselling author**

1. http://www.karyngerrard.com/

More Books by Karyn Gerrard

~Historical~

The Spinster and Mr. Glover (Book #1 Blind Cupid Series)

The Governess and the Beast (Book #2 Blind Cupid Series)

The Copper and the Madam (Book #3 Blind Cupid Series)

Protecting the Duke (The Rakes of St. Regent's Park #1)

The Baron and the Mistress (The Rakes of St. Regent's Park #2)

Knight of Christmas (The Rakes of St. Regent's Park #3)

Duke of Pain (The Rakes of St. Regent's Park #4)

Bold Seduction (of Professor Hornsby) (Book #1 Hornsby Brothers Series)

The Vicar's Frozen Heart (Book #2 Hornsby Brothers Series)

Marquess of Secrets (Book #3 Hornsby Brothers Series)

Beloved Monster (Book #1 The Ravenswood Chronicles)

Beloved Beast (Book #2 The Ravenswood Chronicles)

Marriage with a Proper Stranger (Book #1 Men of Wollstonecraft Hall Series)

Scandal with a Sinful Scot (Book #2 Men of Wollstonecraft Hall Series)

Love with a Notorious Rake (Book #3 Men of Wollstonecraft Hall Series)

The Not So Perfect Duke (The Rakes of St. Regent's Park #5)

COMING SOON! The Viscount of Shadows (The Rakes of St. Regent's Park #6)

~Contemporary~

My Highlander Cover Model (Heroes of Time Travel Anthology Series #1)

Timeless Heart (Heroes of Time Travel Anthology Series #2)

My Wicked Soul (It's Never too Late for Love Anthology Series #1)

That Christmas Feeling (It's Never too Late for Love Anthology Series #2)

Wild Pitch

He's the Wicked Bad (Wicked Men of Rockland City #1)

His Wicked Celtic Kiss (Wicked Men of Rockland City #2)

His Wicked Cold Heart (Wicked Men of Rockland City #3) coming soon!

Sneak Peek of The Not So Perfect Duke (The Rakes of St. Regent's Park #5)

PROLOGUE

COSTA DE LA LUZ, SPAIN
July 1898

IT HAD BEEN SEVERAL years since Damon Cranston, Marquess of Brookton, had any contact with his mother, the Duchess of Chellenham, much less encountered her in person. But here he stood, awaiting her appearance on the veranda of her hacienda. When Damon arrived at his mother's home unannounced, the servants had been dubious about allowing him access to the property. Showing his card and throwing his imperious manner around gained him entry eventually, with a muscular footman keeping watch.

Damn it all, his insides twisted in knots. Feeling like an 8-year-old lonely little boy had him annoyed to the extreme. Holding his temper will be a definite challenge. When was the last time they had met face-to-face? Scads of years. Decades. The chasm between them was insurmountable, at least in Damon's eyes.

His mother breezed onto the patio and stopped cold in her steps. "My God, it *is* you. I would recognize you anywhere," she whispered while removing the scarf from her head. She then turned toward the footman. "Mateo, you may leave us. Bring refreshments, if you please."

"*Si, de inmediato Duquesa*," the brawny footman replied, giving her a bow. He departed directly, leaving them alone.

How astounding to find his mother had retained most of her youthful beauty after twenty-plus years.

Damon stood with his hands clasped behind his back. "I haven't heard from you in a decade, so I thought I would check to see if you are alive." He kept his voice devoid of emotion, as usual.

"As you see. I am well. Come, and sit at the table," the duchess replied as emotionlessly as he had done. Once seated, she asked, "And what brings you here?"

No need for pleasantries or kind words; right to the point. Then so shall Damon.

"I want to know of father's affairs and how many children there are from all his various debaucheries and dalliances."

His mother blinked rapidly but kept her expression neutral. "Before I answer, do you wish to know why I have not contacted you since that lone letter of ten years ago? Of which, you did not reply."

"I don't care to know," Damon sniffed indifferently.

She gave him a plaintive look. The first display of emotion from her. "Yes, Damon. You do. There was no contact before or since that impulsive letter because it was the arrangement I had agreed to."

His brows knitted. "What are you on about?"

His mother sighed. "The only way your father would agree to the separation was for me to leave the country without further communication with you. The duke gave me this cozy villa and a monthly stipend in the settlement. I had to get away, no matter the cost. That cost was—you."

The churning of his guts increased, along with his annoyance. "And when I grew older and came of age, what then? You could have contacted me besides that one time, and I would have assisted with your upkeep. But you did not." The last words ended with a hiss through clenched teeth. "Two sentences in that letter. To say you are well and that you hoped I continued in good health."

"And *you* never responded. Who pays you a monthly allowance?" the duchess shot back. "The duke would have cut you off. Besides, I *made* inquiries through the years and learned that you were following in your father's footsteps by joining a debauchery club and haunting East End brothels and music halls. What is the name, The Rakes of St. Regent's Park?"

She tapped her finger on the table. "I could not subject myself to such again. Not ever. Not if I were to keep my sanity. I barely escaped with a semblance of lucidity, and I had what is called in polite society—a breakdown. Your father threatened me with incarceration in an asylum, and I *had* to leave."

At that shocking moment, the footman entered and laid a tray in front of the duchess. Damon needed a lull in the conversation to process what his mother had divulged. Of course, this was *not* the picture his detestable father painted. The duke had claimed that the duchess no longer wished to be his mother and abandoned him to travel and seek out adventures—with other men.

Who to believe? One was as bad as the other. Or so he had supposed. His mother's abrupt departure had affected him so profoundly that he accepted his father's blatant fabrications. At the time, Damon was 8 years old, an imprudent boy, hurt and afraid. His father was all he had. Of course, he believed the duke. But be damned if Damon would reveal how much his mother's absence had damaged him.

"Iced tea?" She held the pitcher aloft in question.

"Yes."

His mother poured a glass and passed it to him. "Thank you, Mateo. You may leave us."

The footman departed, and Damon took a long swig of the cold beverage. Perhaps it would cool the heated uproar spiraling inside of him.

"There are almond biscuits, called panellets, and citrus sponge cake. Please, help yourself," the duchess offered politely. "Where are you staying?"

Still the gracious duchess.

As if he could partake of any food. Regardless, he reached for a biscuit. "I am staying at the Casa Cádiz."

"You are stunningly handsome. You have grown into the beautiful man I always knew you would be. On the outside. I have no clue what beauty exists within you."

"Do not bother delving deep. I let no one in," Damon replied as he absently nibbled on the biscuit.

The duchess eyed him askance but gave no reply to his dismissive statement. "Now that we have the pleasantries out of the way regarding your father. Inasmuch as I detest the man, it is time I discussed him. It was not a love match at first," she stated matter-of-factly. "But God help me, I grew to love him most desperately. Or it was more of a wild infatuation. Why? Perhaps it *was* his breathtaking golden looks. I was that young and shallow once. Oh, how he took advantage of that vulnerability. He was cruel, the devil incarnate. I assume he still is."

"What, handsome and a devil? Yes, and he has only worsened with age. And yet, you left me in his care. Abandoned me to that overt cruelty," Damon accused. "And his cold indifference." So much for keeping his emotions hidden.

The duchess frowned. "I tried to depart and take you with me. Reach back in your memories."

He sneered. "I banished all memories as far as you were concerned." Perhaps a harsh taunt and not all that accurate, but Damon said it anyway. It appeared he acted as a sullen child, after all. He often lashed out and said things he really did not mean.

His mother visibly winced. "Yes, you were always adept at pushing away and hiding horrible reminiscences. I envied you for that. Even at a young age, I watched how deftly you tucked away your emotions. Hiding them, denying them, just like your father."

"Stop comparing me to that wretched bastard," Damon snapped.

"Not hiding the emotions now. Think, you were 7 years of age. We traveled as far as Euston Station before your father, and his men dragged us back, and he thrashed us both for good measure."

The buried and hauntingly disturbing memory pushed its way through the protective haze and returned in full force. Yes, he recalled it, just as his mother described. His father beat him, the only time he had done so, then made him watch as he battered his mother and—worse.

"Damn you for making me recall that," he whispered dangerously.

"Forgive me. I will not speak of our shared past under your father's harsh and corrupt rule. You see why I departed in such haste? And why I couldn't take you, even if I wanted to? I sent numerous letters, but the duke returned them unopened. So, I waited until you reached the age of majority. I honestly believed that you were lost to me, that you are your father's son." The duchess reached across the table and took his hand. "Are you—his son?"

Was he? It was a chilling thought.

Partly, perhaps, but not deep down. At least, Damon hoped that was the case. What was the decades-old proverb or idiom? The apple doesn't fall far from the tree?

"I don't want to be," he whispered. Damon gave his mother an affectionate squeeze of her hand, and tears welled in her eyes. This was the first time he had admitted this to anyone.

"I am glad to hear it. Avoid emulating the duke in any way." Releasing his hand, the duchess dashed away the tear trickling down her cheek. "Let us change the subject. Why do you wish to trace your half-siblings?"

"Guilt. To know some children have been tossed aside—picks at my conscious. Yes, Mother. I have one, impaired though it may be."

She sipped her iced tea thoughtfully. "And have you taken care of your own dealings?"

"I would never act as recklessly as the duke. That is all you need to know."

"What have you discovered so far?"

Damon stared out over the serene scenery, squinting at the bright sun. "Two half-sisters, or so the claim goes. One refused to meet, and considering the source, I believe the statement was untrue. I have met Olivia Durham. There is no denying it, as she has the same blue eyes and golden hair I imagine all his spawn possesses. We are going to attempt friendship. Perhaps, in time, think of each other as brother and sister. Perhaps we are starting to do so already."

His mother smiled warmly. "I am glad to hear it. Is that the baby adopted by the country vicar and his wife?"

Damon could feel the blood drain from his face. "You knew of her?"

The duchess nodded. "And more besides. I found out about these children *after* my wedding. Your father took great pleasure in bragging about his perfect progeny. You had best pour us a drink, my son. You will need it. And so shall I. There is Brandy de Jerez over on the side table."

Damon rose but gripped the table to steady himself as his legs shook. Such revelations, such unfamiliar sentiments. He wondered if coming here was a terrible blunder. There was something to be said for staying removed from family drama and well above the fray. He would be picking at threads best not pulled.

Well, he had come this far.

After pouring the drinks, he handed one to his mother.

She took a sip, then sighed. "You have an older half-brother by three years; last I heard, he is with the Metropolitan Police. You have a younger half-brother working as a footman at Chellenham Park."

The mouthful of brandy Damon had taken sprayed across the flagstones.

A copper—and a footman? A footman at the country seat?

Damon searched his mind for recollections of a blond-haired footman, but he never stayed at Chellenham Park, and he barely even looked at the staff the few times he did.

God above.

He picked up the serviette and wiped his mouth, then took another mouthful of the brandy to steel himself for the disclosures ahead. "How do you know about these children, and what became of them?" Damon asked.

"Your father kept me apprised of their progress through the years, whether I wanted to hear of it or not. With each quarterly allowance statement, he sent a noxious letter bragging of his conquests and the fact he had illegitimate children in every corner of London and beyond."

Damon glowered, despising his father afresh. "I am sorry you were subjected to that."

"After a few years, I no longer cared. But I read the letters to spite the duke. And to prove to myself they had no effect on me."

"How many more offspring are there?"

"I know of seven, no wait, eight," his mother murmured. "But, as I said, I know there are more, considering the infidelities. At first, your father noted locations and names and even continued their maintenance, at least the boys. But later, he ensured they were taken to an orphanage and never thought of them again. Those are the ones you will never locate. There are no doubt a dozen or more of the poor children. At least, that is what he told me. I doubt the veracity, considering the information came from him."

His mother sipped her brandy. "Your father preferred poor, young, attractive women, mostly Irish, so not all the children you may try to locate will have blond hair and blue eyes."

"Good God," Damon muttered. "Rumor states the Earl of Oakby died of syphilis, along with some baronet the earl was friends with. Why is Chellenham so hale and hearty considering his flagrant behavior?"

His mother reached for a panellet. "I have often asked the same. It is why I kept him from my bed after you were born. You know what he is capable of, and I did not trust him to keep me safe and healthy."

"Do you still have any lingering feelings for him?" Damon inquired. "Forget I asked; it is an indelicate question."

"No, I will answer. Not for a long time. That particular destructive fever left me a year after you were born. I have turned my affections elsewhere."

A man in a crisp white linen suit strode across the flagstones toward Damon's mother as if on cue. The handsome man looked in his mid-forties, and his eyes softened as he gazed affectionately at the duchess. The man leaned down to kiss her cheek.

"We have company," his mother beamed. "This is my son, Damon Cranston, Marquess of Brookton. Damon, this is Antonio De León."

The man held out his hand. "Tony, please. A distinct pleasure."

Damon took his hand and shook it.

"I will leave you, *mi corazón*, to visit with your son. You will stay for dinner, my lord?"

"Yes, thank you."

How astonishing that he would agree so swiftly, but the day was full of surprises, and Damon had the notion there were more shockwaves to come.

De León was about to depart when the duchess took his hand. "My love, could you ask Mateo to bring a pen, ink, and several sheets of paper?"

He brought her hand to his lips and kissed it. "I shall."

After De León left, Damon asked, "How long have you been together?"

"Over nineteen years. Tony is six years younger." She bit her lower lip, pausing as if considering revealing a secret. "You have a younger brother. Promise you will never tell your father."

"I swear it."

My God. A secret, indeed.

"Sebastián is away visiting his grandparents far north of here, but we will arrange a meeting soon if you wish. I am so pleased you are staying for supper. Will I see you again? Will you write? Am I in your life again, my darling boy?"

That is what his mother used to call him.

My darling boy.

It took all his inner courage not to fall to pieces, for a rush of memories threatened to overcome him. The affection she had always shown him, the extra hugs and attention. As if making up for the lack of warmth from his father. Yes, in the past, his mother tried to protect him. But falling to pieces, showing emotion?

It was not the done thing. It was not Damon's done thing.

Regardless, Damon stood and leaned in to kiss her cheek. "Yes, Mother. We will keep in touch. In fact, I will stay a few days. And I want to meet my half-brother. How old is he?"

His mother smiled. "Soon to be 17 years old. And yes, please stay, Damon. I have a guest room overlooking the water. We have so much to catch up on."

"Thank you, I will take you up on the kind offer."

Mateo entered with a tray and sat it before the duchess. She quickly wiped away another tear, then waved the servant away. Damon took his seat.

"Take your coat off, roll up your sleeves, relax in the sun and sip your brandy. This will take some time. I will write down the names I am aware of and note the name of the orphanage. All I know is that it is in the East End." She peeked up from the papers. "Does your father still employ that muscle-bound thug, Silas Browning?"

Damon nodded and removed his coat as his mother suggested. The oppressive heat was starting to make him feel dizzy.

"Question him, for I believe he was involved in this scheme. Also, question any servants working for your father since our marriage. Although, I imagine there are hardly any left."

"Perhaps I will. I do not want the duke to know what I am doing. At least, not right away."

"The people on this list will not thank you for locating them," his mother murmured as she dipped the pen into the ink bottle.

Damon rolled up the sleeves of his shirt and stretched out his legs. "I want to know that they are well, and I will be cautious in my dealings if any need assistance, monetary or otherwise."

"You are stirring up a hornet's nest. Perhaps you should hire an investigative agency," his mother suggested.

A slow smile crept across his face as he thought of the lovely Miss Althea Galway.

"I have just the investigative agency in mind."

www.ingramcontent.com/pod-product-compliance
Lightning Source LLC
Chambersburg PA
CBHW070107030726
47506CB00002B/623
* 9 7 8 1 7 3 8 6 8 4 5 0 2 *